STILLPOINT

A novel of war, peace, politics and Palestine

At the still point of the turning world. Neither flesh nor fleshless;
Neither from nor towards; at the still point, there the dance is,
But neither arrest nor movement. And do not call it fixity,
Where past and future are gathered.
Neither movement from nor towards,
Neither ascent nor decline. Except for the point, the still point,
There would be no dance, and there is only the dance.
I can only say, there we have been: but I cannot say where.

T.S. Elliot

Books by the author

STILLPOINT

A novel of war, peace, politics and Palestine

FINALIST

2013 NEXT GENERATION INDIE BOOK AWARDS

General Fiction

SOMETHING TO PONDER

Reflections from Lao Tzu's Tao Te Ching

WINNER

US NATIONAL BEST BOOKS AWARDS
INTERNATIONAL BOOK AWARDS
Eastern Religion

FINALIST

US INDIE EXCELLENCE AWARDS
Interior lay out and design

UNDERSTANDING

The simplicity of life

WINNER

US INDIE EXCELLENCE AWARDS

New Age Non Fiction

FINALIST

US NATIONAL BEST BOOKS AWARDS
Eastern Religion

NEXT GENERATION INDIE AWARDS
Spirituality

STILLPOINT

A novel of war, peace, politics and Palestine

Colin Mallard, Ph.D.

Stillpoint

A novel of war, peace, politics and Palestine

by

Colin Mallard

Promontory Press

ISBN: 978-1-927559-36-9

Third Edition: October 2013

Interior design and layout by

Raga Man Studio

Cover design: Colin Mallard

Printed in Canada

www.promontorypress.com

Notes to the reader.

This book is a work of fiction. The following events are facts: The destruction of Palestinian villages by the Stern Gang, the Carmeli Brigade, and other paramilitary groups, the attack on Haifa, the siege of Acre, the typhoid epidemic, the encroachment of Settlements on Palestinian land and the conditions in Gaza. So too is the sanctuary at Boston University's Marsh Chapel. Statistics quoted are also factual. For those interested a bibliography is provided at the back of the book. All characters are fictional, except for brief references to David Ben Gurion, Brigadier Beveridge, chief of the British Medical Services, Colonel Bonnet of the British Army, Dr. McLean of the Medical Services and Mr. De Meuron, the Red Cross delegate.

A bibliography can be found at the back of the book.

All quotes from Lao Tzu are taken from the book, *Something to Ponder, reflections from Lao Tzu's Tao Te Ching*, by Colin Mallard.

"Stillpoint" is dedicated in fond memory of

Pierre Elliot Trudeau

15th Prime Minister of Canada
Dreamer, Gadfly
And inspiration

And to my friend

Madhukar Thompson,
the craziest wise man I ever knew.
His unexpected departure was a loss for
those of us who loved him.
Madhukar loved this book in its early stages.
I think he'd be pleased with the result.

Lights along the way

Acknowledgments.

I would like to thank Steve Flawith for reading the manuscript and for his insight, and suggestions.
But then there was bread and sunshine too.

Thank you to Raga Man Studio. You have combined simplicity and elegance in the layout of the book

Craig Shemilt, thank you again for printing our books.
It's always a pleasure!

To Nowick Gray a big thanks for his editorial contributions and the swift return of the manuscript, as well as suggestions.

To Val Walton my editor and friend,
my deepest thanks. Without you, this book would not be what it is.
From the bottom of my heart. Thank you.

Table of Contemts

Alphabetical list of characters appearing in more than one chapter

Abdullah- Hard line Iranian guerilla.

Ali- Father of Nadia, Halal and Jalal, grandfather of Mera

Amal- Nasir's older brother, fought with the guerillas.

Aziz- Friend of Nasir who provides refuge.

Benjamin- Brother of Josef who was killed by Nasir. Married Rachel.

Bokhari- Sufi sage, spiritual master to Nasir.

Cole- Republican Senator who led attacks on Tremaine.

Durrah- Mother of Tariq, friend of Nasir and Samara.

Emerson, Richard- President who dies early in his term of office.

Gabir- Nasir's uncle who tended the sheep.

Goldhirsh, Joseph- Israeli Foreign Secretary.

Hafiz- Member of Nasir's unit who yearned for peace.

Halal- Ali's son who worked in a garage. Brother of Nadia and Jalal.

Hana- Omar's wife, friend of Nasir and Heatherington.

Harith- Hard line Iranian guerrilla.

Heatherington, Chris- British medical officer in Acre, married Nadia, Mera's father.

Herzog, Samuel- Hard line Prime Minister of Israel.

Jalal- Son of Ali, brother of Nadia and Halal. Member of same fighting unit as Nasir.

Joan Merril- Secret Service agent assigned to protect Tremaine.

Josef- Jewish soldier killed by Nasir, engaged to Rachel, brother of Benjamin.

Kersey, Doug- US Secretary of State

Khalil- Guerilla fighter, friend of Nasir.

Lacey- Wife of President Emerson.

Levin, Michael- Prime Minister of Israel.

Levin, Rebecca- Wife of Prime Minister of Israel.

McCloud, Kevin- Ex green beret, friend of Travis.

McManus- Admiral, member of Joint Chiefs.

Mera - Granddaughter of Ali, daughter of Nadia and Heatherington, wife of Morgan.

Makarios, Jonathan - Aide to Tremaine.

Mikel Antebi Husseini- Israeli peace activist.

Morgan, William- (Bill)Vice President to Tremaine.

Nadia - Daughter of Ali and Natalia, married Heatherington, mother of Mera.

Natalia- Wife of Ali and mother of Nadia, killed in attack on village.

Nasir- A Palestinian guerrilla who sought peace and became a sage.

Nevis, Peter- Ex green beret, friend of Travis.

Omar- Physician, Hana's husband, friend of Nasir, Ali, Heatherington and Mera.

Rachel- Wife of Benjamin, engaged to Josef before his death in 1948

Ramirez, Jennifer- Was once mistress to David Tremaine.

Robert Sandusky - Secret Service Agent, assigned to protect Tremaine.

Salim- Nasir's older brother, brain damaged by blows from a rifle.

continued on next page

Alphabetical list of characters continued

Ted- Son of Mera and Morgan, killed in a gang shoot out.

Sandra Tremaine- David's wife.

Tariq- Member of a Palestinian guerilla unit. Friend of Nasir, son of Durrah.

Travis, J. P. General- Chairman of Joint Chiefs.

Travis, Mildred- Wife of General Travis.

Tremaine. David- Vice President who becomes President upon Emerson's death.

Try this coat

flesh on the white bones
of history.

try on this coat
wear it for a while
listen!
see how it feels.

imagine

you were there
living it
the joy
sorrow and injustice.

laughter and tears
tumbling down.

see with the eyes of others
live what others live.
would it change us?
melt our hearts and set us free
of................blindness.

understanding is freedom

but first
the mind must open
an empty mind
zen mind
a beginners mind...knowing nothing.

Now!

The Bus

It was Monday morning, the day after Tishah B'Av. Above the mountains to the east, a fiery sun burned in a cloudless sky. In the shadow of tall buildings, the street was a hive of activity. Local merchants opened their stores, sliding back the iron grates, removing shutters, and wheeling out display carts loaded with produce. Along the street traffic was heavy, impeded by trucks unloading fruit and vegetables from the kibbutzim. Haggling was a way of life in most Mediterranean cities, and Tel Aviv was no exception. Another busy day had begun.

The bus, filled with passengers on their way to work, pulled onto the street and joined the traffic. Its klaxon horns added to the din of early morning. Through an open window a young girl, red hair ruffled by the wind, watched mesmerized by the activity of the shopkeepers.

Above the cacophony of sounds, doves tumbled in play. With a thunderous roar, the bus blew apart. A bright sheet of orange flame shot upward; metal fragments and body parts flew in all direction. The force of the blast shattered windows up and down the street.

A dreadful silence ensued, followed by moans and screams. Lurid yellow flames and black smoke flickered and floated in the twisted shell of the bus. Nearby, two cars lay on their sides, another spun slowly on its roof. Next to the shell of the bus, a large truck leaned at an odd angle, crushing the car beside it. The driver was dead, his head bowed on his chest.

People in the street ran in every direction, some toward the bus. A woman got there first, climbed up the side and pulled herself into the burning wreckage looking for survivors. Within moments others joined her, and as quickly and carefully as possible, they removed the injured before the flames could reach them.

The red-haired girl lay pinned beneath a twisted seat, a shard of metal protruding from a bloody shoulder. Two men carefully pried and pulled at the seat until the girl was freed. A woman bent down and together they lifted the girl off the metal spike. She groaned and passed out as they lifted her over the side to waiting hands and safety. Climbing out of the bus, the woman knelt beside the injured girl. Blood was pumping from the wound, and she knew it would have to be stopped quickly. Ripping pieces from his shirt, a man handed them to her. She glanced up and found herself looking into the green eyes of her husband.

Bunching the piece of shirt, she stuffed it into the bloody wound and quickly bound it tightly. In the distance, sirens wailed. The woman looked around to see where else she could help.

That evening, just before sunset, a well-dressed man on a busy street flicked open his phone and like any other business man in that section of the city, he went unnoticed. What he said did not. With the phone to his ear he waited. He heard a click, and a woman's voice came on the line. "Good evening," she said. "May I help you?"

"Listen closely. That bus this morning—it was the work of

Hamas. We will never allow a dishonorable peace. We are not afraid to die. Allah is great!"

The man snapped the phone shut, turned and hurrying away dropped it in a litter bin. Joining a crowd in front of the synagogue, he adjusted his yarmulke and entered the building.

Samara

Samara adjusted the yoke on her shoulders and set off along the path. The fierce heat of day had yielded to the approach of evening. She loved the daily walk to the springs. It was always a welcome break from looking after her brothers and sister. While she was gone, her mother would prepare the evening meal, and her father would be home by the time she returned.

She followed the trail as it wound along the shore and over the low-lying hills. The ocean sparkled in the slanting sunlight. Beneath the bending palms, small waves brushed the shoreline. The trail turned and followed a shallow valley that led to the foothills. Already the grasses were brown and parched from lack of rain. Clumps of sycamore and poplar dotted the hillsides, offering sharp contrast to the barren terrain.

Samara climbed steadily until she reached a curve where the trail turned south. She walked through a series of knolls before ascending a steep incline. She crested the hill and paused. Below, the trail sloped gently to the well, its pool of water shimmering in the light. Around the water's edge, a sea of green grass offered pleasant relief from the barren land. A cluster of palms stood at the abrupt end of a ridge that extended from the mountain. Beside the palms a steep valley cut into the hillside and vanished from sight.

She could see the old man sitting on the rocks at the edge of the pool, his sheep gathered at the entrance to the valley. He'd been there every evening for the past week. At first she was afraid of him, but as she got to know him, her fear subsided. Each evening he drew water and filled her pots. He wore the traditional clothes of a herdsman, and his hair and close-cropped beard were white. Black bushy eyebrows protruded below a white head of hair. His skin was dark, like hers, but weathered. His eyes seemed to sparkle and emanated both strength and gentleness. She'd learned to avoid the eyes of men, but she could not avoid Nasir's. When he spoke, his voice was soft, rich and soothing. He said he'd lived in the hills all his life. His ancestors had built the well and taken care of it for generations. With the changing seasons he moved the flock from place to place, visiting different wells.

She'd talked with him every evening when she'd gone for water. After their talks, she would hurry home before darkness swallowed her surroundings.

The evening before, she'd told her parents of meeting the shepherd at the well. Her mother stopped eating and looked quickly at her father. Samara caught the look and asked, "Do you know him?"

"What does he look like?" her father asked.

She described him. "Do you know him?" she persisted.

"Yes," her father answered. "Eighteen years ago, not long before you were born, Nasir arrived one evening at sunset. He seemed exhausted. We gave him water and shared a meal. After we'd eaten, we sat around the table relaxing. He looked at me and asked whether I trusted him. I thought it an odd question from a stranger, but I realized I did trust him. Nasir looked at us and told us we were in great danger and must leave for several days until it passed. We asked him to explain, but he wouldn't.

"We packed some food and a few belongings and he took us far into the hills. We walked until dawn. Just as light crept into the eastern sky, he helped us through an opening into a deep cavern. Water skins hung on wooden pegs and sheepskins surrounded the charcoal remains of a cooking fire.

"For three nights we remained in the cave. In the middle of the fourth, we returned home. We arrived at first light and could see at once that something was terribly wrong. Only the almond and sycamore trees remained standing and one small shed where I kept tools and supplies. A door hung on its hinges between two empty holes that had once been windows in an otherwise undamaged white wall. It was the only thing standing of what had once been our home. Craters gouged the earth, and a strange smell hung in the air.

"Nasir assured us we'd be safe. We asked him if he knew what had happened. 'Israeli war planes' was all he'd say. For seven days we worked to rebuild our home. Using the stones and bricks scattered from the explosion we rebuilt walls and framed in the roof using the wood from the fallen trees. It was a lot of work for the three of us and we were exhausted at the end of those long days.

"I was furious over the destruction of our home. We'd done nothing to deserve it. For the first time, I felt an urge to join the guerrillas. I wanted to strike back; I wanted the Israelis destroyed. I wanted things to be the way my father and his father had described them, before the Israelis had taken so much of our land. A long-standing hatred had simmered inside me all those years. Now it boiled over, a silent, barely controlled rage. I wanted to leave, wanted to kill. Your mother begged me not to go, but I wouldn't listen.

"That evening, Nasir went with me to gather water at the well. We filled the pots, and then he told me to sit down. He sat opposite me. For what seemed like a long time he fixed his eyes on mine. At first I was impatient and didn't want to sit, but I couldn't break the hold of his eyes. Eventually I was filled with a strange peacefulness. I think he'd been waiting for this, for only then did he speak.

"'It is not your destiny to go to war. Your wife is pregnant, though she doesn't know it yet. Your first-born will be a girl, a lovely girl. She'll bring you great joy and, like all of us, she has a destiny to fulfill. You'll have three more children and must care for your family. Not only must you provide for their physical needs; you must also nurture them with a loving heart. That love is the gift required of you in this lifetime. Like a pure well, it is not to be contaminated with bitterness and hatred. Do you understand?'

"He'd spoken quietly and, in the silence, his words touched my heart. I did understand. In that moment I saw that only love and understanding could end hatred and the terrible bloodshed of war. As if reading my mind, he said softly, 'We're all brothers, all children of the Exalted One. Even the Israelis: there are no exceptions.'

"The next evening, before he left, we gathered as we had the night he came. 'Suffering comes from wanting things to be other than they are,' he said. 'It is Consciousness Itself, that gave us birth; it is that which brought us together. Each of us is part of a great cosmic dance about which we know very little. Everything unfolds in its own way, in its own time. Out of the all-encompassing silence the divine dream emerges, and like the characters in a play each of us must play a part.'

"Then he said, 'I'll not see you again. One day I'll meet your daughter by the well. When she tells you of our meeting, as she will, tell her of these events. After we meet, a new stage in your lives will come to pass. No matter what happens, never forget that you are deeply loved by some who walk the earth today and some not yet born.' Then Nasir stood and embraced us. I walked with him as far as the well and watched him disappear into the hills.

"A week later a man called Aziz arrived with three donkeys loaded with tiles for the roof. Two goats accompanied him and two chickens rode on the donkey's backs. Nasir had sent him. He stayed with us for several weeks and by the time he left the house was all but finished."

Now, as Samara approached the well, her mind was in turmoil. She felt as if the very stability of the world she'd known was threatened. How could Nasir know the things he knew? She looked up and saw him walking to meet her. Reaching her, he took her hands and looked into her eyes. The turmoil subsided.

Boston University

Tremaine flew to Boston to meet Howard before giving a talk in the evening at Marsh Chapel. It was three o'clock on a sunny afternoon when the car pulled to a stop in front of the university. Tremaine and two agents walked quickly through a crowd of students and into the building. No one recognized him. He went straight to Howard's office.

Tremaine and Howard sat across from each other in comfortable leather chairs, two steaming mugs on the table between them. The smell of fresh coffee permeated the brightly lit space. In one corner a large wooden desk occupied a spacious alcove, while next to it a wall of glass framed the Charles River as it slipped silently to the sea. A red scull with a single rower sliced the calm surface of the river heading upstream. Tremaine was pleased to be with his old friend and former professor. Howard's eyes, alert and soft, held a touch of irrepressible humor. His short hair was white, but he was as slim now as in 1967 when they first met.

"When someone canoes down an unfamiliar river, he must be alert and thoroughly aware," Howard was saying. "It's foolish to blindly hope things will be fine. Waterfalls are dangerous. Global warming is a large and dangerous waterfall and I'm afraid we're asleep in the canoe."

"So how do we wake the sleeper?"

"There's a story I heard many years ago," Howard said. "People were at a party and the room was filled with the sound of voices and laughter. A fire burned in the fireplace and in the centre of the room stood a large glass coffee table with dangerously sharp edges. From time to time guests bumped into the table and cut their shins. They seemed strangely unaware of what had happened. Some tried to steer them away only to be pushed roughly aside." Howard paused and took a long sip of coffee.

"They must have been sleepwalking."

Howard laughed. "You stole my punch line."

"People don't want to be woken up."

"You're right, and as with Socrates and Christ, there can be unpleasant consequences for those who try. Normally I wouldn't advocate waking people up but in this instance it seems the danger of doing nothing exceeds the risk of action. Global warming could render our planet uninhabitable. The sleeper must wake up."

Tremaine watched as a small sailing dingy came about, narrowly missing one of the sculls. "How do we wake people up, that's the question. There's a Zen story I think points in the right direction. 'A man went fishing and caught a fish. The fish was so small he threw it back in the water, and for the first time in its life the fish realized it had been swimming in something.'"

A smile spread slowly across Howard's face. The two men sat quietly and watched the sculls and sailboat on the river.

"The students are the key," Howard said, breaking the silence. "There are brilliant minds out there, and many still open. Students want to learn, to understand. Their minds are not yet closed by life; they haven't fallen asleep."

Again, silence ensued as the two men sipped their coffee.

"Your talk this evening is about green energy and self sufficiency?"

"Mainly. I want to talk briefly about the power of large corporations and lobbyists, which is manipulating the media and eroding our democracy. But the environment is at the forefront. I want America to be a global leader in green energy technology and green manufacturing. I think the majority of Americans want the same thing."

"What about the use of Canadian oil? It's touted as a secure source of energy."

"Oil from Alberta's tar sands?"

Howard nodded.

"At what cost to the environment? And it's certainly not as secure as generating energy ourselves. No one has exclusive rights to the sun, wind, or tides. We'll not be dependent on anyone but ourselves."

"When war broke out in 1939," Howard said, "British industry changed quickly. They had to make tanks instead of cars. We have to take the same kind of urgent action to produce green energy."

He glanced at his watch. "Rose is expecting us for supper at five. I'll take you to the chapel afterwards."

"I've company with me," Tremaine said, nodding toward the door, and the secret service agents on the other side.

"I thought you might, so Rose is making extra. How many are there?" Howard asked.

Tremaine kept a straight face. "The last time I counted there were about twenty."

"What?" Howard was startled. "Twenty?"

Tremaine relented, laughing. "I only brought two with me."

Beyond the window two eight-man sculls were challenging each other. The wind had come up, making the river choppy. The sailing dingy was heeled over as far as it could go.

"I think we've lost the ability to dream," Tremaine said, "to imagine possibilities."

"That may be true but perhaps it's because the problem of global warming seems almost too frightening for us to contemplate, too complex. We're afraid things have spun out of control, beyond our power to do anything. We want government to intervene and have forgotten government is made up of people like us. We've closed our eyes hoping things will work out.

"You and I have been fortunate enough to live and work among students, so we know the importance of open minds and the ability to reason, to think for ourselves. It is that characteristic that makes students so important.

Tremaine looked at his professor. He remembered the same inevitable logic when he sat in his lectures so many years ago. What he'd mistaken then for a childlike innocence he now understood as the 'beginners mind,' something prized by all Zen masters: a mind uncluttered by preconceptions.

Howard stood up and put the mugs on a tray. "Time to go," he said.

After supper the four men drove to the university and entered the chapel from the rear. An arched corridor joined it to the School of Theology on one side and the School of Philosophy on the other. A most appropriate arrangement, Tremaine had always thought. Designed in the tradition of European churches, it had stained glass windows and high Gothic arches.

Tremaine looked over a sea of faces as Dr. Menzies, the President of the University, began to introduce him. Floodlights lit the stained glass in brilliant colors and gave the building a festive air. Was that a hint of sandalwood he smelled, or was it part of a memory from another time, another world? He hadn't been at the university for thirty years.

On October 7th, 1968 at 5:15 in the morning, he'd awakened to the urgent tolling of chapel bells. He flew down the stairs and into the cool night. Police cars lined the deserted avenue in front of the chapel and in the open quadrangle in front of it, more than a dozen unmarked cars were parked haphazardly, some with their doors still open. A small crowd clustered around the entrance to the chapel. Sprinting across the empty street, he pushed his way to the top of the steps. Light spilled through the open doors. Blocking the entrance were members of "Boston's Finest."

The chapel was packed and a woman's quiet sobbing hung in the tense silence. The center aisle was clear and at the end of each pew federal marshals blocked the way. Tremaine watched as three agents emerged from the stairs behind the altar. They half-lifted and half-dragged a young man down the aisle toward the open doors. It was Charles, the soldier to whom Tremaine and four other students had offered the sanctuary of the church. Charles' shirt was torn and a shoe was missing. One of the marshals held him by the hair, pulling his head back. Two more flanked him, holding his arms pinioned, fingers forced back as if they would break. Their faces were flushed with exertion. Charles' black, neatly cropped mustache and hair accentuated the pallor of his face. His dark eyes were large and frightened. A woman's voice began singing "We shall overcome," and more than a thousand voices joined in. The entrance was cleared and Charles was quickly propelled down the steps and forced into the back of a waiting car. Quickly police and marshals filed from the chapel. In moments their cars roared to life and sped into the night, tires screeching.

It was over in minutes. The refrain of the song filled the air and joined with the tolling bells. For five days Charles had sought sanctuary in the church, refusing to join his unit scheduled for Vietnam. He didn't believe in killing. Tremaine and his fellow students, in the tradition of the medieval church, had taken it upon themselves to grant him sanctuary in the university chapel.

Dr. Menzies concluded his introductory remarks and gestured Tremaine to the podium. "Please welcome Dr. David Tremaine, President of the United States." Thunderous applause filled the chapel. With a jolt, Tremaine returned to the present and walked to the podium.

It was well past midnight when the chapel emptied and Tremaine and Howard walked to the car. Howard turned and extended his hand to his friend. "Thank you," he said, "It was as though someone had breached a giant dam. I feel a sense of hope, something I've not felt since the time we set out to end the Vietnam War. The young people are the key. Without them it's not possible."

Swept Away

"They've told you, haven't they?" Nasir asked gently. Samara nodded.

"Come and sit down," he said, leading her to the side of the well.

They sat across from each other, and again she felt the peacefulness in his eyes.

"Who are you?" she asked.

He smiled. "Just a friend."

"How did you know my parents were in danger? How did you know my mother was pregnant with me before she knew? It's not possible, the world doesn't work that way."

"You're right, it doesn't work that way," he agreed.

"But it did, it worked with my parents. How did you know?"

"Sometimes it just happens. Surely you've known things at times and not known how?"

"Do you know anything about me, Nasir?"

"Some things."

"What?"

"That you're a kind and generous person and probably a good cook." He rubbed his nose to hide a smile.

"Nasir, you know what I mean. Tell me, please."

"One day you'll leave your home."

"Of course I will, Nasir. Anyone would know that."

"One day you'll leave your home. You'll leave the ocean here to live beside another one on the other side of the world. Your home there will reflect the peace that comes on the other side of suffering."

"How do you know this?"

"I can't explain it."

Samara was quiet, not knowing whether to take him seriously or not.

"Who knows, Samara, maybe you'll go to the other side of the world, maybe you won't. You'll find out."

Samara watched the sheep as they grazed in the mouth of the valley. She didn't know what to think.

"Samara, these things aren't important. What happens in life, happens. We call it the will of Allah; but it's a poor description, because all there is and all that happens in life is the expression of the divine, in the world of form: hills and trees, suns and moons, rivers, rocks and people."

"Do you have regrets, Nasir? Do you wish you'd done some things differently?"

"When you live in the moment, here, right now, there are no regrets for what might have been. Enjoy the present, Samara. Be thankful for the past as the tree is thankful for the seed that gave it life, for the winds that caressed it and the waters that quenched its thirst."

They watched rays of the sinking sun paint the side of the valley in burnished gold.

"Let's fill the pots so you can make it home by dark," Nasir told her in his soft voice.

He walked with her to the top of the hill, carrying her yoke.

Carefully he set the pots down and stood looking at her. "Have a good evening," he said. "Give my greetings to your parents."

When she got home, Samara gave her parents Nasir's message. She hugged her brothers and her sister as she put them to bed.

She sat for a long time with her parents at the table that night. The certainty with which she'd viewed life was shaken; the world had become a mystery. The light from the lamp cast a warm glow and helped ease the uncertainty lodged in the back of her mind. She kissed her parents and went to bed. Outside a bright moon cast a tapestry of shadows across the uneven ground. In the silence, she could hear the sound of the poplars, their leaves stirred by a vagrant breeze. She'd grown up here, and she loved the isolation.

In the morning, she got up early and helped prepare breakfast. Her father arrived with milk from the goats, just as breakfast was ready.

By mid-afternoon the heat was intense, and they napped. When Samara awoke, it was already late. Her mother was baking bread for supper. Samara splashed water on her face and emptied the pots, ready to go for water.

Kissing her mother, she set out, the pots swaying as she walked. She turned away from the shore and headed into the hills. At the top of the incline she looked back at her home with its whitewashed walls and orange-tiled roof. Nestled in the convergence of low hills it was surrounded by stands of trees, gardens, and the sparkling blue ocean.

Her eye caught a movement on the hill above her home. She saw a cloud of dust. As she listened, she heard the sound of a revving engine. Something was moving fast. Then she saw it: a military jeep with four men inside. With a squeal of brakes, it pulled up beside the house. Above the ocean, two jets screamed inland. They came in low, guns blazing. She saw flashes of flame from their wings. In horror she watched her father racing up the shallow valley from the fishing boat. She saw the puffs raised by bullets hitting the dirt and watched helplessly as they reached him and cut him down, his body jerking with each impact. The strangers dived behind their jeep.

As if in slow motion, she saw a rocket detach from the belly of the lead jet. Trailing fire, it slammed into her home with a loud explosion and burst of flame. The roar was deafening; the concussion from the explosion knocked her down. Her ears were ringing as she pulled herself to her feet. The warplanes were gone. All that was left was the thunderous roar from their engines, the twisted frame of the jeep and the smoldering rubble where her home once stood.

She saw two more jeeps coming down the hill. When they reached the ruins of her home, four men jumped out carrying rocket launchers and hid among the trees. She watched for a few minutes, terrified. Then, with a deafening rush, small rockets lifted into the air. Streaming flame behind them, they vanished beyond the hills.

She picked herself up and ran as fast as she could. As she started up the steep incline, she saw Nasir coming toward her. She flung herself into his arms, sobbing uncontrollably.

“Are you all right?” he asked, looking her over. Then he held her tightly.

Halal

A cold wind came roaring out of the northeast, sweeping ashore. It was the first storm of the season. By early afternoon it had dropped to fitful breezes playing with the leaves of autumn. In mid-afternoon big flakes of snow rocked back and forth like feathers before settling on the ground. Mera put the groceries in the car and walked the short distance to the bakery on Main Street in Camden, Maine. She bought coffee and sat at one of the small tables reading the local paper. When she'd finished she bought a loaf of bread at the counter and turned to go. As she pushed the door open the wind caught it, jerking her into the street.

The snow that had covered the sidewalks a short while ago was gone, whipped sideways by the freshening gale. It covered the northeast side of every lamp post and telephone pole, and the side of Mera's red Toyota Camry. Winter was determined to put an end to autumn, removing all trace of the colored leaves that had lingered in the quiet days of the last week.

Drifts were already plugging the road and she had to punch through them. Snow, flying in every direction, made it even harder to see. When Mera came to the driveway the farm was almost hidden, obscured by nightfall and the driving snow. The light in the yard lit up the house and barn as she approached. She could see Ali had just finished shoveling snow.

He came over and opened the car door for her. She looked at him, his face red and snow frozen to his eyebrows. She loved her grandfather. In his eighties, with a tall lean frame, now slightly stooped, he was still a very active man. He was always helpful, and when her husband Morgan was in Washington, Ali took over the chores.

Arms loaded with groceries, he carried them into the house, stamping the snow off his feet on the porch. "I'll put the car away," he said, "be back in a moment." The door slammed behind him.

Twenty years ago Morgan and Mera had bought this old farm, the kind where the house and the barn were connected by a series of outbuildings. One of them had been a stable and Morgan and Ali had spent a summer converting it into a home for Ali. Over the years Ali had added skylights to it, and large windows on the south side. Mera loved what they'd done. Ali had lived there ever since, his home filled with light.

She heard him on the porch, stamping his feet. He pushed the door open and snow burst past him, vanishing in the heat.

Ali had prepared mushroom risotto. "To warm you up," he said with a laugh. He'd lit a roaring fire in the living room and they ate in front of it. The quiet comfort of each other's presence contrasted with the fury of the blizzard that howled through the eaves of the barn while snow piled up in the swirling yard.

"Grandpa," she said when they finished eating. They were seated in comfortable armchairs on either side of the fire, cradling cups of tea. Light from the fire flickered over their faces. "You told me a long time ago about your son Halal. I was thinking about him the other day. You never told me what happened to him."

Ali had known this day would come. He'd told Mera as a child the stories of his home, the village where he'd lived and the people who'd made up his family. His beautiful bedtime stories were woven together at the edge of sleep whenever he visited his granddaughter. She'd always asked for more and he couldn't turn her down. Years of stories had made him feel like Scheherazade recounting the "One Thousand And One Nights." As long as he could weave their magic Mera had been enchanted and he'd avoided drawing attention to the deaths that a young mind would have difficulty comprehending. "Why do you want to know about it, why now?"

"I'm going there."

"Going where?"

"To visit your village and meet the people who knew you."

"It's changed," he said. "It might not even exist anymore. And as for the people who knew me, they'll be long gone. But why, granddaughter. Why now?"

"I don't know why, it's just time. I loved your stories, I went to sleep and dreamed of the people you talked about. It's as though I know them well—the hills, the towns and the ocean where they lived. Halal and Jalal were my uncles and I don't know what happened to them. And Grandma Natalia, I loved her as well, she was so beautiful and kind. I know they died but I don't know what happened. Now I want to know. Can you tell me?"

Ali sat unmoving and silent. Mera was beginning to think he'd fallen asleep. And then she heard his voice, like a whisper barely audible over the moaning wind. "You're right, Mera, the time has come."

He would never forget the last day he saw his youngest son. "Halal moved to Haifa when he was seventeen. It was over fifty years ago. As a child he was always repairing things and by the time he was thirteen there was nothing he couldn't fix. He was a natural. Bicycles, cars, irrigation pumps; anything! My cousin lived in Haifa and one of his friends, Salman, owned a garage. Business was good, and Salman needed another mechanic. Halal was perfect for the job.

"Salman and his wife Noor took Halal into their home. He was like a son to the childless couple. I got to know them well and Salman and I always found time for coffee whenever I went to town on business."

"What happened to him, Grandpa, when he went to Haifa?"

"He died," he said sadly, "he died."

"I know," she said. "How did he die? What happened?"

Ali wiped the tears from his eyes. After all these years he could still see his son's beloved face when he said goodbye to him that morning at the garage. In the beautiful white harbor city of Haifa in a world forever gone, his son had died.

"He was killed by a car bomb, Mera."

Ali sat still and this time Mera did not rush him but watched his face intently. She loved this courtly old gentleman, her grandfather, the kindest man she knew. How could anyone hurt such a man? she wondered.

Ali's attention had turned to the events forever etched in his mind. "It was October of 1947," he said, "harvest time. Oranges were ripe and we took them to the market in Haifa. An irrigation pump had broken and Halal always repaired the pumps so I took it with me.

"The garage sat back from the road six meters from the sharp face of a hill leading into the mountain behind. The building was made of concrete, open at the front and back, with a flat roof square to the walls. To one side was a gas pump, and on the other a tidy white stone house where Salman and his wife Noor lived.

"It was early evening when I arrived, cool with a fresh breeze coming from the Mediterranean. Noor had prepared a meal and we ate together. Afterward we sat around talking before going to bed.

"The next morning Noor and I sat drinking coffee in the little courtyard at the front of their home. It was a cool cloudless day. Afterwards I went to see how Halal was doing. Maher, the older mechanic, was helping and the three of us chatted as they reassembled the pump. Once his help was no longer needed, Maher went back to the motorcycle he'd been working on.

"Halal had worked for Salman for almost a year, Maher had been with him for fifteen. The older man had seen at once how gifted Halal was and set out to show him everything he knew. Despite their age difference they'd become good friends. As Halal finished the pump we talked about his life in Haifa and a young woman he'd recently been seeing. He'd already met her family. He told me how much he liked them. When he was finished we loaded the pump in the truck and went to find Salman. We found him, a pair of brown bare legs protruding from under a British military jeep. I tapped him with my foot and asked him if he was ready for coffee. He slid from under the jeep and, wiping his hands on an oily rag, turned to Halal and gave him instructions while pointing to an old Austin Seven parked to one side. Someone had used a brush and painted it yellow. Now faded, and the paint chipped, it was covered with dust and innumerable dents. I recognized it as belonging to members of the kibbutz several kilometers away. I mentioned to Halal that perhaps we could meet the young lady he'd spoken of, when he was finished for the day. I can still see him standing there with a big half-shy smile on his face. It was the last time I ever saw him.

"Salman and I walked to the coffee shop, a favorite of ours about ten minutes away. We found seats outside in the courtyard beneath a cluster of low palms. The sun topped the mountains to the east and its warm light flooded the courtyard. I asked Salman what had been happening in the two weeks since I'd been there. I was concerned because I knew tensions had increased between local Palestinians and the new Jewish immigrants, who were arriving by the thousands from all over Europe. The Palestinian Jews, those who'd been our friends and neighbors for years, were not a problem. But the new immigrants were aggressive. They seemed to think they were entitled to the land and we were trespassing on it.

"Salman was worried. He told me that two weeks earlier, just after my last visit, things had suddenly taken a more sinister tone. One night some tires were stolen from the garage and the next night, sometime after midnight, he'd heard a muffled thump and when he looked outside a small fire was burning near one of the trucks parked in the yard. He went out to see what it was and found a burning tire on the ground. It was late, quite late, people had gone to bed. He was just going back in the house when he heard a sharp whistle from somewhere in the darkness up the slope. He looked up in time to see what looked like balls of fire bouncing down the hill. He counted seven and watched as they launched into space from the cliff behind his home, landing in the yard amongst the trucks and cars waiting to be worked on. The balls of fire turned out to be the tires stolen the night before. With help from neighbors they put out the fires before serious damage was done.

"I asked Salman who he thought was doing it. He said he didn't know for sure, couldn't prove anything, but since the flaming tires had come from farther up the hill, he suspected the Jewish immigrants who lived higher in the hills.

"This was just the beginning, he told me. Things got worse. A week later he was repairing some pumps for one of the new Jewish settlements to the east. He'd promised to deliver them that day but it took him longer than he expected. It was evening when he finished. He wolfed down the meal Noor had made and drove to the settlement. It was dark when he turned up the hill that passed through the centre of a large Palestinian neighborhood. The road was steep and he had to gear down when suddenly just ahead of him the road burst into flame. He could see the fire was coming toward him. He turned quickly and pulled over on a small dirt road lined with houses just off the main street. As he pushed the door open he heard people shouting. He ran to join them. When he arrived, some were trying to smother the fire with blankets and carpets, others threw buckets of water on it." Ali paused for a moment and took a long sip of tea. Firelight flickered in the cosy room and wind howled outside.

"A river of gasoline and oil which had flowed down the hill towards the Palestinian homes had been set alight. The fire had ignited the tar in the road and the heat was getting intense. We heard rifle shots and a young lad beside me was hit in the shoulder. I pulled him to safety but a few moments later one of the women with us was killed. Every time we approached the fire more shots rang out. We were forced to watch as the fire spread to two of the homes. Fortunately, it was a calm night with no wind to fan the flames or it could have been much worse. By morning two more houses and a truck had burned.

“Someone was sent to the British garrison at the docks but no one came until morning. I asked Salman what the British had to say about it.

“He said he didn’t know because he’d left and gone home to Noor, afraid to leave her alone.

“I asked him why the British hadn’t helped. The only thing he could think of was that since they were due to leave they were in the process of disengaging.

“When we finished our coffee we started walking back to the shop. Without warning there was a deafening explosion. The force of it knocked us off our feet and shattered the glass up and down the street. We ran as fast as we could and when we rounded the bend we could see a dark cloud lifting into a blue sky. The garage was gone, as was Salman’s home. The force of the explosion had lifted the trucks in the yard and thrown them into the road.

“I talked with Maher shortly afterwards. He’d been working on a bulldozer. He told me that when Halal had finished the Jeep he drove the Austin into the shop. A few moments later he heard him yelling, ‘Get away, get away.’ Then there was a blinding flash and a deafening roar. The bulldozer took the brunt of the explosion and saved Maher’s life. But the blast killed Halal, as well as Salman’s wife.”

“Did you find Halal’s body, Grandpa?”

Ali, suddenly aware of where he was, looked at the shocked face of his granddaughter. Tears were in her eyes.

“No, Mera,” Ali said quietly. “We looked but there was nothing left. Nothing left to bury. He was too close to the explosion.”

Into the mountains

"We must leave quickly," Nasir said. "Come." He turned and headed back along the trail into the hills. Samara followed. She felt dazed, unable to comprehend what had happened. As they came to the top of the incline, she heard the frightening sound of rockets passing overhead.

"We must stay away from the guerillas, not attract their attention." Nasir turned toward her, making sure she heard him above the noise. She nodded. As they passed the springs she noted absently that the flock was gone.

Nasir was moving fast, and she struggled to keep up with him. Finally, they came to a valley leading toward the peaks of the mountains to the northeast. The going was rough, and she could tell by the lengthening shadows it was almost evening. For an hour they climbed steadily.

Above her labored breathing, she heard the sound of gunfire somewhere behind them. She turned to look; Nasir grabbed her by the hand and pulled her toward an outcropping of rocks and stunted oak. She scrambled as fast as she could. At last they reached the protection of the rocks.

Out of breath and lying flat, she looked down in time to see two jets far below glinting in the rays from the setting sun. Hugging the hills, they streaked toward them. In the failing light she saw flashes of fire from the guns on their wings.

The jets were firing at someone further down on the same trail she and Nasir had followed. As they watched, one of the jets exploded in a huge ball of flame. A moment later they heard the explosion and watched pieces of flaming wreckage tumble lazily through the air. The remaining warplane peeled off, and at high speed turned back on its prey. Guns blazed long beads of brightness in the enveloping darkness. Then, as quickly as they'd come, the remaining aircraft was gone. Only silence remained.

Samara and Nasir looked in the direction from which the jets had come. In the distance to the west, a light winked on and off. Above them, a ridge of mountains formed a black silhouette against a carpet of stars. Suddenly three bright lights lifted out of the darkness and arched across the night sky to disappear over a ridge.

"What was that?" Samara whispered.

"Rockets being fired into Israel. Come," he said, "we must be far away by morning. If the planes catch us in the open we won't stand a chance." Nasir knew that in the last six months well armed fighters had arrived from Iran bringing with them hand held surface to air missiles. These had recently been used to attack Israeli jets sent out to destroy rockets being fired into Israel. Samara's family must have been caught in the crossfire when Israeli jets had tracked the jeeps to her home.

Changes

Air Force One leveled off on its short jump from Boston to Washington. David made himself comfortable in the plush leather seat and closed his eyes. He cast his mind back to the events that had brought him to this unlikely position.

For twelve years the Republicans had held the White House and it was assumed they'd continue to do so. No Democratic challenger had been eager to risk the expense, and his reputation, on what seemed like certain defeat.

Richard Emerson, a senior professor at Harvard, was persuaded to stand as the Democratic candidate. It was thought he'd make a good opposition leader, someone who could hold the government to account.

Emerson's choice of Tremaine, a professor of philosophy at a small university in the state of Washington, as his running mate unleashed a firestorm of controversy over both Tremaine's qualifications for such high office and his opposition, in his youth, to the Vietnam War. In both headlines and editorials, Tremaine was described by the Republicans as a traitor, someone unfit to serve. He'd offered to withdraw, but Emerson wouldn't hear of it.

Early in the campaign, Tremaine had been asked

to meet with a group of high-ranking Democrats to answer questions. The meeting included representatives from the youth wing of the Democratic party and took place at a conference hall in Bethesda, Maryland.

The meeting started promptly at ten in the morning with a brief introduction by Emerson.

"I've known Dr. Tremaine for many years and I can't think of anyone else I'd rather work with. He has a clear mind and his expertise and experience would be invaluable. I was very pleased when he accepted my invitation to run.

"Certain members of the press as well as a number of you here today have expressed your concerns over my selection. Rather than trying to explain Dr. Tremaine's views, I thought it better that you have a chance to raise those concerns with him directly. This will give you a sense of the man for yourselves." Emerson took his seat and the questions began.

"It's been reported you had an affair with another woman during your first marriage, which suggests dishonesty on your part. How can we be sure you'll be honest should you be elected?"

"You can't be sure. There's no way I can make you sure. All you can do is see, over time, if my words match my actions. I did have an affair, and as you mentioned it was dishonest on my part. I hurt my wife at the time, as well as myself and the woman with whom I had the affair."

There was a murmur in the crowd. His simple acceptance of responsibility for what he'd done was a surprise.

"Yes, over here," Tremaine pointed to a well-dressed young woman to his left.

"There are those who would argue that you're a poor role model. Having an affair and going through a divorce is hardly a ringing example to follow. After all, the President and Vice President are people we look up to in our society."

"There are people who are divorced and live honorable lives; there are those who are divorced and don't. There are those who stay in marriages when it might have been better to leave. My marriage is blessed with friendship, companionship and love, something I wouldn't change for the world."

"Newspapers report you've taken drugs. Is it true?" The question came from a young man in the front row.

"It's true. I have."

"Isn't your use of drugs a bad example for others, particularly young people, caught up in drugs such as crystal meth, cocaine and heroin?"

"This is an important question. The abuse of a drug, any drug is a problem, including those our physicians prescribe. Drugs are helpful and harmful, that is a fact. I have not taken the drugs you mentioned. Let me describe what happened. In the early sixties, Professors Timothy Leary and Richard Alpert were engaged in LSD research at Harvard. Their research was based on the work of two Swiss chemists, Stoll and Hoffman, who first discovered LSD in 1938.

"I was exploring Western philosophers, and the wisdom traditions of the East. I was intrigued by the Hawaiian kahunas and Toltec shamans of Mexico. It was with the latter that I first came in contact with peyote and ayahuasca. While in India I discovered hashish and from time to time sat for days on a village wall with holy men where a hash pipe made occasional but regular appearances. This intense period of exploration continued for a dozen years.

"The drug experiences opened my eyes much as psychedelics

had for Aldous Huxley. He speaks of it in the book, *The Doors of Perception*, with which I'm sure some of you are familiar. These drug experiences took place at the same time as the Vietnam war. Vietnamese Buddhist monks began to immolate themselves in the streets of Saigon in an attempt to draw attention to what was happening in America's name. What moved them to take their lives in such a painful way? With those acts the monks wove together the strands of war, suffering, death, peace, wisdom and life. These things were uppermost in my mind during LSD experiences in the countryside outside Boston in the summer of sixty-five.

"Under the influence of the psychedelics, the reading I was doing, and the people I met, I came to understand how the description of the world was held together by subtle agreements we shared. In psychological terms, these accepted interlocking agreements are made of commonly held beliefs.

"Each culture has its own set of beliefs, which determine our approach to life. Cultures differ to some degree, yet there is a core of beliefs common to all human beings. All of these beliefs, however, remain largely hidden. All perception, the simple seeing of the reality around us, even our perception of ourselves, is filtered through those beliefs. As a result these beliefs exercise almost total control over human perceptual and conceptual processes.

"Several examples come readily to mind. The belief that slaves were somehow inferior justified the right of one group to enslave another. The same thing occurred in Hitler's Germany toward the Jews and today takes place in Israel toward the Palestinians. When beliefs like this are brought into the open they eventually dissolve in the light of understanding.

"Such beliefs are never brought into question, however, until we're aware of them. How then, do we become aware of them? That is where the influence of psychedelic drugs helps to open our minds. Yet it would seem life has also provided for that need through the wisdom of the sages, people like Lao Tzu, Buddha and Christ." Tremaine took a sip of water.

The silence was interrupted by the rustle of a small group who made a noisy show of leaving.

"Are you not worried about alienating a large proportion of conservative Christian and Jewish voters?"

Tremaine turned toward a short stocky man sitting to his left. "You think perhaps I should be worried?" he asked with a smile, in acknowledgment of those who'd just left.

"I think so."

"Maybe, but I suspect there's a growing population who've already moved beyond the narrow confines of religion. The killing, suffering, hostility and war caused by religion is the primary reason why the Founding Fathers enshrined the separation of church and state. Religion has not made our country the promised land. Many are convinced their beliefs are the only ones that are true, that their God is the only true God, and they are prepared to use violence to enforce that belief. Islam and Christianity may share the same God but that doesn't prevent them from fighting each other."

Tremaine smiled. "Over there." He pointed to a bald-headed elderly gentleman with a white goatee.

"I was a professor at Boston University in the late sixties and, if I recall correctly, you were one of the anti-war student leaders at the time."

"That's right."

“Five of you took over the chapel and offered sanctuary to a deserting soldier. I’ve read some of the articles you wrote at the time and you strongly opposed the war in Vietnam. You advocated resistance to the draft, and desertion by soldiers. If you were President, and thus Commander-in-Chief, what would you do if a young man refused to follow your orders and go to war?”

“Good question.” Tremaine paused for a moment. “First of all, I’d have to be convinced that war was the only option. But, if events arose as they did with Hitler’s Germany, for example, I’d talk to the people, explain what was taking place and ask for their help. Those not prepared to fight would have to help in some other way; as a medic, ambulance driver, or in some form of civil service.

“In fact one of the things Emerson and I discussed at some length was the implementation of a system of national service for all young people. The options would be to serve in the military, the Peace Corps or perhaps, VISTA or similar programs geared to be of help here at home. The general idea would be to foster awareness of service and the joy, yes joy, that comes with it.”

The meeting continued for another hour and when the questions shifted from the personal to the platform, Emerson joined Tremaine. The two of them were able to lay before the committee the platform on which they were going to run.

Later, when they left the meeting, Emerson shook his head. “Well,” he said, “I don’t think the Founding Fathers would ever have envisaged a candidate speaking to a political party on the benefits of LSD. I wonder what we’re unleashing on the American public.”

Tremaine smiled, a tired smile. He wondered as well.

An aid brought him a cup of coffee. He looked at his watch. It was late and he still had more to do when he got back to the

White House. He was tired and perhaps the coffee would help keep him awake. When he finished he set the cup aside, pushed the seat back and closed his eyes. It would be fifteen minutes before they landed.

He found himself remembering the outrage in the conservative press the day after he addressed the Democratic committee. It was the subject of radio talk shows and fodder for TV news pundits. The religious right was incensed; but some, who took time to think about what he said, realized it made sense.

The Republicans subjected Emerson and Tremaine to scathing attacks, attempting to portray them as men bent on undermining family and religious values. The liberal press became less hostile and more curious. They enjoyed the engagements with the Democratic contenders. There was something refreshing about them. Although they seemed to have little hope of winning, they addressed matters of real concern, things other politicians were afraid to touch. They spoke to the concerns of all segments of the population. Still, the general consensus was that they couldn't be elected, so why bother to vote for them?

Six months into the campaign, the Democratic ticket was surprised by the public's discomfort with the Republican Administration, which tried to deflect attention from the CIA scandal in Nicaragua. However, as more information emerged there were whispers of a possible Republican defeat. Some Democratic presidential hopefuls who'd held back regretted not entering the race.

When the Nicaraguan government collapsed in scandal two weeks before the election, few thought much of it. The election, which initially had stirred only minimal interest among voters, had been largely written off by the press as nothing more than a quixotic tilt at the windmills of power. But as revelations from Nicaragua spilled into the papers and dominated the news, the administration's duplicity galvanized the electorate.

Following hard on the heels of this embarrassment, came the hedge fund scandals where hundreds of thousands lost their savings and pension funds were decimated. It appeared that several high-ranking members of the Republican Party had made hefty profits from early trading before the scandal broke. The cost to the country, it turned out, was enormous in both reputation and finances. The Republicans lost the election. Tremaine thought it was probably the scandals that defeated the Republicans, rather than the platform he and Emerson outlined.

The fact was, however, they did have a platform and had campaigned hard and skillfully. They'd examined the current state of government, and given a great deal of thought to domestic and foreign policy as well as the looming environmental crisis—which, it seemed, no one else wished to address. Emerson had, in his own unique way, injected the simple values of common sense, decency and accountability into the campaign.

Since the election, the Democratic administration had worked to restore the integrity of government. At the beginning of the term, they'd faced a constant barrage of criticism that verged on contempt, most of it emanating from a cynical conservative press and the disgraced opposition—after all, both Emerson and Tremaine were political neophytes, academics out of their depth and unfamiliar with the "real" world of politics.

Under Emerson's leadership they began an ongoing conversation with the American people. They understood that in order to bring the changes they envisioned there would have to be a shift from polarized politics and sound bite clichés, to well-reasoned policies that people could understand. Neither the House nor Senate would pass constructive legislation without the collective will of an informed electorate. Emerson implemented a weekly televised version of Roosevelt's fireside chats during which he engaged in a national dialogue on the direction the administration wished to go and the policies and legislation that would have to be implemented. He wanted the populace to be fully aware of the difficulties the country faced and the opportunities that arose from facing these challenges head-on.

He called for the best in people and gradually they responded—tentatively at first but increasingly as they came to trust him. He never considered himself better than others. He was always a good listener, polite, respectful and hard-working. He presented his views in a language easily understood.

Not once had the President and Vice President avoided issues; never had they glossed over difficulties. They were always honest. Tremaine had watched a shift taking place. He saw more and more people had come to respect and appreciate Emerson, even though they didn't always agree with him. They knew, however, that he always spoke truthfully, whether they liked what they heard or not. By quiet example, President Emerson had demonstrated what people could accomplish. They perceived him as someone like themselves, and so they trusted him.

Then suddenly, surprisingly, nine months into his first term, the President was found to have an aggressive and untreatable form of cancer. Tremaine and Emerson discussed what to do after his death. They talked about the environmental crisis, and the influence on foreign policy of powerful groups with a vested interest in maintaining the current incendiary situation in the Middle East.

The end came quickly. Tremaine was called to Emerson's bedside at three in the morning. Emerson looked tired, and it was obvious he was dying.

"David," he whispered, "keep an eye on Lacy and the girls for me."

Tremaine nodded in silent acquiescence, deeply moved. He would miss his friend. As he left, Lacy and the girls entered and the door closed quietly behind them. Lacy told him later that just before dawn, her husband had slipped into unconsciousness and died.

There was a subtle change to the engines as they were throttled back and the plane banked on its approach to Andrews Air Force Base. As they prepared to land, Tremaine thought of the conversations he'd had with Emerson and Kersey the Secretary of State concerning the Middle East.

Haifa

Spring had come suddenly. One week it had been cold with heavy snow, and two weeks later the snow was gone and the dormant plants of winter pushed through the earth in search of the sun. Coaxed into the world of the living, they thrust upward, frantic for life which they somehow sensed was all too brief. Mera and Ali strolled along the docks in Camden, warmed by a sun in a cloudless sky, while a cold wind came sweeping off the Atlantic.

The river flowed beneath the bakery on Main Street, spilling over the weir, and rushed, white foam flying, toward the harbor, where it slowed into a muddy stain pushing against the green incoming tide. It was almost a year since the death of her son, Ted.

They sat on a bench, with the river behind them and the harbor in front. "Tell me," Mera said to Ali, "what happened in Haifa?" The death of Ted had brought home the delicate balance between life and death, and perhaps because of it, she'd probed with more urgency into the deeper layers of her grandfather's story.

"Haifa?"

"Yes, Haifa, Grandpa."

"All right, little one."

She smiled at Ali's use of the phrase. It was what he'd always called her as a small girl, and even now as a woman approaching fifty, he still thought of her as the little one. She watched the subtle change come over him when he opened the door into the past. Somehow he seemed to soften and the quality of his voice became devoid of emotion as though describing events from a great distance.

"We arrived at Haifa just before dawn. More than a hundred of us had traveled all night to escape the carnage and destruction of the attack on our village. We looked over the city shrouded in darkness except for the lights around the market and the harbor, which gave it a warm and friendly appearance. We were exhausted and in shock. Loudspeakers blared somewhere below but we couldn't hear what was being said. We made our way toward the town. It was early in the morning as we approached the harbor. Roads were choked with refugees. Arab leaders directed us, loudspeakers in hand, to the old marketplace near the harbor.

"Moving streams of people became more densely packed. Children were crying, some carried by their parents, some by older siblings; still others clung to their parents' clothing. Many of the children and some adults stared blankly unseeing, in a state of shock. People had slept on the ground, wherever they could find room. Most of them had been there all night, some longer. As the crowd grew, the crush of people forced them to stand and make room.

"The first rays of sunlight burst over the hills to the east and flooded the market and harbor with light. Suddenly the noisy mass of humanity went quiet. Loud amplified shouts came from high up the slopes in the direction from which we'd come. Waves of humanity poured down the side of the mountain. Like a river that had broken its banks it flowed around the houses, filling the roads and trails, an unstoppable mass of people driven toward the harbor.

"Someone was shouting over the loudspeaker, 'The Jews are on their way, get out! Get out while you can.' Explosions and smoke rose above houses in the Palestinian quarter.

"The crush of people became so intense it was getting hard to breathe. Nadia and I lost sight of our friends from the village. They'd vanished in the tide of humanity forced into a space no longer able to hold everyone. Some had climbed into the trees that lined the roads and the square. A lone policeman stood nervously behind the gate to the harbor, the crowd now straining against the fence.

"Then came the sound of mortars. They were being fired from a ridge in the hills and fell just at the back edge of the crowd, driving them toward us. Women, children and the elderly died underfoot in the ensuing panic. Somehow Nadia and I were able to withstand the pressure and stay together. We were being pushed toward the harbor gate when it gave way and thousands surged through, trying to escape the mortar rounds that came ever closer.

"Propelled by the great thrust of the crowd, we broke free and ran for the boats. Somehow we managed to board an old sailing hull with a battered sail of little use. The big single-cylinder motor had been started and we found ourselves with a chugging sound nosing toward the outer harbor and open water. Not another person could have got aboard. There were so many boats we could have walked from one side of the harbor to the other. People hung over the rope railings and with their feet tried to fend off the boats that crowded us. Mortar shells were now landing in the market. Terrified people trampled each other. Some were pushed and others leapt into the water, which was filled with boats and people trying to swim. Some landed in the overloaded boats, others on top of the swimmers, and some on the bodies that were now floating everywhere. We escaped only through the will of Allah. It was not our time to die. Once out of the harbor, we were part of a huge flotilla heading for the fortress city of Acre across the bay to the northeast.

"It was late afternoon by the time we approached the beach just south of Acre. We were so badly overloaded it had taken us eight hours. During the crossing we lost a number of people, who'd died from their wounds. We had no medical supplies, no food and no water.

"We went ashore just south of the city. Palestinians from Acre thronged the beach to help bring people to safety. Coordinating as best they could were the young men, members of the Arab League."

As Ali described the horror of Haifa, Mera found herself looking at the harbor in front of her, crowded with boats and the docks that stretched like fingers into the bay. She tried to imagine the same events taking place here. This peaceful idyllic place she loved, choked with boats and panicked people and the explosions coming ever closer, signaling the approach of death.

The water spilled over the weir behind her, tumbling to the sea, while the halyards of the sailboats slapped in the sharp wind. She reached over and took Ali's hand.

The cave

Samara was exhausted by the time dawn approached. She was following Nasir down a steep ravine into a dark valley when she slipped in loose shale. Nasir caught her before she vanished over the edge. She was trembling.

"Not much farther," he promised.

She looked at him in the subdued light and saw the exhaustion in his face. She got to her feet, and they continued. When they reached the valley floor, the going was easier until they came to a steep rock face.

Carefully, Nasir climbed a goat trail that angled up the side of the wall. In the faint light of dawn, she saw it disappear into a sharply inclined ravine a hundred meters above them.

She worked her way up the trail until she reached the ravine. Nasir was waiting for her. She stopped to catch her breath. The valley floor was lost in shadow, while the grasses on the rim swayed golden in the light of the rising sun.

Samara turned to follow Nasir, but he was nowhere to be seen. She looked up the ravine to a cluster of giant boulders. As she approached, she saw him sitting in the shadows, his back against the cliff.

"We've made it," he said.

She looked around. "Where will we stay?"

"Up there." He pointed.

All she could see were more boulders rising thirty meters above her.

"Come," he said. Jumping from rock to rock, he worked his way up the tumbled boulders. She followed, careful not to fall into the cracks.

Nasir lowered himself through an opening and she followed. She climbed down a steep tunnel that led into a large cave. Light entered indirectly from several shafts at the back. Sheepskins were spread on the floor around a circle of firestones. Leather water-skins hung on poles, and cooking utensils had been placed on a ledge. On one side of the cave were two sleeping pallets with woven blankets.

"Welcome to my summer home." Nasir smiled at her. "We're safe here; it's not easy to find. There's a spring over there." He pointed to the back of the cave, where she could hear the sound of trickling water. "If you want, you can wash. I'll get us something to eat, and then you can rest." Samara went to wash and when she returned Nasir handed her a plate of goat cheese, olives, dried apricots, almonds and dates.

They ate in silence. When they finished, Nasir pointed toward one of the sleeping pallets.

"You can take the one over there. I have to go and check on the flock. My brother is with the sheep and expecting me."

"Don't you need to rest?" she asked.

"Once I make it to the flock I'll get some rest, but I need to be off before it's too hot. I'll be back at dusk. Help yourself to food and water, and when you go out stay in the shadows."

She watched him put dried apricots, almonds and dates in a leather bag slung over his shoulder. "I'm sorry to leave you. Sleep well. You'll be safe here. I'll see you when I get back."

Slinging a water-skin over the other shoulder, he disappeared through the opening. She walked over to the pallet and lay down. She felt hopeless, lost and alone. Before long, she fell into an exhausted sleep.

She watched helplessly as an Israeli warplane came directly at her, guns blazing. She awoke with a scream. For a moment, she didn't know where she was. Then the memories came flooding back and she shook with grief. She ached for her family. Vividly etched in her mind were the convulsive movements of her father's body as bullets from the low-flying aircraft struck him. Sorrow and rage alternated in an endless cycle with the images and thoughts in her mind.

She got up and looked around. It was late afternoon. She drank water, found some dried fruit and nuts and took them with her through the entrance. Sitting in the shade against the rocky face, she had a clear view of the valley below.

What could she do? Where would she go? What was to become of her? There were no answers to these questions. Her eye caught a movement far below. She watched as a tiny figure crossed the valley in her direction and disappeared. She waited and eventually Nasir emerged at the lower end of the ravine. She stood and went to greet him.

Ambush

Samara followed Nasir along a narrow trail leading to the rim above the valley. He helped her up, and they climbed higher into the mountain. Darkness had fallen by the time they stopped.

Nasir spread a blanket on a smooth rock and they sat back to back. A warm breeze brought the fragrance of old cedar. Overhead, the great dome of night was studded with millions of winking lights. An hour passed without a word before Nasir finally spoke.

"Talk to me," he said softly.

Immediately her eyes filled with tears. She told him of her day and the thoughts that bedeviled her mind.

"Let the thoughts come," he said. "They cannot be stopped; so watch them as you would a flowing river or clouds passing across an empty sky. You are not the thoughts; they come uninvited. Let them come and... let them go."

"I hate the men who killed my family."

Nasir felt her anguish and understood. They sat quietly for a while.

"In the morning, you'll meet my brother. You'll see there's something wrong with him; he's simple."

"Was he born that way?" she asked.

"No, a man struck him in the head a long time ago. It left him brain-damaged, but he can still work with the sheep. He's content and has no need to be around people. The silence and the mountains are his home."

"What happened to the man who hurt him?"

"My father killed him."

"Was it a long time ago?"

"Yes, the late forties."

"Nasir, what happened? Can you tell me?"

"It's not something I talk about. But what happened to me fifty years ago is almost the same as what happened to you. Things haven't changed much in fifty years. I once told your parents their gift to life was the love they gave their children. It's their legacy to you. They nurtured you with love and wisdom. In this way, they have molded you for what destiny has in store."

Samara was puzzled but said nothing.

Nasir sat quietly for a few minutes. "My family had been shepherds for generations, and the land on which they raised sheep lay in both Palestine and southern Lebanon. After the Second World War, Jewish immigrants flooded into Palestine and as previous settlers had done, bought land wherever they could. We had no idea of the changes about to take place. The British, who'd broken the hold of the Turks, had ruled Palestine for thirty years and were getting ready to leave. Life went on in the villages as it had for generations. My mother and father had three sons: two older brothers, Salim, Amal and myself. Father worked the flocks with my uncle Gabir, who also lived with us. As my brothers and I became old enough, we helped father and uncle tend the sheep. We were sometimes away for days at a time. My mother spent time carding, spinning and weaving, and working with the land. We had a grove of oranges and a lemon tree, as well as olive and almond trees. We lived in a small valley that sloped from the hills and gave way to the Mediterranean, much like the valley where you lived. Behind the house was a sycamore tree and a small stand of poplar.

"We didn't understand at the time, but our home was just inside the northern border of what would become the new Jewish state. One morning I didn't go with the men who were moving the flock higher into the mountains. I was dizzy and felt sick. For two days I stayed on my bed but by the end of the second day, I was feeling better. We expected the men home sometime before dark.

"My mother and I were sitting at the table. We'd finished supper and were talking by the light of the lamp. I loved my mother. She must have been in her mid-forties at the time. Her name was Fatah. She was beautiful and had a lovely warmth about her, dark almond eyes tinged with green, and jet-black hair. We heard a sound outside and were about to get up, thinking the men had returned. The door burst open and four strangers glared at us, rifles leveled. They tied my hands with cord and pushed me into a chair. I was shaking with fear. I looked at my mother. She was shaking too. Then two of the men grabbed her. The third started tearing her clothes off. They raped her in front of me right there on the kitchen floor. When they finished, they dragged us both outside. I saw the vague outline of a military truck and a jeep with more men nearby. I suddenly realized this was one of the armed Jewish gangs that had been attacking outlying Palestinian villages and homes. They had a reputation for brutality.

"We were dragged toward the jeep and watched as gasoline was splashed inside the house before being torched. The surrounding buildings were soon burning as well. The fire lit up the sky. Above the roar of flames I heard shouts coming from the hills. I knew it was the men returning. The Jews heard the shouts, too. All but the four who'd entered the house jumped in the truck and drove away. The soldier holding my mother pulled his gun and, before I realized what was happening, held it to her head and shot her. I managed to loosen the cord around my wrists, and when he turned toward me I charged, knocking him down. The gun spun out of his hand. I dove on it and turned it toward him. He drew his knife and came straight for me. I leveled the gun and fired. He fell on his face in the dirt.

"A shot rang out, and I felt something strike my arm. It burned and spun me around. Lying on the ground, I saw the remaining gang members crouched beside the jeep, their rifles leveled at me. My father and uncle came racing into view, everything illuminated by the flames from the burning house. The men, so concentrated on me, were unaware of the danger behind them. My father and uncle swung their staves at two of the gang, who went down before they could get off a shot. The third man fired, but Salim, charging from behind, spoiled his aim. The rifle jerked out of his grasp. He grabbed it by the barrel and swung it at Salim, hitting him in the head. He hit him several times before my father killed him."

"That's terrible, Nasir."

"We buried my mother and for the next month we nursed Salim back to health. As soon as he was able he went with uncle Gabir to help with the sheep. My brother Amal, my father and I joined with others to defend the land against the Jewish immigrants who seemed determined to take it from us. The Jews were well supplied with weapons but we knew the hills and mountains better than they did. We were just a small band of men, and though there were other groups like ours, the encroachment continued all over Palestine.

"The Jewish settlements grew and as they did the immediate land around them fell under their control. In this and other ways we were driven off the land. We wanted to stop it but could only slow it down.

"One evening, we attacked a convoy delivering supplies to a settlement. We ambushed the trucks in a narrow valley. We'd learned they were carrying rifles and ammunition, a prize worth taking. Some of the Jews were killed in the initial ambush but others managed to escape and dug in against a low cliff, slightly above the valley floor. Each time we tried to get close to the trucks we were hit with machine gun fire.

"We withdrew and waited for darkness before trying again. Once more the machine gun opened fire. We'd have to destroy it. In the early morning we were able to get close enough to lob grenades over the parapet. It was impossible to know how many of the men were still alive.

"When it was light we approached their hiding place and once more the machine gun was brought into play. We were getting concerned that Jewish reinforcements could arrive at any moment, and the longer the fight went on, the more at risk we were. After some discussion it was decided that Jalal and I would work our way into the hill behind them. From there we could enter a ravine running to the left of where they were hiding. If we could get into the ravine without being noticed we could get close enough to wipe them out. The rest of our unit would keep them distracted.

"Shadows had lengthened by the time we reached the place directly above the enemy position. All firing had stopped. There hadn't been any for the past hour.

"From our position we could count six men below us but

couldn't be sure that was all of them. They weren't moving and two of them sprawled at odd angles. Jalal and I made our way into the ravine, following it until we had a clear view. We counted eight men all told. We watched silently for about fifteen minutes but detected no movement. It was a strange experience; an intrusion almost, into a very personal place where men had breathed their last. We could see that some of them were severely dismembered, probably from the grenades.

"While Jalal covered me with his rifle, I moved over the parapet and started checking them. They were all dead. As I stooped to check the last man he suddenly rose to his feet and lurched toward me. In the low sunlight I saw something glint in his hand. When he fell against me I couldn't get my rifle up. Drawing my knife I drove it deep in his gut.

"As he slid to the ground Jalal came up beside me, his rifle still pointed. The wounded man looked to be about twenty. He had red hair and blue eyes. Blood oozed from the wound in his belly, and the side of his face, badly disfigured, was caked with blood. He looked at us, and we at him. He tried to say something and lifted his hand. We jumped back and saw then what had glinted in the low sunlight. He was holding a silver pen and a piece of folded paper. With his eyes he pleaded for me to take it. I reached down and took it from him. When I opened the paper it read:

Dear Mama,

We were ambushed yesterday and most of the men were killed. Some of us survived the attack but were soon pinned down by enemy fire. About an hour before the sun came up grenades hit us. All of us were wounded, and in the heat of this awful day my comrades died. I'll not live to see another day.

I love you and thought of you and Papa at the end. Give Benjamin a hug for me. Tell him to take care of you, and when the time comes, may he be as good a man as he has been a brother to me.

Please tell my beautiful Rachel that I love her and I'm sorry to cause her grief. I wanted only happiness and joy for her. One day, when the sorrow has gone from her heart, may she find love and happiness with someone who will love her as I do.

It's getting harder to write. I watch the sun sink behind these hills in a beautiful glow and know I'm going with it too. I hope this letter finds you. Peace be with you.

Your loving son,

Josef

"I looked down at the dying boy. His eyes pleaded and his lips gurgled blood. I knelt beside him while Jalal moistened his lips from his canteen. Bending closer I whispered in his ear, 'I'll find your family, I'll make sure they get the letter.'

"I straightened up and, looking in his eyes, so blue and so innocent now, I told him how sorry I was. I don't know if he fully understood, but a deep peacefulness seemed to settle over him. Despite our differences, in the face of death each of us was born of the same earth, and though we had different names and came from different places, we were all children of the same God. We sat with him in silence, a comfort in his dying. Then he gripped my arm, breathed deeply, and when his breath went out, it did not return. I removed his identification and closed his eyes."

Decisions

It was late when David returned to the White House from Boston. It felt strange to think of it as home, even a temporary one. He went straight to the bedroom and pushed the door open. Sandra lay propped against the pillows, reading. She sat up and putting the book down patted the bed beside her greeting him with a smile. Sitting beside her, he leaned over and kissed her. She could still make his heart skip a beat when he looked at her.

"How was it?" she asked.

"Good. I don't know why I bother taking notes; I never use them. It was good to be back at a university again, even just for a visit. Students are more open to exploring ideas, their minds not so cluttered."

"How about you?" he asked, "how was your day?"

"It was good, we got a lot done. We finished the living quarters, and of course, I had lots of help. It's hard to get used to having people around all the time. Lacy Emerson was back in Washington to tie up loose ends and stopped for tea before going home."

"How is she, is she okay?"

"It's hard for her. She's glad to be back on the farm again, glad to be out of the White House and the city. She said she keeps expecting Richard to show up. She'll go into the barn and catch a glimpse of him and when she looks again he's not there."

"How about the girls, how are they doing?"

"She says they're all right. A lot of tears. They talk about Emerson and the things they did together. They've been reading his journal, which is filled with his poems. He started writing in the early sixties when he was a graduate student, and wrote the last poem the evening before he died. Lacy said it's like a window on his inner life. He'd read some of the poems to her, but she didn't realize how many he'd actually written. Every evening for the past several weeks, she and the girls have taken turns reading them."

"What a beautiful way to say goodbye. I'm sorry I missed her."

"We talked about living here, in the White House. She told me she and Richard had difficulty getting used to it, and she thought we would too. She felt like she was living in a museum, and at first was afraid to sit on the antique furniture in case she damaged it."

The image of Lacy unable to sit on the furniture brought a smile to David's face. "So how did they get used to living in the museum?"

Sandra looked up and caught the quickly suppressed smile on her husband's face. She laughed. "It is a museum, isn't it? Anyway, she said they insisted on more privacy and changed some of the procedures and protocols. There was a lot of resistance to begin with. The argument they kept getting was, 'This is the way we do things here.' Pushing through this was hard, she said, but they did have some success. She thought things would quickly revert to the old form and we'd have to begin all over again."

"And she was right!"

"You look tired. Are you coming to bed?"

"I wish I could. I'm going to have a shower and I have to do some paperwork for a meeting in the morning. I won't be too long."

She looked around the room. It seemed almost surreal to be in this beautiful and elegant old house. She remembered the day he'd first spoken to her of the remote possibility of becoming president.

One evening she'd arrived home after visiting one of her patients. David had supper ready and they'd eaten at once. He seemed unusually quiet. She asked him if he was okay.

"I'm fine, but we need to talk. I've got something I want to discuss with you. Let's take Murphy for a walk."

Wrapped in warm clothes, they strolled slowly through the leaves of autumn while their black lab went exploring. A rare cloudless night, the stars stretched full across an inky sky.

"I had a call from Richard Emerson this evening. He's going to run for president."

"He is?"

"Yes, he's now the official Democratic candidate."

"Wow. He doesn't stand a chance though, does he?"

"Probably not, but things can change quickly in politics."

"Why does he want to do that? He's still teaching, isn't he?"

"He was."

"Doesn't he want to teach anymore?"

"He loves teaching, but it's one thing to teach in university and quite another to apply that knowledge to the real world of politics."

"But why would he want to do it?"

"I think he's fed up with what he sees in politics today. He knows how democracies are supposed to work, he understands what the Founding Fathers envisioned and he sees how the purpose of democracy—government of the people, by the people, for the people—is being subverted by powerful special interest groups such as big oil, agribusiness, big pharma and the banking industry.

"He said the government is spending more than it brings in. Political parties are afraid that if they raise taxes to meet those costs they might be voted out of office. But they want to stay in office, so how can they meet the expenses of government without raising taxes?"

"By borrowing money?" Sandra chimed in.

"Brilliant idea, let's borrow money, a long-term loan topped up as needed. We don't need to concern ourselves with repayment right now..."

Sandra picked up. "If we're not able to meet the payments we'll just borrow more and we can pass it on to our kids."

"That's the idea. He said it was time someone injected a sense of reality into the election. He's a brilliant thinker, as you know, and a philosopher. He makes sense. I like his ideas. As he said, 'I couldn't find a good reason not to run. I've nothing to lose, so from that perspective I can afford to speak the truth as I see it.'

"We must have talked for a couple of hours. He explained his thinking and asked for mine. 'Show me where I'm wrong,' he said, 'show me any weakness in my reasoning.' It was, to say the least, a stimulating discussion. Anyway, the crux of the matter is that he wants me for his running mate."

"What!" Sandra exclaimed. She stopped so suddenly he almost bumped into her. "You mean he wants you for his Vice President?"

"Yes."

"What did you tell him?"

"I told him I'd think about it and talk it over with you; see what you thought."

They walked in silence for several minutes. Murphy rummaged through the leaves not far away. Above them, through the bare trees, Orion glittered in the cold night sky.

"What do you think, David? Do you want to do it?"

"I'm not sure. I'd have to take a leave of absence from the University and writing would have to go on the back burner for a while. What do you think?"

"I don't know. It's hard to get my head around it. I'll have to think about it too. There's not much chance you guys could really get elected, is there?"

"No, I think our chances aren't very good. But, Sandra, if I accept the offer, we'll be in it to win."

"But you just said you don't think you could win!"

"I don't, but I can't enter the race from that perspective. I'll only accept Emerson's invitation if we're prepared for the possibility that we might live in Washington, D.C., and even the possibility we might live in the White House, some day."

"The White House?"

"Yes. That's one of the eventualities a Vice President must consider. As I said, I'm not expecting it, but the possibility exists. We have to be prepared for the eventuality of winning, and all it might entail. I don't want second thoughts when it's too late."

An owl called softy from somewhere in the dark.

"When the campaign is over, will you go back to teaching?"

"Of course. But Sandra, you need to think about this. We'll have to give up so many things we take for granted: quiet meals in restaurants, movies, walks, even grocery shopping. Cameras will be following your every move; and I know how you love cameras!"

Sandra smiled, realizing that she, like David, had to consider the possibility that he and Professor Emerson might win. Murphy nuzzled her hand with a cold nose and disappeared into the woods again. If they won they'd have to leave their home, and she'd have to leave the Home Health Agency where she worked.

"Give me time. I need to get used to the idea. How long before you have to let Emerson know?"

"A week."

"Okay."

They talked often over the ensuing week and, in the end, David had called Emerson and accepted his invitation. She'd supported him without reservation.

Since then Sandra had watched events unfold. She ached inside for him when the affair he'd had during his first marriage became public. Vitriolic comments by members of the conservative press made her angry. She'd loved the openness with which he faced the crises as they came and the self-deprecating humor that seemed to render his antagonists impotent. She'd even tried not frowning at cameras.

She picked up her book again and started to read. It wasn't long before she fell asleep.

Natalia

It was early evening when Mera and Ali arrived home. Ali had taken Mera to supper in a favorite restaurant on the harbor in Rockport. On the way home she'd asked him what had happened after he and Nadia had landed on the beach in Acre. But after their earlier conversation Ali was reluctant. "If you don't mind," he said, "I'd rather not talk about it tonight."

Once they were home Ali was so tired he went to bed. He fell into a deep sleep and before dawn woke up feeling cold. The window was open and the quilt lay on the floor. He got up and closed the window, leaving it open a crack, then picked up the quilt and climbed into bed, still feeling cold. He slept lightly. In that in-between state it seemed he was back on the beach in Acre, fifty years ago.

When they came ashore they were cold. The people of Acre had poured out of the city bringing blankets, sometimes covering those already asleep. They brought food as well, aware by now of the catastrophe that had swallowed Haifa. His daughter Nadia, exhausted by the horrors of the last two days, found relief in the peacefulness of deep sleep. Sleep had not come easily for Ali. He lay beneath the silent stars and watched them move across the night sky. A deep sense of detachment came over him and for the first time in his life, he felt like a speck of consciousness moving through space on a giant spinning ball.

The intensely personal events of the last several days had given way to a vast impersonal awareness. If it wasn't for Nadia he'd have died with his beloved Natalia. He'd been stunned by the barbarity of the attack on the village, the vicious cruelty of the men, the sappers who'd dynamited their homes and opened fire on those who tried to flee. He could still hear the harsh voice screaming at them over the loudspeaker, "Get out or die." It was only the location of their home at the opposite end of the village that had saved them from the initial attack.

His mind kept returning, like a silent movie, to those brief moments when by the flames of the burning buildings he saw his wife fall, cut down by a sniper's bullet.

"Listen to me, Ali," she'd said, as he'd sat on the road and cradled her head in his lap, Nadia beside them holding her mother's hand. "Take Nadia to safety," Natalia urged him. "If you stay, my husband, they'll kill both of you." The words came slowly. She was drained, the life force all but spent. "Go, my beloved, save our daughter, please, I beg you." Ali's tears splashed on his wife's face. She smiled and looked at him knowing this was the last time she would ever see him.

Turning to Nadia, she tried to speak. Nadia bent low. "Beloved daughter, go with Ali. Get away from this madness, my sweet one."

Her eyes returned to her husband again. He bent down toward her. "I love…," were the last words she spoke.

They lifted Natalia and carried her carefully into the orange grove. Ali put his jacket under his wife's head and knelt beside her. Nadia knelt on the other side and once more took her mother's hand. He would never forget his daughter's face. Lit by the unsteady light from the flames consuming their homes, the shock and horror was replaced by a wave of sorrow. Nadia lay her head on her mother's chest.

He knew Natalia wouldn't live long; her breathing was almost indiscernible. He looked one last time at the face of the woman he'd loved, and then, bending down, he kissed her one last time. He reached for Nadia's hand and gently pulled her to her feet. For a moment tears blurred the view of the woman they loved as they turned away. "Goodbye my love," he'd whispered,"Inshallah."

Morning came, a cold morning on the beach. Ali watched it push the stars back as the light of a new day suffused the horizon. The beach was covered with people, most of them still asleep. Here and there small groups huddled around low fires. He looked down at the sleeping form of his daughter and wondered what would become of them. He noticed the silhouette of two men walking among the sleeping people. They seemed to be searching for someone—probably for relatives, he thought idly. He watched as they came closer. There was something familiar about one of them. Then he heard the sweet sound of his son's voice calling softly to him, "Father, is that you?"

He stood up and suddenly Jalal rushed toward him, throwing his arms around the father he loved. For several minutes they held each other, oblivious to their surroundings. Then Jalal stood back.

"Nasir," he said, "this is my father, Ali."

Omar's home

One evening Nasir and Samara left the cave and climbed to some rocks, a place they often went to talk. Over the months since the death of her family, Samara wanted to know more about the events Nasir had touched on. "After the death of the young Israeli, you said you went to Acre to talk with Jalal. Why?"

"It was a long time ago, Samara, the spring of 1948. Acre was an old fortified city on the coast, south of Lebanon, where the members of my unit had gone. We, like most other Palestinians at the time, had come to realize that the Jews had every intention of driving us out of Palestine. They wanted to repopulate it with Jewish immigrants arriving from Europe. The Carmeli Brigade and other paramilitary groups had driven people out of their villages; some had made their way to Haifa, others had gone to Acre. The mayor of Haifa was a Jew but he was friendly, a man who treated people equally and with respect. To him all people were the same; all children of the same God. He'd welcomed Palestinians who fled to the city, telling them they'd be safe, but he was overruled by the leaders of the Carmeli Brigade who arrived at the city to finish the job they'd started. Those who escaped from Haifa made their way to Acre by boat.

"I knew something would happen in Acre: I knew Jalal had to find someone. I didn't know who it was but I knew he'd know when it happened. Before dawn, we went to the beaches south of Acre. Clusters of people sat hunched around small fires. Smoke hung in blue-grey layers, as though over a battlefield. In the early light the magnitude of what happened in Haifa became apparent. As far as the eye could see thousands lay sleeping.

"As light flooded the beach we picked our way through the sleeping people not wanting to disturb them. Sometime later Jalal found his father Ali, and asleep beside him, his sister Nadia. They'd escaped Haifa by boat. It was then that Jalal learned of his mother's death."

Samara, who'd been immersed in Nasir's tale, was startled by the unexpected braying of a donkey not far away. They listened for a few moments until it stopped and the soft quietness of night wrapped itself around them.

Nasir continued. "It was afternoon when we got to Omar's house. Once Ali and Nadia were settled Jalal and I went to talk with members of the Arab Legion about the defense of the city.

"Omar Rashid and his wife Hana lived within the walls of the old city close to the Mediterranean. With the arrival of Palestinians on the beaches of Acre they'd opened their doors to those in need of food and a place to sleep. By nightfall twelve guests crowded the small, walled courtyard at the back of the house. Omar was a physician who worked at the Lebanese Red Cross Hospital in the city, and with the influx of injured from Haifa, it was late when he got home. Hana had taken charge, assigning each to specific tasks. Nadia worked in the kitchen, where the women soon performed miracles—food, always ready, for those who came hungry to the Rashids' door.

“Ali and two elderly gentlemen were given the task of getting water and food. Each day, they filled the urns at the nearby well, followed by trips to the market in search of fresh produce, now almost nonexistent. Then, off to the baker’s for bread. Hana’s kitchen was stocked with lentils and rice so everyone was well fed. I ate with them as often as I could.

“The work kept them busy but all too often Nadia found her mind returning to the events of the past week. She talked with me about it. She was frightened, and grieving for her mother. During the third night the city came under attack. Those who’d escaped Haifa recognized at once the terrifying sound of mortars. The explosions were sporadic but continued all night. Close to the sea, the Rashid home was well back from the outer walls to the east and north where the attacks were taking place. Occasionally rifle fire echoed through the streets of the old town. It was hard to sleep. Just before dawn a voice screamed through loudspeakers on the other side of the wall. Nadia awakened, shaking. It was the voice she’d heard the morning of the raid on her village. It was the same voice, the same hatred, the same heart-stopping fear. ‘Surrender or die. Better to die by your own hand than ours.’ At times the voice attacked, at others it surprised. It played with fear and loved it. I wondered, who was the man behind the voice, what had brought him to this place at this time?”

A meeting of minds

When David returned to the bedroom, he found Sandra asleep, the book she'd been reading beside her. Gently, he put the book away, switched off the light and slipped into bed. She stirred and snuggled close to him. His mind drifted back to their first meeting. He'd loved her from the start, although he hadn't realized it at the time.

He'd been invited to Vancouver to speak at the University of British Columbia on a recent book he'd written. Afterwards he rented a car and drove to Whistler. He had the use of a friend's condo for a week, which was in easy walking distance of the lifts. He loved skiing. At the end of the first day, he was, as usual, one of the last off the slopes. The mountain obscured the sun by the time he reached the bottom of the run.

He wandered through the village to get familiar with it again. It was several years since he'd been there. He found it crowded with skiers in bright-colored clothes with red, wind-burned faces and dancing eyes. Laughter, the murmur of voices, and music filled the crisp air. It was one of the things he loved about skiing.

He entered a small English-style pub and ordered a McEwans. Sipping his beer slowly he stretched his legs, glad to take the weight off his feet. His body tingled and his face felt flushed. He enjoyed his beer and listened to the hum of conversations and laughter around him. The pub was packed; yet, despite the crush of people, he felt alone and happy to be so.

She came out of nowhere and asked to sit with him. "No more empty chairs," she explained. She was tall standing by his table, her head bent toward him. Light from the ceiling framed her dark hair with an aura of reflected gold. She wore a red ski jacket over a navy blue sweater that accentuated her unusually dark eyes which seemed to have a quality of stillness about them. There was an ease about her that he liked at once and he was pleased to have her join him.

They talked of skiing and the different areas on the mountain with which he was unfamiliar. He learned she was a nurse working on Vancouver Island. She learned he was a professor of philosophy and psychology.

The waiter came and she ordered a glass of wine.

Before long their conversation drifted to a recent trip she'd made to India and Nepal.

"Have you been there?" She asked.

"I have," he told her, "and I loved it. What did you think of it?"

"It changed my perspective on life. I spent a month in Benares, where people bathe in the Ganges before they die."

"Why did you go?"

"Benares or India?" she asked with a smile.

"India."

"I wanted to get a fresh perspective on Canada and my life. I felt drawn there. I hoped to be of help. I thought people who were poor and suffering would be unhappy. It was a surprise to realize most of the people I met in India seemed happier than my friends in Canada, despite the circumstances of their lives.

"One day when I was in Nepal I watched some children playing. One of them, a little girl of about six, must have had polio. Her legs were shriveled and disfigured. She got around by using her hands and scooting her legs after her. She played with the other children, who included her in their games. All of them were having a great time; I could hear their squeals of laughter. The place where they played had an irrigation ditch running beside it. It was very polluted. Every now and then they'd jump in to cool down.

"I wondered how it would be if the little girl lived in Canada. She'd be sitting in a wheelchair, watching other children play, observing at a distance. It made me realize that the joy of life is not dependent on what we have, on wealth or even a strong healthy body."

Sandra, who'd been sipping her wine as they talked, now lifted her glass and emptied it. "I'll be back in a moment," she said. She stood up and made her way to the back of the pub.

When she returned she took off her jacket and dropped it over the seat before sitting down. As he looked at her, relaxed and smiling, he could feel the energy between them. He'd sensed it when she first stood beside his table; now it was even more obvious.

The waiter appeared and they ordered more drinks.

"Was it hard to readjust to Western life when you came back to Canada?" he asked.

"It was. The last six weeks I spent in a Buddhist convent in silent meditation. Shortly afterward, I was on my way to Vancouver, via Toronto. My father had changed my ticket. He wanted me to spend time with my sister who lived in Toronto and was depressed. So there I was, one day in Nepal, and two days later walking down a crowded street with a sister who was bored with life and upset that she couldn't have everything she wanted. That was a shock. Suddenly the world I found myself in seemed bizarre. I felt like Alice, that I'd stepped through the looking glass.

"India and Nepal had a profound effect on me. I realized that what is of real value has nothing to do with wealth or power, our position in society, who we know or who we don't. For the first time, I saw our culture and society with fresh eyes, the eyes of an outsider. I was appalled by the waste. I felt overwhelmed by it, particularly in the city. It struck me how cut off we are from nature and how we seem to have lost the sense of our own mortality. Here death is hidden, while in India it's not.

"It seemed to me that for many Westerners, there's a deep emptiness. I saw it clearly with my sister. She and her husband have been working for years to get an apartment in downtown Toronto. Now that she has it, she's decided her life is still not perfect. She's talking about leaving her husband, thinking maybe then she'll find happiness. Her joy from acquiring possessions is short-lived. I think for many people there isn't anything in our culture that can fill this emptiness. Nothing; not wealth and possessions and certainly not the religious practices and beliefs found in most churches today."

"Are you pessimistic?" David interjected, with a wry smile.

"No, not really. India showed me what I was missing."

"How do you mean?"

"I think India is the spiritual heart of the planet. To me it's a place of great wisdom, a place where the role of spiritual masters is just an ordinary part of life. People recognize them and have always looked to them for insight and wisdom. There are probably more enlightened men and women in India than in any other country in the world. Why is that, do you think?" She looked at David as she took a sip of wine.

He thought for a moment. "Perhaps it's because, although we have social and cultural freedom, we don't have the same freedom when it comes to ideas and spiritual understanding. From my experience in India, the opposite is true. The power of the caste system is still very strong; there's much less social freedom. But, in the realm of ideas and spiritual understanding, the mind is free to soar, and it does."

"Why do you say we're restricted in the West?" Sandra asked.

"Christianity has always thought of itself as the one true religion. But even within Christianity there has been strife and conflict. During the Spanish Inquisition for instance, those who disagreed with the Roman Catholic Church were put to death. And, in Europe, during the witch hunts, tens of thousands of women were killed. This sent a chill of fear throughout Europe and America which I think still exists today. This is why Westerners are so cautious, afraid of thinking outside the theological parameters of our culture. The belief that Christ is the final and ultimate revelation of God and all others are false prophets closed people's minds to other ideas, other masters and most importantly to the idea of enlightenment itself.

"It's not that enlightenment vanished from the world: it simply vanished from Western consciousness. In places like India, Japan and South East Asia, it is deeply embedded in the psyche of the people. Enlightenment in India represents the pinnacle of spiritual awareness and is based in experience rather than belief, as in the West."

Sandra jumped in. "I see what you're saying," she said. "Besides removing the idea of enlightenment from Western consciousness, the same rigid thinking is one of the causes of the conflict between fundamentalist Jews, Muslims and Christians, in the Middle East. All of them are convinced their theology, their God, their way, is the only true one, and all others are false."

She sat back and finished her drink. David invited her to join him for dinner. She accepted, and they left the pub for a secluded Italian restaurant she knew. They walked in silence as snowflakes floated lazily into the light of street lamps and settled gently on the ground. "Skiing in such a beautiful place does away with any sense of emptiness," Sandra said, almost to herself. "No need to look any place else, it's all here in the mountains."

"You mean skiing is the pinnacle of enlightenment." David tried to suppress a smile.

Sandra laughed. She was deeply aware of the man at her side. When she'd approached his table, it was the only one with an empty chair. She was immediately struck by his unusual eyes and had wondered whether it was the light. As they began to talk she had felt at ease in his presence. She found it easy to share with him things she was still reflecting on, things she hadn't shared with anyone else. She hoped she hadn't put him off by her intensity. It was hardly a normal conversation for a first meeting but it had been fun to talk openly with someone who was interested in more than just the day's skiing.

The nature of belief

Sandra and David arrived at the restaurant and were soon seated at a table for two in the corner. The lights were low and a candle burned steadily between them. The restaurant was almost full. David recognized one of Puccini's arias playing quietly in the background.

When the waiter arrived they selected a bottle of red wine. Sandra and David both ordered goat cheese antipasto with basil and sun-dried tomatoes. Once the order was taken she looked up and caught David's eyes. No words were spoken. She smiled, and he felt his heart jump. It was like the sudden appearance of the sun and he found it impossible not to smile in return.

"Freedom of ideas and religious thinking in India is more prevalent than in the West," she said, returning to the earlier conversation, "and yet it seems to me there's been a rise of conflict between Hindus and Muslims. What do you think is behind it?"

The waiter appeared with their wine.

"Sometimes when life doesn't meet expectations, people think it's because they've drifted away from God and that He is punishing them. How do they get back to God? By following a more literal interpretation of the scriptures, such as found in the Bible or Koran. When this happens there's a tendency to define reality in terms of right or wrong, good or bad, black or white.

This inevitably leads to conflict, and in extreme cases, war."

"When you step back, what do you see going on, between India in the East and North America in the West?" Sandra asked.

David put his wine down. "I think an evolutionary process is underway that will, in the end, bring together the social and cultural freedom of the West with the religious and spiritual freedom of the East. I hope so, anyway."

After dinner, David walked Sandra to her condo and asked her if she'd like to ski with him the next day. For a week they skied together and in long, rambling conversations explored a wide range of subjects.

Friday was David's last day at Whistler. He and Sandra met for an early breakfast and were on the slopes as soon as the lifts opened. They skied all day, stopping only briefly for lunch, exploring the places they'd visited during their six days on the mountain.

In the late afternoon, they came over the crest of a hill and paused. Far below, the valley lay in shadow. Leaning on their poles, they took in the view before them. They'd spoken little all day, just enjoying the thrill and exhilaration of skiing, and the warmth of each other's presence.

"Let's sit awhile," Sandra said, then turned and skied slowly to the lee of some nearby firs. David followed. She trampled a spot with her skis, removed them and drove them into the snow for a backrest. David did the same.

In silence, they watched the shadows reach farther and farther up the valley. In the distance, they could see Whistler Village. Blue wood-smoke curled in layers around the tops of the trees, and the lights of evening twinkled through the gathering dusk.

The remaining rays of sunlight winked out as a golden sun

slid below the ridge behind them. Already they could feel the approaching cold of night. Sandra turned and reached for David's hand. She looked at him and smiled.

"Thank you so much for another wonderful day," she said.

That was the first time he'd known he loved her. He helped her to her feet, and she stood before him, pulling on her gloves. Her face was flushed from the wind and sun, her eyes bright and still. He leaned over and kissed her gently. He wanted to tell her he loved her but couldn't bring himself to say the words. Then the ski patrol came over the hill on their last sweep of the day and the moment vanished.

"Lets go," she said. Stamping into her skis and turning, she launched herself down the hill. David reached the bottom before her and was stepping out of his skis when she came straight at him. At the last moment she angled her skis, spraying him with snow as she came to a stop, grinning.

They went for a drink in the pub where they'd first met, both of them aware their time together was all but over. Finishing their drinks, they went to their respective condos to shower and dress for dinner.

When David knocked on her door an hour later, Sandra was almost ready. She wore a long, full, denim dress with a red sash around the waist. He watched as she pulled on thick, woolen socks and lambskin boots; then taking her parka, she slid her arms into the sleeves. Together they stepped into the cold night, and arm in arm, walked the short distance to the Hokkaido, a Japanese restaurant they'd chosen earlier.

Alone in a small elegant room with rice paper walls and tatami mats, they sat across from each other on small cushions. For a few moments they simply sat in silence. There was a meeting of minds in a quiet inner place. Neither of them wanted it to end. David picked up the conversation they'd had the night they first met.

"I was thinking about this idea of religious fundamentalism," he said. "I suspect it has less to do with religion and more to do with beliefs. I've seen people in politics with the same kind of fanaticism both on the left and the right. It's the same tendency to define things in terms of right or wrong. I think it has to do with the nature of belief itself. It seems to me that belief underlies so many of the problems we've been speaking about. Not specific beliefs, but the characteristics of belief itself. That set me to thinking, what is belief? I mean, what is central to it, what is at the heart of it?"

Sandra thought for a moment, then shook her head. "I don't know. Some beliefs turn out to be true, while others don't."

"That's so, but what I'm really asking is, what is the fundamental nature of belief itself? What could be said to be implicit in all beliefs?"

Again she was at a loss. "I don't know."

"All right. How about this? It's a beautiful sunny day in late spring and you're in your office which happens to be in the basement of a local hospital with no windows. I call and we talk a bit and then I mention the heavy snowfall outside. Would you believe me?"

"I'm not sure."

"Why aren't you sure?"

"Because it was sunny earlier. It seems unlikely that snow would have developed so quickly."

"Then returning to my earlier question, what would you say is implicit to all belief?"

"Uncertainty ... doubt?"

"So what you're saying is that belief is not necessarily true. It represents instead, not knowing. Belief might correspond to truth or it might not. So let's take it a step further. Given the nature of belief, what would you say is the nature of truth?"

"We recognize it as being true, simply a fact; "It's snowing. When I look outside and the snow is falling it's a fact" she laughed.

"That's right. So if that's the case, what is it about belief that makes believers so dangerous?"

Sandra gazed quietly at the flame of the candle on the table. Then suddenly she understood his question. "The believer's sense of identity is tied to his beliefs, and any challenge to them is taken personally. So," she continued, "that would explain why some people become fanatical and, in extreme cases... dangerous."

"That's how I see it."

Sandra looked at the man across from her. She liked being with him, loved talking with him. She smiled, a quick, spontaneous smile.

They drank sake and savored the delights of Japanese cuisine. The shadow of the next day's parting lent richness to the moment. David watched her across the table. She was radiant. The waves of her dark hair shone in the light. She looked up, and their eyes met.

"Let's go to the condo," she said. "I've got a hot tub, and we can ease our aching muscles."

Beneath the old-fashioned street lamps that lined the sidewalk, they walked slowly, hand in hand.

At the condo, Sandra kicked her boots against the step, unlocked the door and went inside.

"Come in," she said. She bent down, removed her boots and socks and hung up her coat. She led him through the living room to an outside deck. Sliding the doors back, they stepped outside.

The deck faced the mountain. A dark ridge of peaks stood against a black canvas of glittering stars. A crescent moon delicately tipped the ridge to the east. On either side, silent firs stood unmoving in the clear, cold night. She pointed to a small bench against the wall.

"You can put your clothes there," she said. "I'll get some towels."

David undressed quickly in the frigid air and slipped gratefully into the tub. It took a few moments to adjust to the hot water. Sandra returned, draped in a large towel secured above her breasts. She put extra towels on the bench. By the light of the stars and the bright snow, he watched as she slipped the towel from around her. For a moment she paused, and he saw the curves of her body. Bending, she slid into the water. Her breasts hung momentarily, full and round, before they disappeared beneath the surface. A breeze stirred the nearby branches.

In the dim light she sat facing him, allowing the heat from the water to ease the tiredness in her body, every muscle slowly relaxing. Suddenly, in the subdued light, David became aware that she was watching him. She moved to him and wrapped her arms around him. He suddenly felt embarrassed. He closed his eyes, and she kissed his eyelids, his cheeks, the tip of his nose.

Fifteen years had passed since that night in Whistler.

Like a fly in a spider's web

Samara and Nasir were sitting with their backs against the rock face where they would sometimes sit as the valley below disappeared, swallowed in the gathering darkness. Samara watched the moon as it slipped into the night sky above the mountains to the east. "What was Ali like?" she asked.

"I liked him. He was tall and slim, a thoughtful man. He didn't say much but when we talked it was obvious he thought deeply about life and the events playing out around us."

"So did things get better?"

"No, they got worse." Nasir replied.

He remembered how he'd hoped that people could return to their villages. But after several days in Acre he'd come to accept what he saw. Things were not going to get better.

It was just before dawn when he went to Omar's home. He stayed there whenever he could. Ali was sitting alone, drinking coffee, unable to sleep. "There's coffee in the kitchen," he said. The crack of a rifle, not far away, echoed between the stone buildings. They listened for more shots but none came. "Where is Jalal?" Ali asked, his voice low. They were seated at a small table beneath the window. A single oil lamp doubled as light for both the kitchen and the courtyard. The glow from the light was warm and comforting; but, beyond it, in the shadows, fear gripped the city. No one in the courtyard could sleep. They'd tried but given up and now lay staring at the receding stars, wondering what would happen next.

"Jalal and the rest of our unit came to help defend the city," Nasir had told Ali.

"How many are there altogether?" Ali asked.

"There's soldiers from the Arab Legion, I'm not sure how many. People from Acre and Haifa as well as four groups like ours. Another two hundred men and boys came here last week when their villages were attacked and they'll fight too."

"'And Jalal is part of a 'unit,' as you called it?' Ali asked.

"He is. There are fifteen of us. We've been together for two and a half years."

"Are the British still in charge?"

"Right now there's no one in charge. What authority there is comes from the end of a gun. If we don't fight to protect the land there'll be no land to protect; and then where will we live, if we survive at all?"

"Can you hold the city?"Ali asked, "or will it fall?"

"I think it will fall unless somehow the Jews are held in check. With the British going though, I don't see it happening."

"What will you do, Nasir?" Ali stretched his long legs.

"I'll do what I can to help, but I'm not sure I can do it using a gun. Sometimes I think life has its own ways, that we're simply actors. What influence can we have over the big events that take place, wars and dislocations, illnesses and deaths? Right now I feel that Palestine is like a fly caught in a web of circumstances over which we've little or no control. The harder we struggle the more tightly bound we become. I don't see a solution. What will happen? Inshallah!"

A warm breeze came suddenly from the escarpments above where Nasir and Samara were seated. It flowed around them as it spilled into the darkness below.

Those days in Acre were a long time ago but Nasir could still recall the shock he felt when he first heard about the outbreak of typhoid. It was the fifth day of the siege. Omar had arrived home at dusk. Smoke hung in the air from the explosions and fires.

"I've bad news," he said when he saw Nasir.

"What happened?" Nasir asked.

"There's an outbreak of typhoid in the city, close to sixty cases so far, fifteen British soldiers included, with six deaths all told."

"When did it start?"

"Three days ago. It's been spreading and I'm sure there'll be more deaths by morning."

"How did it start?"

"We don't know yet."

The discussion was cut short when the shelling suddenly resumed, rattling the windows and dishes. This time it was intense, accompanied by loud and sustained gunfire which crackled over the city, echoing down the narrow stone flanked streets. Then as quickly as it started, silence returned and out of the darkness came the voice. The same voice that came every night and again at dawn setting people's nerves on edge.

"I couldn't understand," Nasir said, turning to Samara, "how so much hatred could be directed at us by people we didn't know. In a matter of weeks hundreds of thousands of people had been uprooted from their homes, and family members, mothers and children killed. Just hearing the voice reminded us that death lay in wait and no one knew who it would take with it. For fifteen minutes the voice ranted, repeating over and over, 'Surrender or die,' and 'Kill yourselves or we'll do it for you.' Then the voice went silent and the shelling began."

Samara sat quietly wondering how Nasir had managed to move beyond the anger he must have felt at the time.

After a while Nasir stood up, stretched and reaching down helped Samara to her feet. They returned to the cave by the pale light of the moon.

Myths

One evening Mera and her grandfather had been invited to supper with her parents. When they arrived they found them in the kitchen. After supper they sat out on the deck drinking tea. Before them a rocky shoreline stretched to the south, and beneath a cloudless sky a gray ocean hurled itself against a rocky shore. A breeze played with the flowers that tumbled from ceramic pots lining the deck. To the north the lighthouse flashed its warning to the unwary and welcomed local fishermen on their return.

Heatherington finished his tea. "We'll do the dishes," he said to Nadia and Ali, nodding to Mera. Mera followed her father through the French doors and into the kitchen.

"I'm going to Lebanon to see Omar," she said, as she ran water into the sink.

"Really. What prompted that?"

"I've been writing to him for years. Do you remember how Grandpa used to tell me stories when I was a little girl?"

"I do."

"Those stories were about his home in Palestine. Since then I've always known I'd go there one day. After Ted died I realized there had been a lot of death in Grandpa's life but he never really talked about it.

I started asking him questions. At first I was upset by what he told me but I still wanted to know. You were in Acre; do you remember it?"

"It's not something one forgets. Those were difficult times for all of us, Mera."

"Why won't Mom talk about it?"

"It was very hard for her. She lost her mother and two brothers as well as her home. Since coming to America she'd rather leave the past in the past. We've talked about it some because we were both there, but it still upsets her, even today."

"Do you mind talking about it?"

"No dear, I don't mind."

"Do you remember the first time you saw Mom?"

Heatherington smiled. "How could I forget?"

"Tell me."

"There's not much to tell."

Mera looked at her father. "Can you tell me anyway?"

He nodded.

"One evening I went with Omar to his home in the Western section of Acre, near the sea wall. I was assigned to Brigadier Beveridge, chief of the British Medical Services. I'd been at the hospital for eight months, which is where I first met Omar. We worked together during that time.

"One of the Palestinian fighters, a man called Nasir, arrived at Omar's a few minutes after us. I was pleased to see him. I hadn't seen him since I'd hitched a ride with a convoy bringing supplies to our troops in Acre two years earlier. The convoy came under attack from a gang of Jewish thugs called the Stern Gang. Nasir's unit happened to be in the area and joined the British in repelling the attack. One of Nasir's men was wounded in the fight and I treated him.

"With the presence of our troops as well as representatives of the International Red Cross in Acre, the shelling had been suspended and for the first time in a week we could breathe more easily. Hana, Omar's wife, and the women served coffee. One of the women was your mother Nadia. She caught my eye at once."

Mera waited, expecting more. "That's it?" she asked.

"That's it."

Mera laughed. "C'mon Dad, you can't just leave me hanging like that. Ali has told me a little about what happened but I'd like to know more about it from your perspective."

Heatherington smiled at this girl child of his, now a mature woman. "We were in a very difficult situation. Typhoid is a frightening disease and so, although I noticed Nadia, my attention was on other things."

"What happened that evening? Can you tell me more?"

"Omar, who knew the people staying at his home, felt it important to keep them informed of the events taking place in the city. 'We had a meeting at the hospital this morning,' Omar told the expectant group. 'Colonel Bonnet of the British Army, Dr. McLean of the Medical Services and Mr. De Meuron, the Red Cross delegate, met with city officials to discuss the typhoid outbreak. The aqueduct that supplies water to the city was deliberately contaminated with typhoid. We can't use it until we decontaminate the whole system. Other wells, including the one we use here, are safe. We've tested all of them.'

"Omar's words came as a shock, adding to the fear each of them felt. The enemy they faced was prepared to use any and all means to kill them. That was a frightening realization.

"'How do you know this was deliberate?' Ali asked in his quiet voice.

"Omar turned to me and said, 'I'll let Captain Heatherington tell you.'

"I remember I took off my hat and put it on the table. I hated having to tell them what I'd found. 'When we heard of the outbreak we were surprised because the conditions in the city, although difficult, were not bad enough for typhoid.' My Arabic by this time was passable. 'Because typhoid is carried by water the first place to look was the source where the city obtained its water. Most of the water comes from a spring eight miles north of here. It flows by way of an open aqueduct. It seemed a probable source of contamination, particularly when I found it flowed between Jewish settlements not far from the springs themselves. I knew that two Jews had been caught trying to infect the Gaza water supply with malaria and so it seemed likely the same thing had been tried here. Similar tactics have been used in sieges throughout history. I took a squad of British soldiers and we searched the area. We found two glass vials, a broken one discarded in long grass right beside the aqueduct and a second one in the aqueduct itself. The contamination was deliberate.'

"Hana, Omar's wife, was very upset by the news. 'Is this the only explanation?' she asked me. I don't think she could believe human beings were capable of such acts.

"'I'm afraid it is,' I told her. 'There isn't any doubt. It was deliberate.'"

"The discussion continued but there was really nothing anyone could do. It was getting late when I left. Nadia had seen me to the door. Just as I was leaving Nasir came out of the kitchen;

he was leaving too and going by the hospital."

Heatherington drew a breath, collecting his thoughts before continuing his narrative. Mera wiped her hands on the dishtowel and stood quietly attentive, but he wasn't seeing her anymore. He saw instead the nighttime streets of Acre, silent for the first time in days, a brief pause before the siege began again.

He and Nasir had walked in silence for several minutes, their footsteps echoing softly in the night. Nasir suddenly stopped and turned toward him. They were two shadows in a sea of darkness. Above them the outlines of buildings were black against the night sky.

"This will not end in our lifetime."

Heatherington nodded his head in agreement. "When I was in Germany at the end of the war I saw how the Germans drove the Jews out of their homes. I saw how they confined them in ghettos and then killed them when the death camps were ready. Jews and the Roma were considered inhuman, vermin, and the best way to get rid of them was extermination. Most of the European Jews that have come to Palestine have seen this. They know how it works, how effective it is. Now they're using the same tactics on the Palestinians."

"But there aren't any death camps here," Nasir said. "It's not the same."

"It depends how you look at it. There are no extermination camps like Auschwitz and Treblinka, it's true, but death is death no matter how it comes. And when it comes to prisons, prisons don't have to have walls. Confinement to an area of land works just as well and the cost of construction is far less."

He knew Nasir was sickened at the thought.

"There comes a time when we have to face facts. Vanilla is vanilla regardless of the color. I'm not that old but I've seen things I wouldn't have thought possible. And knowing what human beings are capable of, I'm no longer surprised. It's not a matter of nationality, religious persuasion or the color of one's skin. We're all capable of Auschwitz and Treblinka. To think otherwise is a big mistake."

"It's hard to hear, hard to believe." Nasir responded.

"For you; but not for me. I've seen it, I know how human beings are. What's happening to the Palestinians is unfair, terribly unfair, but life is not known for its fairness. Repercussions will come for a long time, and as you said, we'll not outlive it."

They started to walk again. Nasir was silent, thinking.

"Acre will fall," he said at last.

Heatherington knew he'd looked at the facts, looked at the events taking place and had seen it.

"The mayor and city officials are frightened by the typhoid, and they believe if they surrender, the Jews will let them stay—who runs the city will change but life will go on as before."

"They're dreaming," Heatherington replied. "It's not going to happen. The British are leaving and London's instructions are clear: Don't get involved. Officially we're neutral. But privately I'd say the facts speak for themselves. The Jews will not let up. I've been in villages they've attacked. They're merciless.

"I was sent to a village three months ago. It had been attacked earlier that morning. When we got there, mid-morning, nothing moved. Bodies were everywhere. What shocked me was, there were more women and children killed than men. The villagers had left so quickly, food was still in the bowls. On the table, bread and coffee was untouched. In some of the homes children's toys were scattered on the floor, trampled underfoot. Children had been whisked away without notice and those who weren't had died. In this village and every single village I've been in since, homes were systematically ransacked. When it was finished sappers blew up the buildings, saving the larger ones, and when I went back weeks later I found those home were being lived in.

"At one village we surprised members of a kibbutz looting the homes. Children were carrying off the toys. Adults were taking furniture, pots, pans, plates and cups; everything to set up home. I saw wheelbarrows filled with other people's belongings, so full it took one person pushing and one on either side for balance. I even saw jewelry being taken off the dead."

Nasir responded, "I talked with Ali and he'd told me how Jewish officials came to his village. They told him they were conducting a survey, gathering information. They were well armed and had asked how many people were in the village, what they did, what ages they were, and what sex they were. They surveyed the wells and springs and plotted them on their maps. They counted the trees in the orchards, even the olive trees. The soil was examined and they took notes. What were the crops and their yields? they asked. The irrigation systems were examined and they even wanted to know how many donkeys they had."

"I've heard the same thing," Heatherington replied. "It's been happening all over Palestine."

They walked for several minutes. Nasir seemed lost in thought. Suddenly he asked the question that was bothering him.

"Why are they so brutal?"

"War is brutal."

"I know, but why deliberately target women and children?

Why do that?"

"One reason only. To terrorize people so they'll leave and never come back. The killing of women and children sends a message: There'll be no mercy, the laws of war governing civilian populations do not apply here. That's why there are so many refugees. People are scared and rightfully so. The Jews want your land; they've convinced themselves it's theirs. They believe it's their God-given right, and in my opinion they'll do anything to get it."

"And when they've driven us out, what then?"

"They'll say you didn't exist, that no one lived here."

"That's not true; we both know it, you and I."

"We know it but future generations won't."

"What do you mean?"

"Today's propaganda will be recorded as history and treated as fact. It wouldn't do to have Palestinians contradict this myth."

Nasir thought for a moment. "How do we live with ourselves when we use war to justify crimes for which there can be no justification?" he asked.

"By pretending they didn't happen, by turning propaganda into history and believing it to be true."

"How would they do it, what would it look like?" he asked.

"First, get rid of the people, destroy their villages, destroy all evidence that anyone lived there. Make a myth, a new one more to your liking."

"What kind of a myth?"

"If I were a Jew I might claim that we've reoccupied the land of our forefathers; that the land was given to us by God. The land was desert, no one had lived there for generations. The soil was poor and through heroic efforts we caused the desert to bloom while fighting off hostile neighbors who tried to stop us. But we persevered against all odds and that's how the great state of Israel was born in modern times."

"They don't have a state. There is no Jewish state," Nasir insisted.

"Not now, not at this moment. But don't forget the British are leaving in a couple of weeks and when we do, Ben Gurion and his friends won't waste any time. Mark my words, they'll declare a new state and there'll be very little anyone can do to stop it."

"What makes you so sure?"

"We've just come through a six-year war. People are tired of fighting; they want families and children, a more normal life. Ben Gurion sees opportunity in this. His policy has always been to establish a reality on the ground. Possession trumps rights. He'll not budge on this and it wouldn't surprise me to see him, and those who follow him, continue this policy once the Jewish State is declared."

They arrived at the hospital and shook hands.

Nasir looked at him. "I haven't wanted to accept this but I think what you've said is probably right."

"What I told Nasir fifty years ago turned out to be true," Heatherington concluded, meeting his daughter's eyes and then turning to the sink to pour himself a glass of water. "I think if you go there, Mera, you'll be disappointed."

"But there's no war going on right now," she replied.

"Not a war in the way we used to think of wars," Heatherington said, "but it's still a war. When you go, Omar and Hana will be glad to see you, but don't expect the same response when you go to Israel."

Mera and her father joined her mother and grandfather on the deck just in time to watch the moon like a giant golden tear lift out of the dark distant Atlantic.

Bhokari

Nasir and Samara had spent several days moving the flock with Nasir's brother Salim before they returned to the cave late one afternoon. They'd collected, as they often did, scraps of wood for the fire. It was all but dark when they arrived. Nasir got the fire going and Samara prepared the meal. Afterwards they sat quietly while the light from the fire flickered on the walls of the cave.

"It's hard to believe you could have killed anyone Nasir," Samara began. "What happened after the death of Josef?"

Nasir poked the fire and put wood on. It flared up, sending sparks dancing in the darkness. "I went to Acre to talk with Jalal. I told him I couldn't be part of the killing. But things were changing rapidly. The Stern Gang and the Carmeli Brigade had attacked Palestinian villages to the East. A lot of people had been killed but some of them made it to Acre, thinking it would be safer in the city. Jalal was staying at Omar's at the time.

"When I got there it was evening and after supper we went for a walk along the western wall. The Mediterranean was below us. For a while we watched the fishing boats as they returned to the harbor. It was getting dark and I turned to look at Jalal. Jalal was gone. In his place sat Josef, the young Jewish boy I'd killed. His blue eyes were moist with tears. I closed my eyes and when I opened them Jalal was staring at me, a worried look on his face. 'You all right?' he said.

"The experience with Josef affected me more than I realized. It was the first time I'd ever killed someone up close and afterward watched him die. I found myself wondering if peace exists, or if it's just a dream, something we hope for, something with which we delude ourselves. I told Jalal this and the words surprised me; they had just come, by themselves, suddenly. They reflected the unresolved questions in my mind.

"Jalal smiled sadly, a smile of recognition. 'I wonder the same things,' he said. 'Are we going to lose this land? Will Europeans replace Palestinians? Will anyone remember us or will we vanish from the minds and memories of men?'

"We sat looking over the Mediterranean, the sound of waves lapping against the wall mingled with the hum of the city.

"'I'm leaving.' I told him. 'I don't want to take another life. Whether there's peace or not I don't want to kill anymore.'

"'Walking away will not bring peace; how can it?'

"'You're right.' I told him. 'Walking away won't bring peace but staying won't either, not for me. If peace exists at all, perhaps it's a state of mind, something not to be found in the events and circumstances taking place; a state of mind we take with us wherever we go. That's the only hope left.'

"Jalal thought about it. 'You might be right, but I know myself well enough to know that I must do what I can to help people: I can't walk away while our land is being stolen, when Palestinians are being killed and injured, when they're being deprived of their homes and the means of making a living.'

"I understood him completely. Jalal had reached a place where he considered himself already dead. Perhaps he already knew he was going to die. He would do what he felt moved to do and if death came, it came. It no longer concerned him.

"I had a long talk with my father and later my brother. They, like Jalal, felt compelled to stay. The same was true of the rest of the men.

"When I left Acre, just before it fell, I'd agreed to take Jalal's father, Ali, and sister, Nadia, with me and find a place for them to stay where they'd be safe. I had the help of a friend of mine, a British captain called Heatherington. Once out of the city I went into the mountains with Ali and Nadia and made our way north. I was thinking about what had happened, the events of the past three years. I saw how hatred and the thirst for revenge had poisoned my very being. And in the days before I left Acre, I had to kill another man. Hatred, I could see, makes monsters of us all.

"I took Ali and Nadia to my friend Aziz and his parents in Sohmor. Afterwards I went into the mountains again. One day the strangest feeling came over me. I felt I had to find someone but I had no idea who. I started wondering when this meeting would take place and who I was to meet. The feeling persisted for months.

"One day I'd climbed high into the mountains. From there the Mediterranean stretched to the horizon. The lower slopes of hills showed green and vineyards draped the undulating hills. Small settlements, whitewashed houses and clumps of trees dotted the landscape.

"As I made my way along a ridge, I noticed a grove of cedars nestled in a broad ravine. I climbed down and entered it. The fragrance of cedar permeated the warm air while the upper limbs sighed, caressed by a steady breeze. It was late afternoon, and birds called back and forth as they do when light begins to fail. I sat resting beneath a tree, leaning against the trunk. I could see into the upper reaches of the mountains, which pushed into a clear blue sky. They glowed orange in the rays of the slanting sun. I watched the changing colors as the shadows lengthened. Suddenly I caught a movement above me and saw an old man ascending from beyond the ridge.

"When he reached the top he stood for a few moments, as though getting his bearings, before starting down the ravine toward the grove of cedars. He wore white cotton pants gathered below the knees, a white, loose-fitting shirt, and around his shoulders a robe, like a thick cotton blanket with a faded red and gray pattern woven in it. He wore a pair of old leather sandals. His skin showed the effects of long exposure to the sun. His hair was white and short and he had a white mustache and closely cropped beard.

"I watched him as he came to the trees. He entered the glade and paused, waiting and listening as though expecting someone. After a few moments, he approached my hiding place. I pulled back and continued to watch. He stopped ten meters in front of me. His movements were fluid and graceful despite his advanced years.

"He carried a stout walking staff which he leaned against a tree. Unrolling a small rug, he sat on it and wrapped his blanket around his shoulders. He crossed his legs and closed his eyes. I noticed his back was straight, relaxed. Dusk fell upon the mountain and the chatter of birds faded away. I made myself comfortable and waited to see what would happen.

"I must have fallen asleep, for when I awoke, a shaft of moonlight came through the trees, illuminating the glade in which he sat. He was as still as I'd last seen him, except his eyes were now open and looking in my direction.

"I heard a voice saying, 'Come and sit with me, Nasir.'

"I couldn't tell if I'd really heard the words, for they seemed to originate in my head. I waited.

"'Come and sit with me, Nasir. I've been looking for you. The Exalted One sent me to find you.'

"Again I couldn't tell where the sound of the voice was coming from, and I remained still and hidden, or so I thought.

"'Yes, I'm speaking to you. No need to hide from me. I know what happened. I know of your beloved mother's death, and that of the young Israeli boy. Come and sit with me. I've been looking for you.'

"I got up and stepped into the clearing. He patted the ground in front of him, 'Sit here,' he said.

"I sat in front of him and felt a strange wave of relief flowing through me. It felt like I'd been lost and suddenly remembered where I was. I sat quietly, suspended in a deep and infinite peace.

"He spoke: 'As sunlight awakens the sleeping plants of winter, it is time for you to awaken. The life in which we live and play our part is a dream, a living dream, dreamed by Allah. When the poison of hatred melts away, the flame of Allah's wisdom lights the way.'

"'What do you mean?' I asked.

"'Wisdom is passed from generation to generation, from the beginning to the end of time. It always happens, though most are not aware of it. In some men and women the heart overflows with compassion. Guided by wisdom it is passed through time, one person to another.'

"We spent two years together. I had many questions at first

but over time they died away. At the end of the second summer he told me to find my brother Salim and uncle Gabir. 'They need your help,' he said. I did go to find them, and worked with them from then on.

"One day word came that my father had been killed, and a month later my brother Amal as well. For six years, I tended the flocks and went to see the Master whenever I felt the need. One night, I had a dream. The Master came toward me; his eyes were soft. I felt a great love for him. Putting his hands on my shoulders he kissed me gently on both cheeks; then standing before me he bowed slightly, his hands joined as though in prayer. Without a word, he turned and walked away. I knew I would never see him again. I never did."

Samara sat in the silence. "Who was he?" she asked eventually.

"His name was Bokhari."

"Did he ease the sorrow in your heart?" Samara asked.

"Only time does that, but what he showed me helped."

Preaching to the converted

General J. P. Travis had a busy week. As Chairman of the Joint Chiefs he'd had a meeting with Tremaine who'd once more stated his intention of opening the military to gays. The Joint Chiefs, who were unanimous in their opposition, set out to enlist the support of pro-military congressmen and senators.

For a week they walked the halls of Congress. Travis was successful in getting the Chairman of the Senate Armed Services Committee, Sam Jackson, firmly behind him. Jackson was a tough man, probably the most powerful of the southern senators; his influence was legendary. Jackson shared Travis' distaste for the new president, for many of the same reasons.

The next day Travis met with Senator Bill Cole, who'd assumed the mantle of opposition leader. Travis knew Cole would support any opposition to the president no matter what it was. He was left with the impression that the man was not honest. He had a way with words; he could twist them to suit his purpose and make those who opposed him look like fools. He had the bluster of a bully.

By week's end, the Joint Chiefs were pleased with the support they'd marshaled. Things looked good and Travis was confident they'd hand the president his first defeat. McManus had spoken with Thad Jamieson, the Secretary of Defense, who'd listened carefully but refused to support them.

"We never expected his support anyway," Travis explained to the Joint Chiefs. "We don't need it."

"You may be right, but it concerns me that we haven't changed anyone's mind. We've been preaching to the converted."

"McManus, you worry over nothing. Tremaine wouldn't dare oppose all of us. What's he going to do, fire us? I doubt that. He can't function without our help, and he knows it."

"I think we need to be cautious," said Frank Williams, Commandant of the Marine Corps. "Tremaine's no fool. He needs our help all right, but we mustn't forget, whether we like it or not, he is the Commander-in-Chief."

Travis was getting angry. "He knows nothing about the military; he's not competent to tell us how to do our job."

"Presidents don't tell us how to do our job," said Williams, "but they do make policy decisions. It'll be the same with this president whether he served in the military or not."

"We'll see," Travis said, calming himself down. He preferred not to pursue this further. As long as they stayed on the topic of gays in the military, they were united; as soon as they strayed to the powers of the Presidency, their harmony vanished.

After the meeting, Travis went home. Entering the house, he yanked off his tie, grabbed a beer and flung himself in his chair. Clicking through the channels, he found a football game and watched the final thirty minutes. Through the window he could see his wife, Mildred, working in the garden. The game ended and he went upstairs and took a shower. When he came down, Mildred was washing her hands at the sink. He kissed the back of her neck. She spun around and flicked water at him.

He laughed. “I just finished my shower—I don’t need another one.”

“We have to leave by six on the dot, I suppose?”

“Exactly!”

They entered the hall at precisely six forty-five. The convention was the largest annual gathering of veterans anywhere in the country. More than two thousand had descended on the city. Travis was the keynote speaker. Dinner was at seven-thirty, preceded by cocktails. He and Mildred circulated. Travis saw McManus, Williams and Air Force General Vince Bradford, all accompanied by their wives.

In some ways, Travis disliked being the speaker. He had to be careful how much he drank, as he didn’t want to make a fool of himself. By the time they sat down for the meal, he was already feeling the effects of the alcohol and was glad to have some food.

After dinner he was introduced, with emphasis on his three tours of duty in Vietnam. The hall erupted with applause, everyone standing.

“I’m glad to be here tonight, glad to be among friends and those who’ve served our nation,” he began. “I don’t have to tell you our military is second to none. It is the finest fighting machine in the world and has at its disposal the most sophisticated weaponry on the face of the earth. Largely because of its might, we’ve been able to live in peace. Because of its power, the threat of communism was held in abeyance until it collapsed. Most of us never dreamed we’d see the changes we have. Who’d’ve guessed the Berlin Wall would be gone and the once-mighty Soviet Union would no longer exist? The world has changed, and the military must change with it.

"We must restructure and downsize our forces and upgrade our technological superiority, and that's not easy. We've all served, so we know how important it is to be alert and ready for anything.

"Given the changing times in this post-Cold War era, we can no longer justify keeping, as we have in the recent past, an army poised for and capable of fighting on two fronts simultaneously. We will instead have an army capable of great flexibility, mobile and able to respond to the threat of hostile forces wherever they appear, as we did in the Gulf War. The new Army will be more agile and more sophisticated than any the world has ever known. Combined with the Air Force, Navy and Marines it will be capable of deployment anywhere in the world, in a matter of days.

"Our Air Force has demonstrated the unsurpassed capability of our fliers, support personnel and the aircraft and weaponry at our disposal. With increasing technology, that high standard will be pushed even higher. In the Navy, as in the Air Force, we're moving more into the area of stealth technology. Modern weaponry will engender less danger for our personnel, while inflicting a higher number of casualties on those who might oppose us.

"But, we're faced with a problem; one that threatens to undermine the strength of our military forces. The heart of any fighting force is its morale. When morale is low, battles are lost and defeat is inevitable. In the last election President Emerson had promised gays and lesbians he'd allow them to serve. He said he wouldn't allow discrimination on the basis of sexual orientation. These ideas were of concern to us.

"Nothing will do more to undermine the morale of our military than to allow homosexuals to serve freely. Gays have organized pressure groups, but we can't allow them to dictate policy. Under no circumstances can national security be compromised.

"Make no mistake, that's precisely the issue here. What we face is a threat to our national security through the undermining of the morale of the greatest fighting force the world has ever known."

The hall erupted in applause and a standing ovation. When the applause subsided and his appreciative audience reseated themselves, Travis continued.

"If you love your country, you must help. Call your senators and congressmen. Write letters to them. Let them know how you stand on this matter. President Tremaine is considering issuing an executive order to implement this policy. We must do our best to stop him. If it is issued, we must be able to override it. We of the Joint Chiefs will do our part, but it will be easier with your support. Organize your fellow veterans. We need your help. Thank you."

Once more, the hall was filled with applause. Travis made his way from the stage back to the table. All around him veterans stood clapping, cheering, patting him on the back and offering words of encouragement. He felt good. While he was speaking, he noticed members of the press at the back of the hall and along the sides. His speech would appear in the morning papers.

He and Mildred left the gathering at midnight. As they came out of the hotel, they were met by a crush of reporters, cameras, microphones and flashbulbs. Already his speech had signaled the beginning of a war between the military and the new president. The members of the press, smelling blood, were ready.

"What will you do if the President issues an executive order? Will you obey it?"

"I think he knows he can't sustain it, so I don't think he'll issue it," Travis responded.

"Do you speak for the Joint Chiefs? Do they feel the same way?"

"Yes, to both questions."

"Is this a clash between the military and a civilian president?"

"No, this has to do with our national security."

"Is it not the task of the President to determine national security?"

"When it comes to military matters, the military will have a strong say in national security."

"But the President is the Commander-in-Chief, surely he's the one with the final say."

"That is the case but at the moment we have a president with no experience. He'll need help. I'm sure he'll consider carefully the advice his military advisors offer."

"Is this a dig at the President?"

"Don't make something out of this that isn't there!"

"What's it like to be under the direct authority of a man who has not served in the military, someone opposed to the country's involvement in Vietnam?"

Travis, realizing he was being drawn into quicksand, brought things to an end.

"Goodnight, ladies and gentlemen," he said with a salute.

With the help of his military aides, he made his way to the waiting car through the blinding flashes of the cameras. Nearing the bottom of the steps he tripped and, but for one of his aides, would have fallen. Quickly he helped Mildred into the car, got in himself, and closed the door. He was glad of the sudden quiet.

"Take us home!" he ordered.

Common ground

The next morning Tremaine was in the Oval Office at dawn. At eight o'clock he returned home. When he opened the door Sandra was singing in the kitchen. She had a beautiful voice and he loved to hear her sing. She was still in her nightgown.

"Ready for breakfast?" she asked, flashing a smile at him.

"I am. I'm famished."

"Travis made front page headlines this morning," she said, bringing him a cup of tea

"So what did he do?"

"He gave a speech last night at the veterans' convention." She handed him the paper and went to butter the toast, "I don't think he likes you very much."

"Could be. I think he has a hard time taking direction from someone he considers a draft dodger. But, he's an honest man and I'd like to be able to work with him."

David unfolded the paper. The headline read, "PRESIDENT UNDERMINES MORALE!" He read the comments of the reporter who'd written the article, and the questions and answers that followed Travis' speech. On the second page, he read the text of the speech itself.

Sandra watched her husband, absorbed in his reading, his breakfast getting cold. She had to voice her indignation. "Travis can speak his mind; he has a right to. But the press should tell the truth and report the facts. They don't. They're more interested in conflict than truth. Clever analysis and opinions seem more important than what actually happens. If they reported the facts people could make up their own minds"

David put the paper aside and ate his cold toast. "Words are such a web and we love to weave them," he said. "The press is a barometer of a country's health, and should be the people's watchdog."

"Why don't you offer to speak at the Press Club? Why not beard the lion in his den? Talk to the press."

David put his cup down. "That's an interesting idea, I'll ask Jonathan to look into it."

At precisely ten o'clock the secretary ushered Travis into the Oval Office. Tremaine looked up from his writing desk.

"Have a seat, Travis. I'll be with you in a moment. Help yourself to coffee."

Travis walked to the sofa and sat down. He poured coffee, stirred in sugar, and looked around. He noticed the newspaper on the desk.

Tremaine pushed his chair back and joined Travis, who stood, and the two men shook hands. He sat opposite Travis and poured himself a cup of coffee.

"I like coming here ... the coffee's good," Travis smiled.

Tremaine smiled too, appreciating the good humor. He hoped to keep Travis on board. Maybe the man is just testing the limits, he thought.

"What's the word from the Joint Chiefs? Will they support a change in policy regarding gays?"

"No they won't."

"I've heard the Joint Chiefs are now a lobby group."

Travis looked at Tremaine and caught the smile. "We are," he said, appreciating Tremaine's humor. "I'm afraid we don't support your proposed change and intend to do all we can to stop it."

"Fair enough."

"I think we have enough strength to override an executive order."

"You may be right."

"So what will you do?"

"I'll issue one anyway."

"Why?"

"Because I believe it's the right thing to do. As I see it all human beings are born with the same rights."

"That may be true, but as I said before, the army is different. I don't think you can win this."

"Well, General, you would know, a war is rarely won in the first battle."

"I get your point; but then what?"

"If the executive order is overridden, then the issue will go before the Supreme Court. I'm confident the Court will support my position. If it doesn't, then so be it. The matter will end there."

"That will take a long time. In the meantime, gays will be excluded."

"Emerson made a promise during the campaign, and he wanted it kept. I agree with him on this point. I gave my word, too. There's too much prejudice in the world. What divides us is the intransigence of our ideas."

"But with these people, it's not just ideas. What they do under the guise of sexual preference is immoral; it's not natural."

"I understand your opinion on the matter. It's opinions themselves that divide. If we do away with ideas of right and wrong, moral and immoral, all that remains are the actions themselves."

"How can you say that there's no such thing as right and wrong, moral and immoral?"

"These are just words. Words are labels, concepts. They create divisions where none exist. Look, Travis, right and wrong change over time and between people. The idea of morality changes, too. For some people, it's immoral to dance or go to movies. For others it's immoral to engage in violent acts or serve in the military."

"There must be some sense of morality people can agree on."

"I don't know what it is. Do you?"

Travis thought for a moment but couldn't think of anything.

"Perhaps the closest we come," Tremaine suggested, "is the idea of the sacredness of life. But who wants to live ninety years if you have to spend the last fifteen in bed suffering from bed sores, with tubes down your throat, your heart monitored by a machine and unable to take care of yourself?"

"I wouldn't."

"Nor I. Yet some consider it immoral to allow people to die without taking extraordinary measures to save them. There comes a time when the quality of life is such that death is welcome."

"I understand your point, but I still don't see how we can live without morality or a sense of right and wrong."

Tremaine chuckled. "Trees do, and, as far as I can tell, so do dogs, cows, bears, lions and tigers. So it seems obvious that it is possible to live without the need to define everything in these terms."

Travis was uncertain how to take Tremaine. Was he serious? "I don't follow."

"Trees make no judgment about the wind. They don't call gentle breezes good and limb-breaking winds bad. When a cougar stalks a deer, the deer doesn't think the cougar's immoral, it just tries to escape. And when a bear chases a man, just like the deer, the man doesn't think the bear immoral, he simply tries to escape. Life goes on without regard for human judgments of right or wrong, moral or immoral. Actions take place, that's all. If we see the various actions as they are without making judgments about them, we still respond. Such action is spontaneous and appropriate."

"But people respond in different ways."

"That's true, of course, and their actions will be appropriate for them."

"What about people like Hitler? He thought he was right, but what he did was wrong."

"Hitler and his supporters believed they were ridding the world of a scourge. Others believed otherwise and opposed him, and fortunately that perspective prevailed. I say fortunately, because I could not have supported him either, and that would have been my point of view. Despite the different points of view, all sides involved in the Second World War believed God was on their side and their enemies were wrong. Good and bad are judgments we impose on events. They're not absolute, they're relative."

"I see what you're getting at. But surely we couldn't just sit still and let Hitler do what he did?"

"No, that's my point; you and I couldn't. We'd take whatever actions we could to stop him. That, however, is not a question of right and wrong. It's simply actions and reactions taking place."

"But surely there must be some guidelines concerning right and wrong."

"I haven't found any, Travis.

"I'll have to think about what you say. One thing still puzzles me though."

"What's that?"

"You want to implement a policy that others oppose. You think your idea is right and we think ours is as well. How can something like this be resolved?"

"Right and wrong are perspectives; those perspectives meet like waves from different directions, and what happens, happens. The truth is, my perspective might not be better than yours. Sometimes ideas are ahead of their time. New ideas are not always welcomed when they first appear; vested interests benefit from keeping old ideas in place.

"For many years, the Church could not accept the idea that the earth was not the center of the universe. Openness to the idea had to come first. Only then did the perspective change. If we're interested in discovering truth, we have to be open to possibilities and aware when fear causes us to be closed to ideas other than our own.

"In the case of gays in the military, I want to articulate this position and remove all the false assumptions upon which the present policy is based. I welcome you to do the same. I don't mind differences, Travis. I welcome them."

"I'll give it some thought."

"Good."

Tremaine offered Travis more coffee, but he declined. He seemed to be thinking about something. He poured himself another cup of coffee. "I'd like to change the subject if you don't mind."

Travis nodded, "Go ahead."

"I read the reports on your speech last night and the comments to the press afterward. We need to talk about it."

Travis put his cup down and sat forward, uneasily.

"There are certain things I find distasteful in what you said, things I find inaccurate and provocative. Your continuing as Chairman of the Joint Chiefs is contingent on your following my instructions on this matter."

Travis was taken aback. He had trouble dealing with Tremaine. The tone of the President's voice was calm but firm. He couldn't read the man. There was no animosity from him, and yet Travis felt a great discomfort in the pit of his stomach.

Tremaine watched Travis closely. He saw the General's discomfort, the small beads of perspiration collecting above his lip.

"What I don't like is the constant reference to the 'greatest this' and the 'greatest that.' It's your opinion that we have the greatest army, isn't it?"

"Yes."

"Is it a fact?"

"Yes."

"Be careful, Travis. Are you sure? How do you think the British, the French, the Russians, and the Israelis feel about their military capabilities?"

"They probably think they're very good."

"Wouldn't some, if not all, claim to be the best?"

"You might be right," Travis said with a wry smile.

"Talk is cheap. It alienates our friends and confirms the beliefs of those who already dislike us. I've traveled outside the US and I know how people of other countries feel about Americans. We jump in and enforce our will against a weak neighbor, and refuse to do so with a strong one. We're more than willing to use our aircraft, missiles and bombs on those we consider enemies. I sometimes wonder where our concern for others has gone. We're motivated almost entirely by self-interest. Needless to say, we are not well liked. Even our allies don't much care for us at times. Why is that, do you suppose?"

"I don't know. It hadn't crossed my mind."

"I suspect it's because we think of ourselves as somehow special. If a plane crashes somewhere in the world, what gets reported? Not how many people are killed but how many Americans are killed. It's this kind of arrogance, combined with our lack of concern for our fellow human beings, that contributes to our reputation and the hostility aimed at us.

"Are you familiar with the Chinese sage, Lao Tzu?"

"No."

"Twenty-five hundred years ago, he said, 'The wise ruler of a strong country does not parade his weapons in public nor make boastful remarks.' Why? Because he knew pride often precedes a fall. The history of civilizations bears this out."

"I think it's good to be proud of what we do, proud of being American."

"By pride I'm referring to arrogance. Arrogance blinds us to the facts. Lao Tzu also said, 'There are three great treasures in life. Mercy, economy and daring not to be ahead of others.' What did he mean? He explains: 'Courage arises from mercy, generosity from economy and leadership from humility.' He must have lived in a time much like our own, for he went on to say, 'Today, men have little mercy and try hard to be generous, they tell others how humble they are and always find a way to be first.'"

Travis felt there was an uncomfortable truth to Tremaine's

words. The conversation with him was both unsettling and somehow stimulating.

Tremaine sat and watched Travis. He looked up to find a pair of eyes smiling at him.

"Travis, I know I've introduced new ideas, new ways of looking at life, but these things are important. We need to use our minds, we need to think clearly if we're to get beyond repeating the same old things that don't work. A Zen master tells the story of a man who went fishing. He caught a fish but the fish was so small he threw it back in the water. For the first time in its life the fish realized it was swimming in something. We need to see what we're swimming in, our assumptions and the cultural beliefs we're not even aware of; the things we take for granted. When we become aware of them it changes everything."

Travis nodded. He felt as though he'd glimpsed something, something so obvious he hadn't noticed it before.

"Coming back to your comments in the newspaper. I have no objection to you speaking your mind on anything, but I want you to do so with honesty, simplicity and humility. As Chairman of the Joint Chiefs, you represent the American people. I want you to represent them in such a way as to not alienate others.

"Are you prepared to serve me, to follow my orders and direction, to speak the truth as you see it and in no way sabotage the orders and instructions once given?"

Just then the sound of a dove came through the French doors. Tremaine looked up and saw by the sun it was almost noon.

Travis thought for a moment. "May I speak frankly, sir?"

"I expect it. Go ahead."

"I haven't liked you at all. I've detested what I thought you stood for. To serve under a man who opposed a war in which I fought and in which so many lives were lost seemed like some kind of perverse cosmic humor. I couldn't support you because I felt I was betraying the young men I knew in Vietnam. I disliked you and considered you unfit to be President. When I walked in here this morning my opposition came from this perspective. Talking with you has made me realize this is not a good place to work from. I may not always understand you but I think I can work with you. Most of what you said makes sense. I still can't say I'll support your policy regarding gays, but I will oppose it cleanly."

"Thank you. I appreciate your honesty." Tremaine smiled at Travis. "I still need to know the answer to my question, though."

"I'll give you the benefit of my experience. I'll advise you to the best of my ability. I'll speak the truth as I see it, whether you agree or not. I'll accept and respect your decisions and policies once they're made. I may oppose them when they're being formulated, but once that's done I'll support you. If I find I can no longer do so, I'll tell you, and offer my resignation. Does that answer your question?"

"It does. Thank you. That's the kind of support I need."

Tremaine stood and Travis followed suit. Tremaine extended his hand, shaking Travis' firmly. "Welcome aboard," he said, smiling, and clapped the General on the shoulder.

Enough!

Benjamin and Rachel found their places at the table. The families had gathered to celebrate their grandson's Bar Mitzvah. Days had been spent preparing the hall; the food had taken a week.

After the rabbi's blessing Benjamin stood up. "I read this letter at Daniel's Bar Mitzvah." He looked over at his son. "And now I will read it at Alexander's," he said, smiling at his grandson. "It was written by my brother Josef who died fifty years ago fighting for the land God gave us." His hands shook as he began reading from a paper which had been creased and re-creased many times. It was obvious he knew the words by heart.

Alexander stole a quick look at his grandmother Rachel who sat stiffly beside her husband Benjamin. She looked grim. It must be hard, he thought, to listen again to the words of the boy she'd loved, the young man she was going to marry. Alexander knew the story well. Josef had written the letter when he was dying after his convoy was ambushed by Palestinians. His grandmother Rachel had married Josef's brother, Benjamin, a few years after his death. Alexander had never heard her speak about what happened. He'd asked her once but she had just turned away.

Benjamin finished reading the letter and then, carefully folding it, put it back in his pocket. He looked at the faces in front of him, the faces he loved. "Josef gave his life for us," he said, "in the hope that we'd once more live on the land given to us by the God of our forefathers, this land called Israel. He'd be proud of our accomplishments, proud that we'd made the desert bloom and created a modern democracy where all men and women were equal. He'd be proud that we've driven our enemies off the land, never to return." He raised his glass. "To Josef, who died fighting for what we now enjoy."

Alexander raised his glass with the others and took a sip. It had a bitter taste. At that moment a rocket slammed through the roof. Bricks, mortar, wood, metal and tiles hurtled in every direction. Dust and smoke filled the air, swirling in the light of the sun now pouring through a hole in the roof. For a moment he didn't know where he was, his ears hurt and the taste in his mouth was awful. In a state of shock he saw his parents kneeling beside his grandmother sitting in the debris beside his grandfather.

As the ringing in his ears subsided he could hear his grandmother's words. Tears had made streaks through the dust and blood on her face, but it was the words that struck him. "It must stop," she said. "Fifty years ago my Josef died and still there's no end. Now Benjamin is dead too." It was then Alexander realized she was holding the hand of his grandfather. She stared straight ahead. "We've got to put an end to this carnage," she said. "Even if we kill all the Palestinians and take the rest of their land we'll still face the hatred of our neighbors and they'll still want to kill us. This hatred destroys those we love most; it is destroying us as a nation. Fifty years ago it took my Josef. When I first met him he was alive and filled with light but in the two years I knew him I saw darkness come over him. The fighting, the cruelty was eating away at him. He was a good man; he believed what we were doing was wrong. He hated the killing, he wanted an end to it, but he couldn't escape what was expected of him. And now my husband is gone as well, the two loves in my life, taken by the same madness."

Her eyes turned toward her grandson. "Alexander, it's up to you. We have failed. We've possessed the land but it has cost us our soul. It's up to you, your generation must find a way to live in peace: peace for us as a nation, peace with our neighbors, and above all peace with ourselves."

She closed her eyes. Then she opened them again. "It has to stop," she said "Fifty years..."

Lebanon

Mera landed at Beirut a little after noon. Omar met her at the airport. He was about five foot ten, thin, with white hair, dark skin and gray eyes. He wore beige slacks, a white shirt and sandals. "Not working today," he said with a laugh. He extended his hand, and Mera, with a big smile, brushed by it and wrapped her arms around the slight frame of the man she knew so well but had met only once. A porter took her bag and followed them to an old Toyota Land Cruiser that looked like it had just come off the showroom floor.

Omar guided the Land Cruiser out of the parking area and headed south along the coastal route to Tyre. He'd come to the US only once since he'd arranged for Nadia and Ali to leave Lebanon fifty years ago. On that trip he was in Boston for a medical conference at his alma mater, Harvard, where he'd received his medical degree in 1943. He'd been twenty five at the time.

During that trip he'd gone to Maine and spent several days with Ali, Nadia and Heatherington at their home just outside Rockport. It was 1956 and Mera, four years old at the time, had little memory of the event.

Omar and Ali had become friends during the siege of Acre, and after the city fell Omar had stayed in touch. Heatherington immigrated to the US in 1949 after leaving the army and opened a medical practice in Rockport. Ali and Nadia arrived shortly afterwards in 1950. A year later Heatherington and Nadia were married.

Heatherington had never forgotten the first time he met Nadia in the days following the fall of Haifa. He'd been aware of a deep attraction to her, which, even though they'd not talked of it, he knew was reciprocated.

Omar drove at a leisurely pace, and Mera, who'd never seen the Mediterranean before, marveled at the white sand beaches and the blueness of the ocean. She watched mesmerized by a land so different from her home but a land which had played such an important part in the lives of Omar and her parents so many years ago. They'd just turned inland when the phone rang. Omar looked at Nadia. "I'm on call," he said. She noticed a cell phone plugged into a holder on the dash. Omar pushed a button and a voice came over the radio. A brief but intense exchange took place in Arabic, then the line went dead. Omar pushed down on the accelerator and the car surged forward. "There's an emergency at the hospital so I have to go there at once."

"What is it, Omar?" Mera could tell from his face it was serious.

"A woman was just brought in. Her child was playing in a field while she was working. A cluster bomb exploded and the child was killed. The mother was taken to the hospital in poor condition. The doctors want my help. I have a lot of experience with these kinds of things," he added.

"I didn't know you still worked, Omar."

"You could hardly call it work," he smiled. "It's what I love. I'll be doing it till the day I die."

"Where did the bomb come from?"

"The last war with the Israelis lasted a month. They dropped four and a half million cluster bombs."

"What are cluster bombs?"

"They're like a shopping bag filled with little bombs. When it hits the ground it explodes, scattering them over a wide area. Then when something or someone touches them they detonate. They kill animals as well as humans. The Israelis like them because they don't destroy buildings, which might be useful to them if they invade."

"You've been doing this all your life. Aren't you tired of the suffering and death?"

"It's my job, it's what Allah has required of me in this life. The people living here need physicians to help with the wounds to body and soul. I do the best I can to give the body a chance to live, but there are times when my job is to just be with people in those moments when the body stops breathing and life ends; to hold them and say goodbye. There's still a lot of violence here, a lot of danger and suffering. I'm an optimist; I still hope that somehow, someday we'll learn to live in harmony again, although it won't happen in my lifetime."

It was eight o'clock when Mera arrived at Omar and Hana's home in the hills east of Tyre. A smiling Hana threw her arms around Mera, making her welcome; and somewhere not far away a father howled with grief for a wife and daughter now gone.

"Omar, what happened to the voice?" Mera asked. They'd just finished breakfast and the three of them were sitting in front of the white arches surrounding the patio. Roses hung in red profusion. They watched as the light of early morning climbed the terraced valley below. Scents of rose and honeysuckle, teased by the first breath of day, ebbed and flowed like waves on a scented shore.

"How do you know about the voice?" Omar asked.

"When I was a little girl, Grandpa told me about his life, about Natalia, Halal and Jalal. He was a great storyteller and described the village and the people in it, the harvesting of oranges and olives. He told me about Halal, who was always looking for things to fix, while Jalal was always looking for ways to help.

"The village seemed like such a beautiful place. It was easy to idealize. When I got older I asked more questions. Ali would tell another story which led to further questions. One day I realized I didn't know what happened to Halal and Jalal, or even my grandmother, Natalia. Since then he told me everything.

"I learned about the voice but I don't know what happened. Grandpa didn't either. He told me the last night he heard it he'd not slept well; the shelling and small arms fire had continued all night. About two hours before dawn everything went quiet, and he'd drifted into a deep sleep. He came awake with the approach of morning. He said he watched the stars begin to disappear. He'd even forgotten, for the time being, where he was. Then the hated voice shattered the silence. He heard a sharp crack from a rifle, the sound echoed over the city and when it faded the voice was gone, cut short."

Omar was quiet. Mera's account had taken him back in time. "Jalal told me about it." He eventually said.

"Can you tell me?"

Omar paused for a moment. "We hated the voice, it was frightening to listen to, frightening to think someone could hate so much. Jalal said Nasir had learned the movements of the voice and early one morning they'd gone to put a stop to him. Nasir was a very good shot."

"Nasir killed the voice?"

“That’s what Jalal told me.”

“How did it happen?”

“Nasir had tracked him and learned his movements. He’d watched him broadcast the same hatred from the same place. The building had been well chosen, with stone walls and windows invisible from the old town. But in one place, Nasir noticed the fortress wall took a sharp turn around a large rock promontory before resuming its northerly direction. At that precise place, the only point along the northern end of the eastern wall, a single window was visible and it was from that room the voice broadcast his hatred.

“Nasir had arrived before dawn. The light in the window went on and with binoculars they could see the voice. He bent over the microphone and again his poison shattered the dreams of the sleeping. Nasir took careful aim, the sharp crack of the rifle reverberated over the city and the voice went silent. It was Nasir who killed the voice.”

“Do you know what happened to Nasir?”

“After he and Heatherington got your mother and Ali out of Acre he went north into Lebanon. Ali and Nadia stayed at the home of a friend’s parents just east of Beirut. Nasir became something of a recluse, living in the mountains. He came to see me and helped arrange for Ali and Nadia to come with me to America. He told me later he was tending his family’s flock. He was a bit older than me so I don’t know if he’s still alive.”

“And what happened to Jalal, do you know? I always felt it was something Ali didn’t want to talk about. He said he didn’t know.”

“For me that was one of the saddest parts of my life. Jalal was the most kind-hearted and generous man I have ever known. In the two years I worked at the hospital I came to know him well.

He had Ali's quiet thoughtfulness and innate kindness and the soft rich warmth of your grandmother."

"Your grandmother," Hana interjected, "was a lovely woman, so spirited and so kind. Natalia and I were good friends, and when I first saw you I thought for a moment you were Natalia." She smiled at Mera. "You and your grandmother are very much alike."

"Jalal disappeared," Omar said. "We've no idea what happened to him. When Hana and I left Acre I went to find Nasir and asked if he would help. We tried everything we could, but all the leads we found dissolved into nothingness. It was as though Jalal had vanished from the face of the earth. Every now and then something reminds me of him. The fragrance of roses in springtime brings the memory of the first time I saw him, and when I'm surprised by the unexpected kindness of strangers, I think of him."

The following morning Omar drove Mera to Beirut airport for a flight to Jordan. From there she'd take an even shorter flight to Ben Gurion airport in Israel.

Mera hugged Omar as she said goodbye. "I'll see you in a week," she said.

Omar nodded. "Be careful Mera it's a dangerous place and the Israelis are very jumpy."

She waved as she went into the secure area. It was the last time she saw Omar.

Interrogation

"Do you know where I can find the remains of the village of Damum al Khirbat?" Mera had asked the young man she'd mistaken for a park ranger.

"I'm sorry, lady, but I've never heard of it. I'll ask my supervisor. I'm sure he'll know."

He had a strong New York accent. She watched as he walked toward a truck where three young people loaded garbage. She removed a flask of water from her bike and, taking a long drink, sat down at a picnic bench in the shade. She could hear bees humming. A man in his mid-fifties came out of the visitor center and threw bags of garbage in the back of the truck. The young New Yorker had a brief conversation with him, pointing in her direction.

Mera was tired. She'd spent the last two days on a rented bicycle looking for Ali's village but had not been able to find it. She watched absently as the older man became animated; the conversation had suddenly turned serious. He looked again in her direction. Signaling the three young men, he got into the truck with them and they drove away.

When the young man walked back over to her, Mera could see he was sweating.

"Have a seat," she said, nodding across from her. "I'm Mera," she said, "and you?"

"Jason Leopold," he said disinterestedly.

"From New York, I bet."

Jason looked at her and allowed a brief smile. He was a big man, solid and probably six foot six.

"What brings a New Yorker to these parts?" she asked in a friendly manner.

"We came to work in the park. We collect garbage and clear debris. We do tree spacing and planting, as well."

"Are you part of a group?"

"Christian Zionists!"

"And what do they believe?"

"That's my business, lady," Jason said coldly. "Why are you here?"

Mera was taken aback. "I'm sorry," she said, "I didn't mean to pry."

"Why are you here?" Jason asked again.

"Years ago my grandfather and mother used to live in a village that's supposed to be nearby."

"Damum al Khirbat?"

"Yes."

"Are you Palestinian?" the young man suddenly demanded.

"No, I'm an American ... like you."

Looking at Jason she realized his friendly and helpful attitude was gone.

"Why are you here, why are you really here?" His voice had hardened.

"I told you," she said. "My grandfather and his family came from here, they lived in the village of Damum."

"Not possible!" Jason snapped.

"And why is that?" Mera asked.

"This was desert, no one lived here. This forest was planted in the 1950s, and there were no villages here."

"I'm sorry, Jason, that may be what you believe, but it's not true." Mera couldn't keep the irritation out of her voice.

"Your parents and grandparents were Palestinians, so you're Palestinian too," Jason insisted.

Mera laughed; she couldn't believe what she was hearing. "No, I'm not Palestinian. As I told you, I'm an American. My mother and grandfather were Palestinian, but I'm American, I was born there."

"Then why are you trying to find this village?"

"I already told you, my grandfather and mother used to live there. They talked about it, how beautiful it was. I hadn't expected it to be covered in forest."

"It's not here, I told you."

"Maybe, but it used to be."

"Stay here." Jason turned away. Pulling out a cell phone, he wandered over to some trees on the other side of the picnic area. She noticed a bicycle leaning against one of them. She watched him again engaged in an intense conversation. Why was he so hostile, she wondered? She didn't like it. Jason finished his conversation and, snapping the phone shut, shoved it in his pocket. He grabbed the bike and wheeled it toward her. "Come with me," he said.

"Where are we going?" Mera asked warily. On the other side of the visitor center she saw a group of cyclists mount up and slowly disappear between the trees.

"Let's go."

She hesitated.

"You wanted to see the village, didn't you?"

"I thought you said it didn't exist?"

"Do you want to come or not?" Jason demanded.

She didn't like the feel of this but she wanted to see the village. They cycled out of the picnic area and followed the main track. Ten minutes later they turned onto a narrow trail that twisted down a steep hill before emerging on a gravel road. Jason looked back to make sure she was keeping up. They turned right and rode a short distance before rounding a corner into a large maintenance area. Mera felt a sense of relief when she saw a police car parked in front of a long low building. Two female police officers stood beside the car talking to the man Mera took for Jason's boss.

Jason rode straight toward them and stopped. As she got off the bike the two women flanked her. "Please come with us," one of them said, in accented English. "We have some questions to ask you, but first we need to see your passport."

The next several hours had not gone well. Mera was transported to Haifa, and once at the police station, she was put in an interview room where she sat alone for two hours before one of the women and a male officer entered.

The woman introduced the officer. "This is inspector Liel Leibovitz," she said.

The inspector nodded and turned his full attention to Mera.

"Your name is Mera Morgan, is that true?"

"Yes."

"You are American?"

"You have my passport so what do you think?" Mera had had a frustrating and long afternoon and her patience was wearing thin.

Liel did not like the sarcasm in her voice. "A simple yes or no will do for now." His voice, though quiet and polite, was firm. "Why are you here; what brings you to Israel?"

"As I told the young man, I came here to find the village in which my mother and grandfather lived."

"And the name of the village, if you please."

"Damum is what they called it."

"It doesn't exist."

"But it did."

"The important thing for you to understand is that it does not exist." Liel's voice was still irritatingly calm and polite.

"That may be the important thing for you but not for me. This was the home of my family. I wanted to see where they lived."

"Who sent you?"

"No one sent me. I came of my own accord. I've already explained."

"Where is your husband?"

"He's at home."

"And where's that?"

"In America."

"Where, madam, where in America?"

"In Maine, on the northeast coast. We live on a farm."

"Do you support Hamas?"

The question was unexpected. Mera suddenly felt off balance.

"Madam."

Mera looked at the man across the table from her. He was about her age. A big man dressed in a white short-sleeved shirt and dark blue slacks. His hair was dark brown, almost black, with streaks of gray, and he had dark piercing eyes that made her uneasy.

"Madam, I asked you a question. Are you refusing to answer me?" Liel asked, his voice rising.

She didn't trust him, he had some kind of agenda. "Do I

support Hamas? That's what you want to know?"

"You heard me. That's the question."

"All right. There are things Hamas does that I think are good."

"Such as?"

"They care about their people, they provide a voice and that's important. They offer services as best they can; food, clothing and furniture to help meet the needs of people. They share the Prophet's concern for the poor."

"And is there anything you don't support?"

"I don't support violence whether on the part of the Palestinians or Israelis."

"What exactly do you mean, Mrs. Morgan?"

"I mean, I don't think the ends justify the means."

"Explain."

"To resort to violence in an effort to obtain peace cannot work."

"And why not?"

"If what we're interested in is peace then it doesn't work to use methods that contradict those objectives. When we use violence how can there be peace? Violence infects our thinking, and like a disease, changes us."

"And where do you stand on the issue of the Palestinians?"

Mera sensed the danger. "You want my opinion?"

"Yes. What else would it be?"

"You want my honest opinion?"

"Of course. Are you going to lie to me?"

"No, I won't lie to you but I don't see what this has to do with anything. I came here to visit the home of my mother and grandfather, that's all."

"What was your grandfather's name?

"Ali."

"Ali what? What was his family name?"

"Tarabulsi."

"Lebanese, then?"

"His family comes from southern Lebanon, yes."

"Now back to my question, where do you stand on the Palestinian question?"

"In relationship to Israel?"

"Of course."

"I think what's happened to them is disgraceful. Driving them from their homes, destroying their villages, stealing their belongings and killing them is a crime usually referred to as ethnic cleansing."

"Are you saying the Palestinians have been mistreated?"

"Mistreated is too mild a word for what has happened to them. I think all human beings deserve a place to call home, a place where they can live with freedom and dignity, have children and raise them, without fear."

"And the Jews don't deserve the same thing?"

"I didn't say that."

"But it's what you meant."

"Certainly not. I said all people and that's what I meant, all people; unless of course you don't fall into that category." Mera was so exasperated she couldn't restrain herself.

"What do you mean by that? You think we're somehow less than human, is that what you're saying?" The inspector sat up and leaned forward. He seemed on the verge of losing his calm façade.

Mera was tired and hungry. She knew she'd done nothing wrong and she disliked having suspicious minds make something of her she was not. "Mr. Leibovitz, I'm tired of being kept here against my will. I've done nothing to harm you or anyone for that matter. I have no evil intent. I consider this harassment. I came here to visit the village of members of my family, that's all; and what I find is that your government has tried to erase the memory of my family and others like them. First you stole their land and drove them into refugee camps and then you pretend they never existed, even going so far as to rename villages with names from the Bible. This shows me you'll do anything to avoid facing the truth of what you've done to the Palestinians.

"You say you want peace with your neighbors. I don't believe it; your words are not borne out by your actions. To have peace of mind both as a person and as a nation you'll have to own up to what you've done. Peace will not come without the truth first being told. Now you have my opinion, that's all I have to say. I want to call my husband. You have no right to hold me here!"

"You have no rights here," Leibovitz said, dismissing her request. "Palestinians have no rights here and that includes you."

"I've told you, I'm an American. My mother and grandfather were Palestinian but I am American. This is bullshit. I want to call my husband. Failing that I wish to speak to someone at the American embassy."

"You want, you want! You can want all you wish but it will do no good. This isn't America, this is Israel. You have no control here." Leibovitz stood and, turning to the female officer, said, "Lock her up for the night. Get her some food. We'll talk tomorrow." With that he left the room without looking at her.

"What were you doing at schools in Gaza?" It was only eight o'clock and the interrogation had already begun. Mera had eaten very little and could not drink the bitter coffee she'd been served. She'd asked for tea but there was none. Liel, she noticed, was wearing a light gray cotton suit.

"What makes you think I was at a school in Gaza?"

"I know where you went and who you met. Why were you there?"

"I brought a gift."

"Why?"

"Why not?

"Are you a teacher?"

"I used to be."

"I suppose you think all Palestinians are perfect, they teach compassion and consideration for others."

"I think that would be too much to ask of anyone."

"But you were hoping."

"That's probably true."

"And what did you find?"

Mera hesitated.

Liel continued. "Was it shocking to find young children being taught to hate, taught to believe that Islam was the only true religion? That martyrdom was glorified and suicide bombers were loved by God?"

"I found that in the religious schools, not in the government and UN schools."

"That's the difference between Israelis and Palestinians. We're civilized, we don't teach hatred to young people."

"You may be more civilized, and even that's questionable, but somehow a lot more Palestinians end up being killed than Jews. If what you do is civilized I want no part of it, just as I want no part of teaching children to hate, or that it's somehow glorious to prepare young minds for martyrdom."

"You surprise me, Mrs. Morgan. How will you know who to support?"

"I support life, I support fairness and justice. I do not support hatred and violence. I understand, however, that when people are cornered, when their livelihood and families are threatened, with no hope and nothing to defend themselves with, they'll use suicide as a weapon of last resort. We both know this."

"You sound disappointed by what you found at the schools; you sound confused."

"Mr Leibovitz, the one thing I'm not, is confused. Now, I have a question for you. Do Israeli schools teach the children what you've done to the Palestinians? Do they understand ethnic cleansing, that this is what you've been doing to the Palestinians and are still doing? Do they know how you've robbed them of their land, pillaged and destroyed their homes, deliberately killed women and children? Do they know how you've tried to remove all trace of their existence? Do they know the facts or have they been taught propaganda? Do they understand why Palestinians would hate Jews?"

Leibovitz smashed his fist down on the table. "Enough! I'm the one asking questions here." Leibovitz was now pacing back and forth. There was a knock on the door. "Just a moment," he said to no one in particular and stepped outside. Moments later he reentered. "The interview is suspended." He looked directly at Mera. "Take her back to the cell," he said to officer Ilana.

"Here are your belongings."

Mera stood at a counter in the police station, Ilana beside her.

"Make sure you have everything. Here's your passport." The clerk had emptied a packet of Mera's belongings onto the countertop. She pushed a thick register at her and said, "Sign here!"

Outside the late morning air was warm, with a lazy breeze that brought with it the sweet smell of honeysuckle. The policewoman drove her to her hotel. Mera sat in the back seat behind a metal grill. Surprised at the rapid change of events, she tried to talk to her.

"What happened? Yesterday you locked me up and wouldn't let me use a phone, and then all of a sudden you let me go without explanation. What changed?"

Ilana didn't reply. She shifted in her seat uncomfortably and kept her eyes on the road. Pulling up to the hotel entrance, the officer put the car in park, and shutting the engine off, turned to face her.

"Why didn't you tell us of your husband's position?"

"You didn't ask!" Mera smiled at her. "Thanks for the ride," she said as she got out of the car.

Insight

"How will it be resolved?" Mera was sitting in the hotel lobby.

"I wish I knew."

She looked at the man across from her. He was in his late twenties.

"There's got to be some resolution to this problem," she insisted.

"Maybe there is, but at the moment and with this government, I don't see it."

Mera had seen the notice on the bulletin board: two days of meetings for a group called "Israelis for Peace and Justice." Mikel Antebi Husseini, Presenter, read the plastic name tag of a casually dressed man who took the seat across from her.

"You're right but the government doesn't listen. They don't like peace activists. We represent Israel's conscience and they wish we'd shut up."

"And they've not succeeded in your case."

"No, but there are costs: harassment, jail time, even death. People don't want to know what's happening. Why did the Germans allow the extermination of six million Jews and do so little to stop it? It's the same reason the Israelis allow the removal of more than a million Palestinians from their land and do nothing to stop it. They don't want to know. Not knowing—they don't have to do anything about it."

Mera thought for a moment. "There hasn't always been animosity between Jews and Palestinians. In my grandfather's village there were Jewish families who'd lived there for as long as he could remember. They were part of the village, it didn't matter whether people were Jews, Christians or Muslims back then. They celebrated together, got married together and had children together. People were simply living. The gulf between us is just words: Strip away our beliefs, strip away our culture, strip away our clothing and we stand before the same Creator, naked and the same."

"My family" Mikel responded, "is from Jerusalem. My great grandfather was a friend of Albert Antebi, they were neighbors in Jerusalem until 1915. We were Palestinian Jews and our families had always lived there. In his letters my great grandfather described neighborhoods that sound like your village. People got along."

"What happened, do you think?"

"Too many Jews lived in fear, strangers and minorities scattered over many nations and cultures. They wanted a country of their own, a country where they were free to be Jews, where they could live in peace free of prejudice, free of bigotry. They wanted a place where they could live in peace, but it hasn't happened. Violence does not bring peace, it brings more fear: it is the repercussions of our own violence that we fear. The ends do not justify the means. It's time we faced reality."

The lobby was full, people coming and going and a steady hum of conversation. Mera sat back in her chair. "My experience in Israel..." She paused. "Let's just say it's not what I expected. It's not a safe place. There's no peace here."

"That's how I see it as well, but those in power still believe the Zionist ideology, as have all Israeli governments: establish a presence on the ground, build houses, settlements and military outposts, link them with roads that only Israelis are allowed to use. Establish that reality on the ground and it's hard to roll back, despite UN resolutions and pressure from the Americans.

"Isn't that ethnic cleansing?"

"It is, but incremental, not too noticeable to the rest of the world; so we keep on going, eating away at Palestinian land, and no one is serious about stopping us. Israelis think from this context. They'll continue to live with the status quo for as long as it's comfortable to do so."

"And so far it's comfortable."

"Yes, up to a point. But there's another problem. We have a lower birthrate than Palestinians, so over the years the number of Palestinians increase relative to the number of Jews. Despite immigration policies aimed at bringing more Jews here, we're faced with the eventuality that a majority of people living in Israel will one day be non-Jewish. This is seen as a serious danger to the continued existence of a Jewish State. That's why so many policies in Israel, both stated and unstated, are designed to drive Palestinians out. But where can they go? There's no place for them to go. They're not Syrians, Egyptians or Lebanese. They can leave and go to Gaza, which only becomes more crowded, and we still keep nibbling away at the land. What is the result? More and more people living on less and less land. Follow this to its inevitable conclusion and the result is death from disease and starvation. Ethnic cleansing becomes genocide."

"You make it sound hopeless."

"I don't think it is hopeless, I have to believe that one day this will change, but I don't see it happening soon."

"Where does your hope come from?"

"What disturbs Israelis so much is a deep intuitive understanding of justice, something I believe all human beings share. They know they've not acted with fairness and justice toward the Palestinians and this is where the shame and guilt comes from."

"Apart from people like you it doesn't seem to have much effect."

"I'm afraid so. There's a kind of racism embedded in government policy. As I said, this has become the norm, it's the context from which Israeli governments operate, it is the context from which the majority of Israeli Jews operate as well."

"So Palestinians leave?"

"Of course! Wouldn't you?"

"What do you think will happen?"

"In my more optimistic moments I think some benevolent power—I used to think it might be America—will see what's happening and step in, put pressure on the government and it will come to its senses."

"And in your more pessimistic moments?"

"I hate to think of it, so I don't. The alternative to optimism feels like annihilation and I don't want to go there."

"So what are you trying to do, you and members of the peace movement?"

"Criminals like to commit their crimes in the dark; metaphorically, that is. They don't want anyone to know what they've done. On one hand they do their best to destroy and hide the evidence, and grease the palm on the other hand." Mikel smiled at the unintended play on words. "So what are we trying to do?" he continued, "We're trying to bring awareness to Israelis of what is happening. So far, as I've said, they don't want to hear, so what we're left with is bringing it to the attention of the rest of the world. That turns out not to be as easy as it sounds."

"What can be done to stop the building of settlements? Mera inquired. "That's clearly a violation of international law and strongly disapproved of by the UN."

Mikel smiled sadly. "Settlements are one of the major ways Israel takes land from the Palestinians. Britain and America don't approve but they do nothing about it. They talk, but that's about all. For settlements to stop it will have to cost Israel more than it gains, and so far that's not the case."

"What about Arab nations, can't they do anything?"

"They have no power and, they're afraid. They'll never take a concerted stand against us. They tried in the past and it cost them dearly. They lost land.

"You've probably noticed settlements tend to be built on high ground, hilltops and ridges? Some of them allow rivers of raw sewage to flow into the Palestinian villages below; ruining orchards and olive groves, and contaminating the ground water. Some settlements have industries that create toxic waste as well, which is also released onto Palestinian land."

"Surely the government would put a stop to that. Wouldn't it?"

"You'd think so. But the government does absolutely nothing. This is how things are in Israel, it never stops; this kind of behavior is the norm and we Israelis take it as such. But underneath it, I think, I hope, is a deep sense of guilt and shame. What we've done and continue to do to the Palestinians is criminal."

Mera sat contemplating what Mikel had told her. It was depressing. She couldn't see a way out for the Palestinians and yet she understood why they would not leave the land they'd lived on for thousands of years. Why should they? Where would they go?

An American entered the lobby in a heated argument with a bus boy. They went out into the parking area. Mera noticed his New York accent, which reminded her of Jason Leopold, the Christian Zionist she'd met in the Olfer forest the day before. "Do you know anything about the Christian Zionists?" she asked Mikel.

"Why?"

"I met one yesterday. He was part of a group of young people from North America."

"And they were probably working in the Olfer forest?"

"That's right."

"The Christian Zionists who come to Israel believe that they, like the Jews, are God's chosen people. The term they use is "ingrafted" gentile Christians. They're fanatical supporters of Jewish Zionism; they contribute financially to Israel and come here to plant trees and look after the public lands. The Israeli government loves this kind of support. Imagine what a gift it is. They help cover the Palestinian villages that have been destroyed."

"I was just in the Olfer forest looking for the village my grandfather and mother came from."

"I assume you didn't find it?"

"I didn't."

"I'm not surprised. Israel has done everything it can to hide the crimes it committed during the war of independence. They destroyed thousands of villages and drove three quarters of a million Palestinians out of their homes in a period of less than six months. Why do you think we've planted so many trees?"

"For environmental reasons, to help stop desertification."

Mikel laughed. "You must have read the propaganda at the visitor centers."

"I did. I spent two days looking for the village but could find nothing except rubble and old foundations. I realized I might not have enough time to find it so I left some flowers by one of the foundations. A park ranger, if that's what they're called, asked my name and took a photograph of me doing it."

"Did you talk to him or anyone else?"

"I did, but no one had ever heard of the village."

"They wouldn't. That's one of the reasons they use foreign help in the forests. Christian groups in particular have rosy and unrealistic views of the 'Holy Land.' They believe the myths in the Bible, they think they're back in biblical times, and to reinforce this there's been a systematic attempt to rename many villages with biblical names. This also covers up the fact that Palestinians once lived there. I bet they told you the land was empty, a desert before they planted the trees, no one lived there."

Mera was surprised; it was as though Jason and Mikel had read the same script.

"The Zionists, like all Christians," Mikel continued, "want to believe what they've been taught about the Holy Land. This adds legitimacy to the myth that this is the homeland of the Jews."

Mera suddenly understood why her questions about Ali's village had led to her arrest. She looked at Mikel; he seemed very knowledgeable.

Just then a smartly dressed man approached. "Mera Morgan?" he asked politely.

Mera looked at him and realized he worked at the hotel. "Yes."

"Would you mind coming with me, please," he said with a slight bow and then stood back waiting.

"What's it about?" she asked.

"We'll talk in my office," he responded gesturing toward a door to the left of the reception area.

"I've enjoyed our talk. It's been very informative." Mera had turned to Mikel as she got up, "Thank you."

Mikel stood up. "Here's my card; perhaps we could stay in touch," he said. Mera took the proffered card. "It's been a pleasure meeting you," he continued. "I hope you have a good visit."

Mera shook his hand and turning followed the man across the lobby. As she approached the desk she felt a sense of shock when her eye caught the English headlines of a newspaper on the stands. "Morgan Confirmed as Vice President," it said and beneath it was a picture of her husband. Moments later she was ushered through a door, along a short hall to a large comfortable office.

A smartly dressed man and woman stood up as she entered identifying themselves as Shabak agents. Her bag was standing beside the desk. She felt disoriented as if she was suddenly living in a twilight zone. She had the distinct feeling of being caught in the strong cross currents of international politics where personal interests and freedom meant nothing.

Five minutes later Mera reached Omar by phone. The Shabak agents had left the office and she took the opportunity to use the phone.

"I won't be coming back," she said, her voice unsteady. She'd reached Omar at home. Hana came on the line and Mera felt a wave of sadness knowing she might never see these two loving people again. "A lot has happened since I saw you," she said. "The Israelis are putting me on a plane that leaves in an hour for Washington. They say it's for my protection." Mera briefly described the events of the last week: her visit to Gaza, her attempts to find Ali's village, her arrest and interrogation, her release and then her apprehension.

"I'm shocked but not surprised," Omar replied when she was finished.

"We heard about Bill's confirmation," Hana added, "that's why they want you out of the country."

Hearing Omar and Hana's voices had brought tears to Mera's eyes. She had been looking forward to seeing them again. They were the ones who somehow, miraculously it seemed, had remained true to the pictures her grandfather had painted. Now she had a better understanding of what he'd gone through and the kind of suspicion and hostility that was now the norm in this sun-drenched and fractured land. She was glad to be going home. She started to speak again but the line went dead.

The door to the office opened and the two agents re-appeared with a hotel porter. The porter picked up her bag and left the room. The agents approached her and without a word took her by the arms. They frog marched her through the lobby to a waiting car. She caught a glimpse of Mikel, a look of alarm on his face. Once outside she was placed in the backseat of a car its engine idling. The women agent got in beside her while the other agent got in beside the driver. With a screech of tires the car sped across the parking area and onto the road, heading south.

Mera felt afraid, utterly powerless, much as she had when she was being interrogated. She was angry. The thought crossed her mind that it would be easier for the Israelis if she just disappeared.

As the car sped south she sat quietly. She was not going to give them the satisfaction of knowing how afraid she was. The female Shabak officer looked at her. "What were you doing in Israel," she demanded. Mera sat back in the seat closing her eyes and said nothing.

It seemed like a long time before she felt the car slowing. When she opened her eyes she saw the airport signs and breathed a sigh of relief.

Nasir and Hafiz

Nasir sat quietly, his back against an old cedar. He had a clear view across the hills that fell away to the Mediterranean in the west. To the east, the hills gave way to the mountains. It had been over a year since he'd taken Samara into the mountains. She'd taken it upon herself to prepare meals for Nasir and his brother. It was good to have the presence and skills of a woman in their lives again, something Nasir had almost forgotten. She was good with animals too, and had quickly learned to work with the sheep. His brother had become fond of her.

Two days ago, he'd learned Khalil wanted to see him. They were to meet at the old cedar grove. Samara wanted to know where he was going, but he preferred not to involve her. She packed his skins with nuts, dried fruits and cheese. He left, saying he'd return in two days. She was afraid. He could see it in her face but he also knew she was brave and would be fine.

Many years had passed since he'd first begun to meet with the men and women who sought him out. The train of events began innocently enough. One evening in Tyre several years after the death of his father, he'd gone to pick up supplies. He walked beside the ocean watching the fishermen around their boats. The pungent odor of fish hung in the still air. Suddenly, he'd seen his friend Hafiz coming toward him. Nasir hadn't seen him since he left Acre thirty years ago. Hafiz had aged; he looked worn out. Nasir watched his old friend approaching. He sensed the bitterness and sorrow in him, etched in the lines of his face. When Hafiz came closer, Nasir spoke.

"Hello, old friend."

Hafiz stopped and looked sharply at Nasir. As recognition and joy lit his face, he flung his arms around Nasir, kissing him on the cheeks.

"Nasir, Nasir, how are you, my friend? How many times have I thought of you and wondered if you were still alive! I was with your father and brother until they died. They told me you were in the mountains."

"I've been tending sheep in the mountains with my brother ever since I saw you in Acre, just before the city surrendered. "

"Do you have time, Nasir? Can we sit and talk?"

They found a place where they could sit quietly and drink the strong coffee both of them loved. Hafiz poured out the sorrow of his soul.

"Sometimes I think war is such folly. It costs so much and when it ends, you settle for less than you had when you started. In the meantime, you can't really live. In some ways, you become a brute, bent on destruction: no room for enjoyment and love and no possibility of raising a family. Most of the men I've known are dead. And after all these years, the Israelis are stronger than ever. The harder we fight, the more powerful they become.

"For so long, I've hated them and everything about them. I've killed them whenever I could. When I was young, hatred filled me like a fire that gave me strength! Now hatred has gutted my soul.

Joy is gone; death is a familiar friend. I find myself welcoming it, for life is so empty and full of suffering."

"Hafiz, my friend, I know what you're talking about. The longing for peace is still there even after all these years.

"When I went into the mountains, I found myself with doubts similar to yours. They nearly drove me crazy. I had to find an answer to them. But first I had to get away from the madness of war. Only then could I get a perspective on what was going on."

"What happened? How did you get away from it?"

"Growing up and tending the sheep with members of my family gave me familiarity with the mountains. Though I didn't realize it at the time, the mountains were a place of solace for me, a place where I could feel their stillness and their age. At night, I looked at the stars and wondered at my role in this vast unfathomable universe. For months I wandered alone, except for occasional meetings with my brother and uncle, who tended the sheep. I felt the poison and the horrors of war slowly seeping out of me, as though absorbed by the mountains themselves. I had not, for a long time, thought of the God of our forefathers, yet one day I found myself pondering this mystery again. I didn't welcome such thoughts, because the idea of God presented problems I didn't want to face."

"What do you mean?"

"For me, the idea of God implies the idea of justice, a time when the scales would be rebalanced. But when I looked around, there seemed to be very little evidence of justice. Then came the questions. If there really is a God, if Allah really does exist, how can there be so much suffering, so much hatred, so much death? What about right and wrong? Why does my enemy prosper after stealing our land? Why must an innocent young Israeli die for something he's too young to understand? Why are my enemy and I so alike, creatures of flesh and blood, love and hate? How did we arrive here on the same planet, a tiny speck of dust in the vast expanse of space? What were the chances of that happening?"

"What did you discover?"

"Those questions tormented my mind. At the same time, a subtle feeling grew deep within me. Somehow, I felt at home on this planet, in these mountains, beneath the stars. I couldn't explain it; I just felt it. I sensed there was something I didn't understand, and this lack of understanding created the disturbance I was feeling. I was tormented with doubt about the existence of God. Eventually I came to realize that what I believed meant nothing at all."

"I don't understand. Why did it mean nothing?"

"Because what I believed didn't have any bearing on the truth or falsity of anything."

"I still don't understand." Hafiz, who'd been fingering a polished stone, placed it on the table before him. Nasir recognized it from the days they'd fought together. It was his friend's good luck stone.

"I saw that my belief or lack of belief in God made no difference. I thought I should believe in God, that believing was the right thing to do. I was even afraid not to believe. I lived with these thoughts and feelings for a long time. Then I realized the most important thing of all was to know the truth for myself."

"What was the truth?"

"That I didn't know whether God existed or not. That was the truth! That admission was just a beginning. Until then, I'd either believed that God existed or that he didn't. As long as I believed one or the other, I couldn't find the truth." Nasir sipped his coffee and thought for a moment.

Hafiz looked at his friend and felt a sense of calmness that hadn't been there in the days when they'd fought together. His black hair was turning white; dark, imperturbable eyes were set in a dark face. His body was lean and strong. Not a trace of bitterness or pain of any kind seemed present in the tranquil expression of his friend's eyes. Hafiz wanted to know more about him. What had he found? Patiently he waited.

"We believed that by fighting the Israelis, we could force them to leave the land and go back where they came from. That was our belief. It hasn't worked. They believed they could destroy us by wiping out our villages, by driving us out of our homes. That belief proved false as well. When people give up belief, reality is all that's left. As long as we're locked in our stubborn and self-righteous beliefs, we'll continue to kill each other."

"What can be done, then? We can't convince anyone of this, can we? We can't stop them."

"No, we can't. They have to realize it for themselves."

"So what can be done?"

"I don't know."

They'd talked many times following that meeting. Hafiz wanted to leave the guerrillas, but he was under tremendous pressure to keep the group intact. He was an experienced fighter and knew the terrain well. The younger fighters looked to him for advice. For him to leave would be a great loss.

Nasir remembered the last meeting they'd had. Hafiz had come into the mountains and they met at a prearranged spot. Nasir had waited then, as he did now for Khalil. As usual, they talked late into the evening, sharing the bread and cheese Nasir had brought with him. Nasir heard Hafiz's voice beside him as they gazed at the hills below. He absently fingered the polished stone he always carried with him.

"My brother, you've helped me find a measure of peace. I don't know whether I'll leave the men I'm with. At first I wanted to, and yet I feel I must stay with them. They're younger and less experienced than myself. I've tried to speak to them about my deepest thoughts. They don't want to hear—they think I'm crazy. In their veins still beats the thrill of war, of living on the edge, of believing in a righteous cause. As you know, my friend, that edge brings exquisite appreciation to life because we don't know how long it will last. It can be snuffed out at any moment.

"I feel my time is near. I look over these hills that I've loved for so long and feel their beauty as never before. I'm thankful to sit beneath the moon and feel that, despite the suffering, I'm part of the earth and part of the stars. My belief in Allah has vanished. In my heart something stirs that I've never wished to speak of before. I mention it now only because I feel you'll understand and be pleased."

Nasir put his arm around his friend's shoulders. "I understand," he said softly.

"When I die I want you to know there's peace in my heart. The events that play across this planet are far beyond my comprehension. I no longer feel I have much choice, if any, in these matters. I feel like an actor playing a part in some great drama, the end of which I cannot know from here."

Nasir sat silently, a deep compassion welling up inside him. He understood clearly what his friend meant. Nasir had come to understand that separation was in reality, illusion. Though he couldn't explain his understanding, he felt at one with his friend, with all human beings, with all forms of life. He knew that the illusion of separation was somehow essential to the functioning of life in the world in which they lived. It was something he had no name for. It was something he just knew.

When the time came for Hafiz to depart, Nasir walked with him for several kilometers. They embraced, kissed and parted. Nasir never saw him again.

Months later, a young man called Idries found his way to Nasir's camp. He was tired and hungry when he arrived. Nasir fed him. Over coffee, he learned that Hafiz was dead. He'd been killed in a missile attack. Hafiz had spoken to Idries of Nasir many times. Before he died, he'd asked Idries to find him.

"He asked me to give you this stone. He said, 'Tell my friend I died well because I learned to live well. I'm tired of the bloodshed and glad to leave at last. Tell him I've cherished our talks and felt the silent stirring in my heart, even in the most terrible of times.'

"Then he said, 'The heart of the messenger is open. The fruit is ripe. More will come.' He said you'd know what he meant."

From that time on there were those who sought the shepherd in the hills. Some found him; some did not. His reputation spread like a quiet whisper on a gentle breeze. He'd been known as a fierce warrior, a man who one day turned his back on fighting to find peace in the silent mountains, tending his family's sheep. For years, those who tired of the bloodshed and hoped for another way came to see him. He talked with them in ones and twos, sometimes more. He met them in the hills and mountains, in villages and towns and, occasionally, in Beirut.

Nasir looked down over the hills and waited for Khalil.

Backfire

On the flight back to Washington Mera reflected on her experiences in Israel. In the year before his death Ali, at her insistence, had provided more details allowing her a greater understanding of the events that had molded his life. But even that information had not prepared her for the reality she'd found. It had shaken her to the core.

When the plane touched down at Dulles airport it was five in the afternoon. She was hoping someone would come to meet her but she had not been allowed to make any more phone calls before she was put aboard the plane. When she finished with customs she took an escalator to the baggage terminal and, emerging from the restricted area, found herself suddenly mobbed by a crush of reporters. Flash bulbs blinded her and for a moment she felt disoriented. It reminded her of a feeding frenzy; they were shouting so loud she couldn't make out what they were saying.

"Mera Morgan."

The voice coming from behind surprised her. She turned to see two men, customs officials, she thought.

"Come with us," they said and, taking her by the arms, hurried her away from the gaggle of reporters. She tensed immediately, recalling the police in Haifa and the Shabak agents at the hotel. Were all people in authority like this, she wondered? She was escorted along a maze of corridors and through a door into the bright sunlight of a low hanging sun and two waiting cars. Sandra was beside one of them.

Mera felt a wave of relief as she walked toward her. Sandra opened her arms and held her. Then turning toward the open door, she said, “We have to go.”

“My bag, I don’t have my bag.” Mera pulled up short.

“It’s taken care of.” Sandra said.

Once they were seated, the car moved toward a gate that opened as they approached. They quickly reached the highway and sped away, the second car following behind.

“I didn’t think the Vice President’s wife would attract so much attention!” Mera commented.

Sandra laughed, “It’s a bit more than that. David phoned me on the way to the airport. Senator Cole gave a press conference this afternoon demanding the resignation of the Vice President, and your arrest when you landed at the airport. You,” she said, touching Mera on the arm, “are a Palestinian spy who was thrown in jail in Israel and only released because of your connections. You and the Vice President are part of a Palestinian conspiracy against the beleaguered people of Israel.”

Mera felt sick. “Why would he make up such lies?”

“He doesn’t like David and he’ll do anything to make things difficult for him.”

“Why?”

“It’s just politics, I think.”

“I’m really sorry, Sandra.”

“Mera, don’t worry about it. This has nothing to do with you.” Sandra tried to change the subject. “You must be exhausted,” she said.

“What does David think?” Mera insisted.

"He said to tell you not to worry. He's not concerned about it; he'll talk with you tomorrow."

Sandra took Mera to her new residence. "Bill will be home shortly," she said. "We didn't know you were coming until an hour ago."

When Bill got home he and Mera had a long talk and she learned more about Cole's press conference and his accusations. They made her angry. "Why would the Senator make up such lies?" she wondered aloud.

Sandra and Tremaine came early for breakfast. The four of them sat comfortably around the table.

"We got a phone call last night from Barbara Walters," Tremaine said. "She asked if she could interview you. I told her it was up to you. I had no objections."

Mera, who'd been thinking about Cole, suddenly brightened. "I've watched her interviews," she said, "I trust her." She thought for a moment. "I'll do it."

"You don't have to do it if you don't want to," Bill said, looking at his wife.

"I want to, I've made up my mind, I want the American people to know that what the Senator is saying is a load of shit."

There was a moment of shocked silence. No one had ever heard Mera swear before, not even Bill. Suddenly they burst out laughing.

The following evening Mera was interviewed live in prime time. She described her trip to Lebanon and Israel and what had led to her arrest. Barbara asked her about her family connections to the Middle East and she talked about her grandfather and the stories she'd heard as a child. She explained how as an adult she'd learned about Haifa and Acre and the loss of a grandmother she'd never known. In the telling of Natalia's death tears suddenly blurred her vision. Quickly she wiped them away and continued. It was the only display of emotion she showed, in an otherwise calm and thoughtful presentation. The American people heard, many for the first time, the story of a conflict that began many years ago and was still going on, largely unreported.

The following day Cole was asked by Fox News what he thought of the interview. "We've no way of verifying what she had to say," he said dismissively. "A lot of it was second-hand; fairy stories an old man told a gullible child, stories by a man no longer alive. These stories shouldn't be taken seriously. It's obvious the village never existed. If it had she'd have found it."

The next day Nadia had gone to get food from the grocery store in Rockport. When she came out she was surprised by a reporter who wanted to know about her experiences in Palestine. Nadia, as she had done all her life, refused to talk about her past. The press jumped on her refusal, wondering in print and on the television news what she had to hide.

Heatherington, incensed at the treatment of his wife and daughter, called a press conference of his own. He corroborated what Mera had said and from his personal experience added details she wouldn't have known. As a British officer serving in Palestine at the time, he had credentials that even Cole's minions couldn't fault. Heatherington had been inundated with questions, and each one he answered in detail. Once the press realized that Cole's accusations were false, that he'd misrepresented the facts, the story fell off the front pages.

Tremaine was pleased with the outcome. The attack on

Mera had backfired. Instead of undermining Morgan and the Administration, it had done the opposite. In addition, Mera had given people a brief glimpse through a window into another time.

"You visited Gaza as well as Israel, didn't you?" David asked. "What did you think of it?"

They were sitting in comfortable chairs on the porch at the front of the Vice President's residence. Tremaine had called Mera earlier and asked if he could come for a short visit.

"It's a place of extremes," she replied. "Employment is a problem for both young and old; it's hard to find work and it's very difficult for the Palestinians to leave Gaza to work elsewhere. Some are able to find work in Israel, but because the border is often closed without notice, it's hard for them to maintain their employment."

"How do you mean?"

"Employers in Israel need employees for set hours but it's not possible because of the difficulties crossing the border."

"But some Israelis do employ Palestinians?"

"Some. But Palestinians have been painted as suicide bombers and that goes a long way in preventing employment. Sometimes there's good will toward the Palestinians, but sadly this is unusual. As I found in Israel, the pervasive view of Palestinians is one of disdain and mistrust. The Israeli government seems to encourage this."

"I'm curious, what made you want to go to Gaza?"

"For twenty years I put aside ten percent of my income. Since I'd been a teacher, education was important. I wanted to help in Gaza if I could. I knew that what I could contribute was just a pittance given the need."

"So what did you do, take money with you?"

"I did."

"Why not just send it?"

"I've always wanted to go to Palestine, and since I knew I would go sometime, I wanted to see the schools for myself and give the money personally."

"You took cash with you?"

"No," Mera laughed. "I took a certified cheque made out to the Ministry of Education."

"What did you see?"

"What I hadn't anticipated was that the Israelis, besides limiting access to Gaza, also control access to water. They can turn it off at will. The same goes for food and medical supplies. Sewage is a problem too, since with all the attacks on Gaza the system has been badly damaged. To repair it is impossible, as the supplies needed are not allowed across the border. In places there was raw sewage running between buildings and gathering in pools."

"You'd been in touch with the Ministry of Education in Gaza before you left?"

"Yes. They tried to prepare me for what I'd find. I'd also been in touch with UN officials about their schools, so I had some idea of what I might come across. But words can't prepare a person for the reality that's Gaza."

"What is somewhat surprising to me, given the circumstances, is how many children get an education. What was your sense of it?" Tremaine asked.

"I was surprised to find there are over six hundred schools in Gaza."

"And this includes government schools, UN schools and

religious schools, is that right?"

"That's right. Almost all of the schools are badly damaged; in fact I didn't see any that weren't. There are not enough schools for all the children wanting education. So, many schools run two shifts a day."

"And higher education takes place outside Gaza?"

"That's right. What I understand, however, is that getting permits to leave is so difficult and frustrating, few are able to take further studies."

They were interrupted briefly when a maid brought a tray with tea and scones, and quietly placed it on the low table between them. They thanked her and she disappeared. David buttered the scones and Mera poured the tea. When they were finished the conversation continued.

"What is the biggest need in Palestine right now?"

"Peace," Mera responded at once. "Peace is what both the Palestinians and Israelis need. But for the Palestinians the need for peace is greater, so much greater."

"Why do you say that?" David said, surprised. "Why is it greater for the Palestinians?

"The inequality of power means that the lives of Palestinians are always at risk. They lack proper food, for instance. I saw statistics that point to the fact that one fifth of all children are iodine-deficient, and iodine is essential for healthy brain development. And sixty percent of children suffer from anemia."

"This is very sad, I hadn't realized how bad it was."

"I hadn't either."

"What else?"

"I'll give you one more statistic, that as far as I'm concerned, illustrates the reality. A 1998 Israeli 'incursion,' they called it, killed almost 300 students and 10 teachers, and wounded over a thousand more. This means that thousands of students lost family members and are having to deal with the trauma and anxiety associated with those deaths. How many Israelis were killed? It's hard to get accurate statistics on this but conservative estimates suggest that for every hundred Israeli children who die, a thousand Palestinian children are killed."

David had seen statistics himself and he knew Mera was being conservative. "Sandra told me you went to one of the religious schools and were upset by what you saw."

Mera looked at Tremaine. "You're right; what I saw made me angry. I had promised myself I would simply observe, and I did. It was hard to keep quiet."

"Go on," David urged her.

"It's going to be a rant," she warned him.

"That's all right," he laughed. "I know all about rants, I've had a few myself."

Mera smiled at his comment. "I saw children being taught to hate, taught that Jews were evil and that it was Allah's will to kill Jews and those associated with the West, particularly the 'Great Satan' America. The children were already being prepared for so-called martyrdom."

"How?"

"They were told that Allah loves suicide bombers; that those who died killing the Jews would live in paradise. When I hear this kind of thing it brings me to the edge of hating. These children are under the spell of fire-breathing clerics. Young minds are being warped by the little minds of bigots. They construct their own God, their own twisted interpretation. Their God is a God of anger, a God of vengeance and cruelty. In this case the idea of man 'made in the image and likeness of God,' is reversed. God is made in the image and likeness of man—the image of those ignorant and heartless fools.

"I don't see any difference between fundamentalist Christians, Muslims or Jews, when they spew the same hatred. The God they create is a false God as far as I'm concerned.

"It's as if the clerics who preach hatred and the Israelis who still think they can banish Palestinians from what's left of their land, are working together to keep the conflict going. A peace negotiation is followed by provocation, followed by rocket attacks or suicide bombings, and then comes retaliation; and peace is now a distant memory.

"The Israeli government stokes this fear; milks it for all it's worth. Preaches about the necessity of being strong. This is how they conduct their election campaigns... and win every time. And so this sad, sick cycle continues, time after time after time. I don't believe this is what ordinary Palestinians want. They want peace, they want to work, they want to raise their families and enjoy life. I believe it's the same for Israelis. And yet Israeli governments are more in line with the fundamentalists, and out of step with many of their citizens."

"Are you suggesting that the government practices a form of secular fundamentalism?"

"I think that's a good way of describing it." Mera replied, "I read a quote recently by David Ben Gurion, the first Israeli Prime Minister. When he was asked back in the 1940s how he'd deal with the Palestinians who were driven off their land..."

"Referring to 'the right of return'?"

"Yes, that's right. His response was: 'The old will die and the new generations will forget.'"

"It hasn't happened, has it? Palestinians haven't forgotten."

"No they haven't." Mera thought for a moment. "I'm finished," she said, "I'm all ranted out."

David looked at Mera. She gave the appearance of a calm middle-aged woman but underneath there was a fierce core. "You don't like intolerance, do you?"

"I certainly don't," she snapped.

"Do I sense an intolerance for it?" he asked, his face straight.

She laughed.

Morgan

Vice President William G. Morgan strolled the grounds of his new home at One Observatory Circle. It was the first time he'd done so since he and Mera moved to Washington. The residence was located in the northeast quadrant of a large circular park at the US Naval Observatory. It was one of a number of buildings within the grounds.

Mera found Washington a big adjustment. She'd grown up in Rockport, Maine and missed her friends and the farm. She'd gone to Washington with her husband on many occasions, but was always happy to return to the old seaport she loved.

Morgan would also miss New England, its people and their down-to-earth practicality.The change from Senator to Vice President took some getting used to.

He'd not known President Emerson well, although years before he'd taken political science from him at the University of Maine. He'd been impressed with the man then. He'd been impressed again when Emerson became President.

Morgan liked Tremaine and his approach to life. He had a direct way of seeing. He didn't fight with life, but saw how it was and responded without judgment. Morgan had listened to him during the presidential campaign and thought about what he said. Where difficulty existed Tremaine saw possibility; his mind worked that way, by itself it seemed. Emerson and Tremaine had made a good team.

The interviews Morgan had with Tremaine had been lengthy and substantive, lasting more than a week. Overall, they'd been a delightful surprise. Morgan found Tremaine a relaxed and attentive person with a mind free of preconceptions. The President's questions had been probing and far-reaching. He wanted to know Morgan's views on the Middle East, his observations and conclusions. He'd explored in considerable detail the family's historical connections to the Middle East.

They'd talked about a wide range of topics including the environment, violence and poverty, kindness and generosity and the idea of service to others. Tremaine wanted to know why Morgan thought the way he did; ideas he had concerning the resolution of difficulties facing the country. He said, "Some accuse me of being a philosopher and not a practical man. My response is that philosophy sets the tone, expresses a fundamental approach to life and our role in it. Philosophical understanding is embedded in all cultures and all ages. It is the context from which all behavior springs. It is, therefore," he insisted, "eminently practical." Tremaine reminded Morgan that public service was a high calling when it expressed the sincere, unselfish desire to serve. Morgan's conversations with Tremaine had rekindled a sense of anticipation and hope.

He approached a stand of trees near the residence and could hear the sound of birds gathering high in the trees for their end-of-day ritual. All about him the cacophony of their cries was a pleasing welcome.

As he came out of the trees he could see the house, and a

glimpse of Mera through the window, working in the kitchen. He could still remember the pained look on the cook's face when Mera told him she liked cooking and was not about to give up "her" kitchen, no matter where she lived, no matter what position her husband held.

For twenty-nine years they'd been married. Twenty-nine years of joys and sorrows, hopes and disappointments. Life had been rich and rewarding. He and Mera had three children, two boys and a girl. Marian, the youngest, had married a fisherman, and together they crewed their forty-foot fishing boat off the rugged coast of northern Maine. Ross, the eldest, was an accountant in Cambridge. Ted, their middle boy, had entered medical school three years ago at the University of California in San Francisco.

Morgan crossed one of the several access roads within the grounds. The thought of his son Ted brought a rush of emotion. During a mid-semester break, Ted had gone to visit his friend Damien in Los Angeles. The two of them went to play basketball in a park near Damien's home and by all accounts, it was an enjoyable reunion with high school buddies. They played for a couple of hours. With slaps on the back and firm handshakes, they went their separate ways.

Ted and Damien had walked five of the seven blocks home when they rounded a corner and found themselves caught in the crossfire between two rival gangs. Ted died on the way to hospital. Damien received a gunshot wound to his thigh.

Ted's death was a terrible shock and they'd sought comfort in the presence of Mera's grandfather, Ali. They sat with him in silence and it soothed them. They walked with him; at times together, at times alone. When they needed to talk, he listened.

His questions when they came were soft, and because of them, knots unraveled and peace returned. Ali had taken them by the hand and ushered them through the valley of the shadow of death, a valley with which he was all too familiar.

Ultimatum

Day after day, night after night, Israeli jets flew into Lebanon, destroying everything that moved within thirty kilometers of Israel's northern border. Troops, tanks and guns pounded villages into rubble. Gunboats patrolled the western shoreline, destroying fishing settlements and sinking any boat they found. A flood of humanity streamed north toward Beirut.

Squads of Hizballah guerrillas fired hand-launched missiles across the border into northern Israel. They moved quickly, never staying in one place, sometimes taking cover in the tide of humanity flowing north. Syrian and Jordanian troops mobilized along the borders with Israel. Lebanon appealed to the UN Security Council for help.

David had spent the last six hours in discussions with members of his cabinet. "I need a break." He stood and stretched, then turned to Secretary of State Kersey. "Doug, I'll meet you back here in an hour." He pushed his chair in, and went out into the fresh air. He set out at a brisk walk through the Rose Garden. The intense heat of the day had subsided, and the warm air bore the fragrance of roses.

When he returned to the briefing room, Kersey was waiting for him. "I think it's time to talk with the Israelis in person," David said to his Secretary of State.

"I agree," Doug said.

"You'll go to Israel tomorrow."

A week later Prime Minister Michael Levin and his Foreign Secretary, Joseph Goldhirsh, entered the Oval Office. Doug Kersey and Bill Morgan were with Tremaine. They shook hands all around and made the introductions.

"Have a seat." Tremaine nodded toward the sofas on either side of a coffee table where coffee and pastries had been placed. "Coffee, gentlemen?"

They accepted. Tremaine poured coffee and passed the pastries. When he'd finished he sat back and waited. He'd never met the Israeli leaders before. They looked tired.

Looking around the men in the room Tremaine noticed through the window a red rose hanging from a trellis. Caught in a shaft of sunlight, it bobbed back and forth. Looking at the Israelis he could see by their posture they were tense, their knuckles white from gripping their mugs.

"Well gentlemen, let's get under way." Tremaine turned toward Levin. "Mr. Prime Minister, you requested this meeting, so please begin."

"Mr. President, we do not accept your proposals. In fact, as a nation we're insulted by your lack of faith in us. The change in policy explained by your Secretary of State, Mr. Kersey, is not acceptable to us."

"I'm sorry to hear that, gentlemen. No insult was intended. What specifically do you object to?"

"First of all, we object to your interference in our political affairs. We have a right to defend ourselves in whatever way we see fit. We're a country at war, a country at war since its birth.

We've had to defend ourselves from hostile neighbors, and our citizens are under threat and subject to terrorist attacks all over the world. When provoked we will strike back; it's how we're able to survive. The only thing our neighbors understand is strength. They're afraid of it, and that keeps us safe."

"Mr. Levin, I don't accept your reasoning. For years preceding the formation of Israel as a state your forebears used violence and intimidation against the local Palestinian population, eventually driving them out by a variety of violent means. This still continues. You and your countrymen seem to think force gives you the right to do what you wish, and until now you've succeeded. You say you want peace with your neighbors, but until the underlying causes of this conflict are acknowledged and addressed there can be no lasting peace..."

Angrily the Prime Minister interrupted. "Rockets slamming into a hall filled with innocent people is not an expression of peaceful neighbors, no matter how you look at it!"

Tremaine ignored the anger. "So far you've lived by threat or force; but violence hasn't brought peace, instead it has made peace less and less likely. You are a powerful nation, powerful in the ability and willingness to unleash deadly force on a mass scale. But, in my opinion, the constant use of force threatens your neighbors: neighbors for instance like Iran. They believe they must develop nuclear weapons as well—a frightening prospect for the rest of the world. Your war with your neighbors threatens us and the well-being of every person on the planet."

"We wouldn't threaten anyone if we were left alone; we simply respond to the threats of those who would destroy us."

The tension in the room was palpable. "Perhaps it would be worthwhile looking at the facts. In 1947 Palestine was partitioned to accommodate the influx of Jewish immigrants from Europe. Palestinians had not been consulted and had not agreed to their land being taken away from them. But setting this aside for now, both the UN and the British government supported a two-state solution. Two states, it was thought, would solve the problem. But really how could it? Perhaps if no one had lived on the land, it might have worked; but the land was populated, largely by Palestinians; it was their land."

"It was only their land because our people were driven out of Palestine by the Romans after the fall of Masada. Then..."

Tremaine held up his hand. "That was two thousand years ago. A discussion like this could go on indefinitely and it's not going to help. We must deal with what's happening now."

Levin nodded and seemed to relax. "What do you have in mind?"

"This is a general statement and it summarizes our perspective on this matter. If we take the suggestion of the United Nations in 1947 as a starting point, it set out that the Palestinian portion of land was 43 percent and the Jewish portion 57 percent. I'm not suggesting that we agree with this, or that it was fair, but we need to start from somewhere.

"Today Israel controls 78 percent and the Palestinians 22 percent. Even that doesn't accurately describe it because Israeli settlements are being expanded as we speak. As far as our government is concerned this is illegal and we will not in any way be party to it anymore. I understand your need for defense but taking another quarter of Palestinian land since 1947 would seem more like aggression than defense."

"What exactly are you saying?" asked a tight-lipped Goldhirsh.

"What I'm saying is that we will no longer contribute to

what we see as a crime against humanity, namely an ongoing and systematic form of ethnic cleansing."

The color had drained from the faces of the Israelis. A shocked silence ensued. Tremaine waited, not in a hurry.

"What do you have in mind?" Levin asked, his voice tense and tightly controlled. "How do you see this happening?"

"I don't know how it will happen, I only know it must." Tremaine paused to let his words sink in. "Without it there'll no peace," he added.

"What land are you speaking of?" Goldhirsh interjected.

"Let's put it this way. If you do not stop the settlement expansion by noon on September 15th we will withdraw all financial support for your government and no longer guarantee your loans."

Levin was incredulous. "You can't."

"I can and I will."

"We have signed agreements, it would be illegal."

"That may be so, but if we continue to support your government as we have up to this time, we would be complicit in the crime of ethnic cleansing. We will appeal to the International Court of Justice for an opinion concerning the legality of our continued financial support under these circumstances."

"They couldn't rule on this," Levin said, "without first determining whether ethnic cleansing and therefore a crime has taken place."

"That is correct."

The Israelis sat in stunned silence. "The American people won't allow it," Goldhirsh spat the words out.

"What you mean is that the Jewish lobbies will not allow it," Tremaine ventured. "The American people are a fair people and

I'm convinced that once they know the facts they'll understand what we're doing and support it."

"You won't get re-elected," Goldhirsh stated flatly.

"May I ask you a question, Mr. Goldhirsh?"

Goldhirsh glared at Tremaine.

"Are you suggesting you'll encourage Jewish lobbies to influence the elections by campaigning against those who support our stand?"

"You said it!"

"You opened the conversation this afternoon by suggesting outrage at what you called our interference in your political affairs. And now you're telling me this is what you'll do?"

Levin stood up. "There's nothing to be gained by staying here and listening to this," he said to Goldhirsh who also rose from his chair.

"Gentlemen, before you leave, perhaps you should fully understand what we propose to do."

The Israelis looked at Tremaine.

"Please sit down," he said. "I want to clarify what I've said so there can be no misunderstanding."

The Israelis sat down.

"As I said, if settlement construction continues anywhere in the occupied territories, anywhere on Palestinian land or land in dispute, beyond September 15th we will no longer provide any financial assistance or guarantee any of your loans."

Levin had recovered from the initial shock of Tremaine's declaration and responded, "What precisely do you mean?"

"We will no longer support you. There'll be no military and economic assistance, no grants for research and business development. Nothing! We're serious about this. I'm seeking legal opinions on these matters from the Supreme Court as well as from the International Court of Justice in the Hague. I need to know you understand what I've said."

"We understand you quite well," Levin responded, not even trying to keep the sarcasm from his voice.

"Do you have any questions?"

"Not for the moment."

Then I'll not keep you any longer," he said, standing.

"You can't do it." Levin said, shaking his head.

"We'll see," Tremaine said. "We'll see."

Tremaine turned to Goldhirsh. "This has to stop," he said quietly, taking the man's hand.

Goldhirsh held Tremaine's gaze. "As you said, Mr. President, 'we'll see.'"

Tremaine turned and put his hand on Levin's shoulder. "Prime Minister, you and I know, only truth can resolve this mess. All of us must face the facts of what we've done. It won't be easy but perhaps it will help when we stop believing our own propaganda. The problem with propaganda is that it can leave us blind to important facts that to others are obvious."

When the Israelis had gone Tremaine walked to the window and looked out across the garden. Large black clouds threatened the city. Lightning flashed, and thunder rumbled. Morgan and Kersey looked at each other.

Moving on

"Why do we have to go?" Samara asked when Nasir told her they were leaving the following day.

"Because we must," was all he would say.

"I like it here," she protested.

"I know."

"I'm sorry for asking, Nasir, but can't I stay?"

"No. Your destiny lies elsewhere." Nasir refused to be drawn into further discussion.

And so, with a sense of sadness, Samara left the cave that had become her home. With Nasir, she climbed into the mountains until they reached a rocky outcrop where they paused and caught their breath. Below them, the familiar valleys snaked down the side of the mountain to the distant ocean in the west. Nasir turned and walked east and Samara followed, until they came to a shallow valley where a spring had pooled and around it the grasses grew in wild profusion. Not far from the spring, they stopped beside a shallow depression surrounded by an outline of stones, marking the grave where they'd buried Nasir's brother Salim. Nasir had planted a small cedar in place of a headstone. Standing before the grave they bowed their heads and silently recalled Salim, who for almost sixty years had cared for the family's sheep.

After a brief rest, they continued along a faint trail

that led through the mountains. Several hours had passed when the sound of a shot broke the silence. Nasir reacted instantly. Pulling Samara off the trail, he raced up the incline and leaped to a ledge. He turned, grabbed her by the hands and pulled her up beside him. Breathing hard, they lay side by side, peering down at the trail below. Nothing moved.

From their hiding place, they had a clear view of the surrounding area. If anyone came along the trail, they'd see them. Holding his breath, Nasir listened, his ears tuned for the slightest sound. The sighing of the ever-present wind was all he could hear. Half an hour later, they cautiously moved on.

"We'll stay above the trail," Nasir explained.

"What do you think it is?"

"Guerrillas. It's safer to avoid them."

The memory of her family's deaths made Samara shudder. For half an hour they moved slowly, keeping the trail below them. Climbing around a rock face, Nasir glimpsed a movement below. Instantly he froze. Samara held her breath and watched. Beneath them, a man had crawled off the trail and sat propped against the shattered trunk of an old tree. His head fell forward. His hands hung limp at his sides, and blood stained his shirt.

"Stay here, Samara. I'm going down to see what's happened."

Before she could respond, Nasir slipped away. Quickly, yet cautiously, he worked his way toward the wounded man. The sun was low, and the shadows in the depressions served as hiding places. He checked the surrounding area for signs of life before creeping closer.

Nasir studied the man. Black hair, wet with sweat, was plastered to his forehead. His eyes were closed, his breathing ragged and fast. He wore camouflage pants and a long-sleeved khaki shirt. His feet were bare. A dark stain spread down his shirt from a wound in his upper chest. Suddenly, the man's eyes opened. With a jolt, Nasir recognized Tariq, a friend of Khalil's. Nasir stood up and Tariq's head turned toward him. Recognition spread across his face, and the light returned to his eyes.

"Nasir, is that you?"

"It is." Nasir knelt before the wounded man and examined him.

"I'm not going to survive this, am I?" Tariq whispered.

Nasir looked into Tariq's eyes. "No, my friend, this is the end for this body."

Standing, he waved Samara to join them. In moments, the young woman was at his side, breathless. While Nasir cradled Tariq in his arms, Samara unslung her water skin and carefully guided a small stream of water to the man's dry lips. His eyes caught hers, and a faint smile crossed his face. "Thank you," he whispered.

"What happened?" Nasir asked.

Tariq shifted his gaze from Samara and looked out across the desolate slopes. "Iranians joined our unit about a month ago." Nasir and Samara strained to hear him. "We captured a young Israeli girl two nights ago. I was ordered to kill her. I refused. The Iranians brought me here today. One of them shot me."

"Was Khalil with your unit?" Nasir asked.

"He was, but he was sent ahead. We were to rendezvous in Bent Jebail."

"Is that where he is now?"

"I think so," came the hoarse voice.

Samara again raised the water skin to moisten Tariq's lips. His eyes focused on her momentarily. Once more the hint of a smile spread across his ashen face.

Nasir adjusted Tariq's position. "It's almost over, Tariq. Soon you'll leave this place of suffering."

"Will you see my mother for me?"

"Yes." Nasir bent his head to catch the words.

"She's a good mother. Please tell her for me..." The words had come slowly. The eyes stared, no longer seeing. Nasir knew that in Tariq's mind his mother now stood before him, her arms tenderly encircling the son she loved.

Samara watched intently, her heart still pounding. She felt the bond of love between the two men and watched through her tears as consciousness faded from Tariq's body. With a slight shudder, he gave up his last breath.

Samara and Nasir stopped for the night, far from where Tariq had died. It was late and, exhausted, she fell asleep at once. She woke once during the night and realized Nasir was gone. Long before dawn, he shook her by the arm.

"We must leave at once," he whispered.

In moments she was ready.

"What's happening?" she asked.

"There's an Israeli unit nearby. They must be looking for the young girl Tariq mentioned. We must get as far away as possible."

Samara had trouble keeping up with Nasir. They climbed a ridge and descended the other side into what seemed like a shallow valley. Against the stars, she could see the outlines of the surrounding mountains. She could tell they were moving east. They stopped only once for a brief rest.

"Where are we going?" Samara asked when she'd caught her breath. They sat on a low hill where they would know if someone was coming. If patrols operated in the region, Nasir did not want to run into them.

"Once we reach the head of the valley, we'll climb back into the high country again. From there it's not far to the village of Rachaf. I have friends there."

Dawn found them standing before an old wooden door, the entrance to a small and tidy dwelling on the outskirts of the village. Nasir knocked softly. They heard movement inside and light appeared in the window. Finally the door scraped open and the sleepy face of an elderly man appeared. He had a stubble beard and a shock of white hair standing on end. As he looked out into the faint glow of early morning, his eyes lit up with recognition.

"Come in, come in."

Inside, an oil lamp sat on a wooden table, shedding light into the small tidy room.

"Please, have a seat."

Nasir and Samara sat in the chairs at the table.

"Samara, this is my old friend Aziz. Aziz, this is Samara."

Aziz gave her a radiant smile. The smile and the disheveled hair struck her as funny. Aziz, understanding the source of the humor, joined in with a chuckle.

He moved quickly to get coffee brewing. Soon the aroma filled the room. From an old barrel, he took out dates and placed them in a wooden bowl. Bananas, along with a loaf of bread, a round of cheese and a knife were placed on the table. "Eat," he said.

The Mango Tree

Samara woke up. From the slant of the sun's rays, she knew it was late afternoon. Outside she heard the murmur of voices. When she opened the door Aziz was sitting on the step. He patted the space beside him. The warmth of afternoon had peaked and passed and cool currents of air wafted down from the tops of the mountains. Nasir sat on his blanket beneath an old tree, its gnarled, leafless branches twisted at odd angles. In front of him, four men sat cross-legged, engrossed in conversation. A breeze sighing through the branches accompanied the melodic sound of voices. The scene bore a dreamlike quality.

A man was speaking, "I've been searching for truth many years," she heard him say. "I was told you're a holy man, a sage, one with whom I can speak concerning matters of the spirit."

"I am merely a shepherd who takes care of his flocks, I have done so since I was a boy," Nasir replied.

"Why are you hiding from me?" responded the man.

"Why are you hammering on my door?"

"I told you, I seek truth."

"Would you know the truth if it were before you?"

"Of course."

"What truth do you seek to know?" Nasir asked. "Is it to add to your storehouse of knowledge?"

"To acquire real knowledge, spiritual knowledge, is the only undertaking worthy of a man."

There is arrogance in that man, Samara thought to herself.

Nasir continued. "Real knowledge cannot be acquired, it happens spontaneously, and only to a few. It's the gift of Allah."

The man recoiled as though he'd been slapped. "Why do you say such things?"

"Because they're true," came the quiet response. "You said you'd recognize truth when it was before you, so, painful as it is, start with this."

"You insult me."

"No, what takes insult is not real. Who you truly are lies behind the mask you present to the world."

"What are you talking about?"

"You wanted to know the truth. I've taken you at your word." Nasir paused for a moment as though collecting his thoughts. "When does a mango drop from the tree?"

"When it's ripe, of course."

"The understanding you seek is not something that can be forced. Like the mango, a person cannot fall from the tree of illusion until the necessary ripeness is present."

"How can I bring this about?"

"You, can't; it comes only as a by-product of living."

"I've lived a long life. Maybe not as long as you, but more than this man beside me."

"Wisdom, the ripeness of which we speak, is not a matter of age in the way that you understand it. Who can measure the unfathomable experiences of the ancient soul? How many times has it dressed to enter this vast hall of life for the feast of the senses? Your time will come, my brother. Never fear. Walk abroad in the world and, no matter what you do, pay attention. Find the happiness that does not disappear. One day, when the time is ripe, you'll sit before the one who will shake you into wakefulness. Then you'll know the truth you seek."

"It was a mistake coming here today."

"No mistake. From deep in the dream, you heard the voice of Allah and responded. It is reassurance that is needed by the sleeper enmeshed in life's dream. Now you may go your way, relieved. Go back into life. Live life to its fullest."

Nasir stood up and, reaching down for the man's hand, helped him to his feet.

"Aziz, give him dates for his journey." Nasir embraced the man, who suddenly seemed uncertain. Samara watched as he walked slowly up the road and disappeared. She wondered: was it sorrow she sensed in those stooped shoulders?

"I'm sorry I brought him," she heard one of the men saying.

"It was something you had to see for yourself," Nasir replied. "These teachings have nothing to do with making converts to Islam. Who can improve on the handiwork of Allah? Trying to convert anyone comes from pride and lies, from the belief, whether realized or not, that you know more than the Creator whose dance it is: a dance set in motion before the beginning of time."

"I'd heard him say many times how much he wanted to know the truth. He's always reading. He's a learned man, while I'm not. I wanted him to meet you. When I told him of you, he was excited. I didn't know where you were, so it was coincidence that brought us to Aziz's house. I thought he might know when you'd be back, and there you were."

"Tahir, I know that in your heart are generosity and love, but you must understand what I said about the mango. Until the person is ripe, the presence of a master does no good. Those who are compelled to seek Allah cannot help themselves. They don't choose to seek. How could they? It is the action of destiny, the love of the Creator for Itself that brings about the sacred search."

"But what about the mullahs who teach that the only way is the way of the Prophet?" one of the young men asked.

"A wagon wheel has many spokes, surrounded by a wooden and steel hoop. At the center is the hub, where the spokes are attached. In the center of the hub is a hole around which everything else turns. The spokes come from the four corners of the world and arrive at the center. The center is nameless and formless.

"Out of necessity, we have given it names: Allah, Yahweh, Vishnu, or God, It's all the same. The spokes represent the many paths that lead there. The farther they are from the center, the more distinct and separate they appear. At the outer limits, beliefs are rigid. Those found there believe their particular spoke represents the 'one and only true way.' Those close to the hub already sense that all spokes lead to the same place; their beliefs are less rigid. Those who find themselves at the hub have discarded belief altogether. They understand that all spokes, though coming from different places, arrive at the same hub. When this is known, it's not long before each one dissolves into the formless center. This is the end of the journey, the union with the Holy One, which words cannot describe."

"Why is there so much conflict at the outer edges of the spokes?"

"Because the world is divided into right and wrong. This division is a misunderstanding, something placed over creation, like a blanket, by the mind of man himself."

"I don't understand."

"What we see around us can only be seen by the combination of what is and what is not. The tree can only be seen against the background that is not tree. This is known as duality. Everything has two aspects to it; inside goes with outside, beauty with ugliness, good with bad. As two banks define a river, so duality gives rise to the appearance of the world. Believers in religions the world over have not understood the nature of reality. They've tried to find good without bad. They struggle and strive, prisoners of their own beliefs, unable to see the obvious truth that is always there."

"How foolish we are."

"Yes, in a way. On the other hand, nothing is out of place. All is as it is and so brings about the divine dance known as life. This is the way it is. This is life; it could be no other way, nor should it be."

"Then why are we here?"

"Because you could be no other place and, perhaps, because the fruit is ripe."

Paper

"I want a copy right away," Senator Cole barked into the phone. "No, I don't give a damn how you get it, just get it. . . . No, in my office by tomorrow morning . . . . Yes. . . . Yes, I know. No, you don't need to be concerned. No one will know. No, we'll keep you out of it. . . . No, you don't have anything to worry about. . . . Okay, goodbye."

As Senator Cole put the phone down, a cynical smile spread over his face. He picked up a cigar. Biting the end off, he spat it smartly into his wastebasket, a skill he'd gained over years of practice. Flicking a lighter, he puffed until a cloud of smoke billowed above him. He pulled out the writing tray at his desk, put his feet up and leaned back in his expensive leather chair. Life was good.

A man in his late fifties, Cole had dark gray hair, thinning on top. He wore dark framed glasses with thick lenses. At five foot ten he seemed short for his two hundred pounds. The cold gray of his eyes was ameliorated by a wateriness that sometimes gave an onlooker the unsettling feeling he was crying. He had a reputation for getting his way and was known to be savvy, even unscrupulous. He knew what he wanted, and was not easily swayed by the opinions of others. After the decimation of the Republican administration, he'd assumed leadership of the party.

There was talk he'd been involved in the hedge fund scandal, which had brought down the previous administration, but no one had been able to prove anything. As minority leader, he kept a tight rein on his fellow Republicans.

He'd hated Emerson with a passion and had made it his mission to disrupt him in every way possible. When Tremaine assumed power, he'd continued the same policy. Tremaine was a maverick and more difficult to handle than Emerson.

It was Cole who'd ordered his henchmen to dig into Tremaine's past. Whatever he could use he'd leaked to the press. Several times, he was sure his revelations would ruin the man and force his resignation, but time after time, the President slipped away unscathed. The press had gone soft, he thought. Never mind, he was a patient man. Sooner or later, Tremaine would slip up. No one could be that smart or that good! Besides, he had a lead on something now. If it proved true, Tremaine would have to step down.

The phone rang. Cole picked it up.

"Yes, Midge, put him through. Hello, Cole here.... Senator Smythe. Thanks for getting back to me. I understand you want to look at the budget that's coming down. . . . I know it's not down yet. . . . Yes, I know, but I don't want any surprises. You know what I mean? We vote as a block, no breaking ranks . . . . I don't give a damn. If you break ranks with us, you won't get your grain subsidy bill into committee. . . . Good. Then we understand each other. . . . I'll be in touch. . . . Bye."

Cole put the phone down and, leaning back, lit his cigar again and puffed hard. Through the clouds of smoke, a low shaft of sunlight struck a wilted bouquet of flowers and fallen petals on the corner of his desk. It had been another busy day. Four days it had taken. He'd been on the phone with every Republican on the Hill. He was satisfied, certain he had them in line. They'll follow my lead, he thought. My troops are disciplined. Pressing a button, he spoke into the intercom.

"Midge, did that memo get sent to McClelland?"

"Yes, it went out yesterday."

"Anonymously?"

"Yes, of course."

"Good. I'm finished for the day. I'll be back in the morning at nine. Have a nice evening."

"I will. You too," came the disembodied voice.

Two days later, Mark Turner, the president of McClelland, sat at his desk. Finishing the letter, he threw it on the table. He was furious. He buzzed for his secretary. An elderly woman with white hair and a pleasing smile pushed the door open.

"Mary, where's Angus?" he demanded.

The smile vanished from her face. "He went out to lunch with the Canadians. He said he'd be back by three." She looked at her watch. "He should be back soon."

"As soon as he gets back, send him in. I need to talk to him right away." Mary nodded and left. She'd known he'd be upset, but she hadn't expected such a strong reaction. Turner was not by nature an angry man. He tended to be quiet and self-contained. Fifteen minutes later, Angus walked breezily into the office. Mary gave him the message.

"What's it about?" he asked.

"He received a letter saying the President is about to issue an order that all Government offices must use recycled paper."

The news was a jolt to Angus, too. He knocked on the door and pushed it open.

"Come in, come in," Turner muttered impatiently.

Angus walked to the desk. Turner indicated the letter.

"Read it," he said.

Angus picked it up and sat down. Quickly, he glanced over it and tossed it back on the desk.

"If it's true, it's bad news," he said.

"You're damned right it's bad news," Turner sputtered. "We've got to find out, and quick. Who would know?"

"There are several people I can think of."

"Get on it right away. Find out all you can and get back to me. If it's true, we've got to put a stop to it."

"Right. I'll get on it at once. I'll have to go to Washington. I can't do it from here."

"I don't give a damn how you do it, just get it done."

Angus knew by Turner's voice he was dismissed. He talked briefly with Mary, giving her instructions. "Call me at home when you've booked the flight. I'm going to pack and let my wife know."

Turner swiveled in his chair and looked out over the city. In the distance, above the haze, he could see the mountains of the Olympic Peninsula. Damn, he thought, this couldn't come at a worse time. The Canadian sister company, Crown McClelland, had just settled a contract dispute after a lengthy strike. On top of that, the Canadian government had increased the stump rate for Crown Lands. Only the steadily increasing purchase of paper by federal government bureaucracies had enabled them to afford such a settlement in the Canadian operations.

If the government was going to use recycled paper, McClelland's mills were not equipped to provide it. Existing contracts with the government were up for negotiation in April. They could lose business to the smaller companies, some of which had already developed the capacity to make recycled paper. Turner shook his head. We can't let this happen, he thought. Angus is good. He's got powerful contacts, but this is going to cost more money and we could still lose it all.

Turner gazed through the window. The Olympic Mountains had assumed the dark violet haze of late afternoon. All his life he'd sought out the mountains when he was troubled. They calmed him. A niggling thought insinuated itself in his mind and he tried to put it aside. Perhaps we've been greedy and shortsighted. Perhaps we've taken the land and the trees for granted. Fifty years ago, when he first started in the forestry industry, no one had ever thought that the vast wilderness would someday be unable to meet the demand for trees.

The same thing was happening to the tropical rain forests. Have we abused the land and now the time has come to pay the piper? He didn't want to think about it. The problem was beyond him; it was not for him to deal with it. Soon those matters would be in the hands of a new generation. He was a businessman entrusted with running a company. His stockholders expected him to make money. He had a duty to the workforce as well. Besides, if his company didn't do it others would.

He pushed the thoughts to the back of his mind. It wasn't up to him to set policy or resolve the world's difficulties. Business was business. Turning around, he reached for the desk lamp and switched on the light. Its opaque green glass shielded his eyes, and light fell on the papers scattered across the highly polished wooden desk. Slowly, he sorted them and put them away. Standing, he pushed his chair neatly in place, took his coat from the rack and walked out of the office. "Good night," he muttered.

Mary watched him go as the door swung shut behind him.

Friday evening, Angus left the Hill and caught a taxi to his hotel. He sat back and relaxed, thinking of all the meetings since his arrival two weeks before. He was satisfied the company would be safe. He looked out the window, watching the people pass by, not really seeing them. Tomorrow, he'd catch a plane. By evening, be home. Sunday he'd go fishing. He smiled in anticipation. He was glad to leave the city.

Jennifer Ramirez

Presidential Aide, Jonathan Makarios stood in front of Tremaine, they were in the Oval Office.

"Jennifer Ramirez?" David was incredulous.

"Yes," "Are you sure?"

"Positive. She held a press conference in San Francisco an hour ago. It's all over the news. The press is clamoring to hear from you. The switchboard is jammed with calls."

David slowly spun the chair around, leaned back and looked out the window. His mind drifted back to the day he'd first met Jennifer Ramirez, some twenty-one years ago. He'd been attending a conference in San Francisco. They had an affair for two years. It had been one of the contributing factors in the end of his first marriage. David had broken it off with the hope of working things out with his wife, but it hadn't helped. That was the last time he'd seen Jennifer. He'd tried to get in touch with her after his divorce, but had been unsuccessful. When he finally reached her mother, she told him that Jennifer had gone away. He had no idea that she'd had a child—his child. He was stunned.

"What are you going to do?" asked Jonathan.

"See if you can get in touch with Jennifer for me, will you? I'd like to speak with her."

David turned to face his friend. "Schedule a meeting

with the press for seven this evening, " he said quietly." He wanted to talk with Sandra before then.

Jonathan nodded and left the office. David turned and gazed into the world beyond the window, wondering about the daughter he'd never seen.

An hour later, David and Sandra were sitting in the Solarium.

"Have you tried getting in touch with her?" Sandra asked.

"Jonathan couldn't get through. She'll only talk through her lawyer. I'd like to talk with her and help her in any way I can. I don't want to make things difficult. The press is reporting she left her job and moved away after the affair because she was pregnant and hurt. How do you feel, love? What do you think about it?"

"It was a long time ago," she said thoughtfully, "before you and I met. What happened, happened. She was someone you loved and, it seems, someone who loved you in return. How could I not understand that?"

Jennifer sat on the edge of her seat and watched the television. Her heart was beating fast and she felt a lump of fear in her throat. What had she done? She watched as David stepped to the podium in the Press Briefing room and listened as he spoke.

"Twenty-one years ago, I had a relationship with a woman named Jennifer Ramirez, a woman I loved. For two years we were lovers and friends. I cared for her deeply although I was married at the time. My actions hurt my wife and brought suffering to all of us, and for that I am sorry. I left Jennifer in the hope of restoring the relationship with my wife, but it didn't work. When Jennifer and I parted, I didn't know she was pregnant. I didn't know until today. If I'd known, I would gladly have supported the raising of our daughter. I don't have anything else to say, but I'll take some of your questions."

"Yes," Tremaine pointed to a young man in front of him.

"I imagine you have regrets ..."

"If I have any regrets," Tremaine interrupted, "it is that I didn't know until now of my daughter's existence, and I was not able to be a father to her while she was growing up. Those years are gone and nothing can bring them back."

"Your behavior has brought embarrassment to the government and the people you represent. What do you have to say to the American people?"

"Some might feel embarrassed by my behavior, but think about it: why should they? What does my behavior have to do with them? It's not a reflection on them. They're not somehow less because of what I did, nor are they better for other things I've done.

"What happened with Jennifer happened. It can't be changed. Life has many twists and turns. We never know what's going to happen, and yet through it all, hopefully we become less judgmental and better able to enjoy life."

Tremaine pointed to a woman reporter on his left.

"You got this woman pregnant and failed to provide for your daughter. What makes you different from any other deadbeat dad who refuses to take care of his kids?"

"Call me what you will. The fact is, as I've already said, until today I was unaware that Jennifer had a child. I'm happy to contribute to the expense and care involved in raising our daughter. Had I known, I would have done so earlier. I'll do everything in my power to make up for the years that have gone by."

Tremaine pointed to a young man at the back of the room. "Yes?"

"I assume you'll have blood tests to determine whether you're the father or not, so my question is, will you make those tests public?"

"Your assumption is incorrect."

"You mean you're not going to have a paternity test or you're not going to make the test public?"

"I'm not going to have a paternity test."

"Why not? Don't you want to know if the child is yours?"

"If Jennifer says I'm the father, that's good enough for me."

"And what if you're not?"

"I loved Jennifer. She was my friend, and we were lovers. Why would I not accept her word for it?"

"Will you remain in office, or will you step down, as some are urging?" The question came from a rather large woman to his right.

"As you suggest, there are those who will urge me to step down, but how can I? I pledged myself to serve the people to the best of my ability. I'm still the same man I was during the election. I haven't changed. The commitment made then remains, and it's what I'll continue to do."

"As President, you're a role model whether you like it or not," the woman continued.

"Yes, what you say is true, a role model no doubt. But what kind of role model? Not a role model that fits everyone's picture, that's for sure."

"So may I ask what do you consider a good role model?" The woman persisted.

"A good role model is someone who was dishonest and learns to be honest; someone who was judgmental and learns compassion; someone filled with pride who learns firsthand the need for humility; someone who knows a lot and learns how little he knows. These attributes are far more important to me than the popular pictures we hold, the conventional wisdom, so to speak."

"There are those who hold strong Christian views who make up a large portion of the electorate and don't agree with what you've done. In their minds, to have an affair, and a child out of wedlock would be reason enough for you to step down," said a tall woman to his left.

"May I suggest that those who truly understand the teachings of Christ will not have a problem with my behavior. Why? Christ was criticized by the Pharisees for consorting with the impure, those who did not follow the letter of the law, the outcasts of society. He went by what was in the heart, not by appearances. One of his disciples, Mary Magdalene, is believed by many to have been a prostitute. What did Christ say to those who tried to stone the woman caught in adultery? 'Let he who is without sin cast the first stone.' No one moved, not a single stone was thrown. Why? They knew they were no different from the woman.

"If we don't allow for the fact that people make mistakes and can learn from them, we're lost. There is no hope. Not one of us here, not in the entire country for that matter, can claim to have lived a life without mistakes. The question is, did we learn from them? That's what really counts."

Jennifer turned the television off. She couldn't listen anymore. Her mind went back to her last meeting with David. He'd flown down to San Francisco for the weekend. On that Saturday, they'd wandered along the beaches looking for shells. It was autumn, and there was frost in the air. They'd stopped for lunch, their faces burning in the warm air of the little restaurant still open on the strand.

Afterward, they'd taken a long walk in the park and stopped for coffee. It was evening when they arrived back at the apartment. Over dinner, he told her he was going to stop seeing her. He couldn't keep living this double life and felt he owed it to his wife to try again.

That night had been the last they'd spent together. After breakfast, she'd driven him to the airport, wished him well, and meant it, even though she was so miserable she wanted to die.

She'd spent the day walking the beaches, and in the evening she went to a bar and got horribly drunk. She woke up the following morning in a young man's bed. As she lay there, the memory of the preceding night came back to her. She'd had sex with a stranger and done nothing to prevent pregnancy. Nine months later, Susan was born. Jennifer wished the child were David's, but knew she wasn't. When her mother jumped to the conclusion it was David's child, she'd not dissuaded her. She'd almost come to believe it herself. Good God, she thought, what have I done?

After the press conference, Tremaine returned to the Oval Office. He sat looking through the window, listening to the ever-present sound of distant traffic. He picked up the phone and asked Jonathan to come in. Jonathan entered quietly.

"I have a meeting scheduled with Kersey and Morgan for tomorrow afternoon. Push it back to Friday morning. I'm going to talk with Brock and Prescott about recycled paper."

Sandra and Cole

The Boston Globe

FANCY FOOTWORK

President Seeks to Restore Tarnished Reputation

Presidential aide Jonathan Makarios tried unsuccessfully to arrange for the President to address the National Press Club in New York on May 15. This move was seen as an attempt by the President to restore his tarnished image following the disclosure that he'd not supported his daughter born to Jennifer Ramirez, a woman with whom he'd reportedly had an affair. Public opinion polls showed a decline in the President's approval rating of fifteen points, down to 41%. This equaled the rating he received during the election campaign following the revelation of the use of drugs when he was a student.

Senator Cole, the leading Republican spokesman, was quoted as saying, "The President has betrayed the trust of the American people. A man who's admitted to such indiscretions cannot be trusted with the governance of the country. He's an admitted drug user, who avoided the draft during the Vietnam War and counseled others to do the same. He's a womanizer and the father of an illegitimate child. Only with the recent revelation was he compelled to assume the financial obligation for his daughter. His interest in addressing the National Press Club can be seen as nothing more than a cynical attempt by a desperate man to restore his image.

Cole hinted that there'd been talk amongst ranking Republicans concerning impeachment proceedings. Not since the Nixon presidency has government been so badly shaken by such scandalous behavior. On a related matter, Harvard University President Dr. James Channing confirmed that President Tremaine would address the faculty and students of the University on May 20. When asked whether the press would be invited, Dr. Channing responded, "Of course." In light of the refusal by the National Press Club, Dr. Channing's invitation can only be seen as a slap in the face of ordinary Americans.

Sandra crumpled the newspaper and threw it across the room. "You hypocritical bastards!" she muttered.

Cole returned to his office following a late breakfast. The day's newspapers lay on the desk. Lighting a cigar, he leaned back and slowly leafed through them. A smile of satisfaction spread across his face when he came to the Boston Globe article.

The phone rang. Tossing the paper on the desk, he leaned forward and picked it up. He sat back and made himself comfortable before putting it to his ear.

"Yes. ... Who? ... Sandra Tremaine! Here? Now?... At your desk? ... Yes, I'll see her, but keep her waiting, I'll let you know when I'm ready."

Cole bolted out of his chair, grabbed the newspapers and stuffed them into a drawer. He emptied the ashtray and, taking a handkerchief from his pocket, dusted off the desktop, being careful to sweep the stray ashes into the trash can. From the bookshelf he selected three books and placed them strategically on the desk, titles visible: Political Theory for the 21st Century, The Role of Contemporary Women in the Modern World, and

Enlightened Self-Government: Its Theory & Application. He placed a pad of paper directly in front of him next to which he placed a pencil. From the shelf beside the door, he took photos of his wife and children and placed them prominently on the desk.

He sat down and spoke into the intercom: "Send her in."

Cole pored over his notes, jotting furiously and pretended not to hear the door open.

"Senator Cole, Sandra Tremaine is here to see you," his secretary announced.

The senator glanced up with a contrived expression of surprise. He walked around the desk and extended a sweaty hand.

"Mrs. Tremaine, Mrs. Tremaine, what an unexpected pleasure. Have a seat, my dear." He motioned to a large, black leather chair and Sandra sat down. The stale smell of old cigars permeated the air.

As Cole walked around the desk, Sandra's eyes swept the office, taking everything in, including the books on the desk.

"What can I do for you?" Cole asked as he sat down.

Sandra sat in the high-backed chair and steepled her fingers. Deliberately, she crossed her legs, all the while keeping her eyes fixed firmly on Cole. She saw a flicker in his eyes, but he'd caught himself, conscious that she was watching him.

"I see you've been reading," she said quietly.

"I beg your pardon?"

"I see you've been reading," she indicated the books with a slight nod of her head.

"Yes, I like to keep abreast of things." Cole was pleased with his clever use of words. He'd never met Sandra before, and at least part of his surprise was genuine. She wore a white blouse under a navy blue jacket and a red tartan skirt. She was indeed an attractive woman, well built and shapely.

Sandra chose to ignore his covert language. "I take it you believe in the equality of men and women?"

"Of course, of course."

"Then why hide behind your desk?"

"What? What do you mean?" Cole was taken off balance. What was she talking about? Her dark eyes seemed to bore into him. He wanted to turn away, but she wouldn't let him. He was beginning to sweat.

"Look, Mr. Cole, I'd appreciate it if you'd demonstrate your belief in the equality of human beings by sitting over here, across from me. That wouldn't be too much to ask, would it?"

"No, no, of course not." He waddled from behind the desk and, pulling a chair into place, sat in front of her.

"Thank you. I want to deal directly with you." She let the statement hang for a moment.

Cole sat back in the chair and tried to recover his balance. He felt self-conscious. "How can I help you?" He had to get something going; the silence was unnerving.

"I read the quote from you in the Boston Globe. I had to see you in person. I had to know what kind of a man would make such statements."

"What do you mean?"

"Senator, you've violated your public trust. By your words, you are doing your best to discredit my husband. You lie."

"How do I lie?"

"You make him out to be something he's not. There was a time when holding public office was a way for gifted leaders and legislators to provide service to their countrymen. It was a high calling, a calling which no longer receives the respect it once did."

"And what's that got to do with me?"

"It's people like you who give politicians a bad name. It's people like you who undermine the ideals of service. You manipulate facts and distort reality, making it appear to be something it isn't."

"What makes you think that?" Cole demanded.

"I know my husband. Your comments couldn't be further from the truth."

"You can't prove that!"

Sandra laughed. "I don't need to. You and I both know the truth, although I'm sure you'd never admit it."

"Its men like your husband who don't belong in politics." Cole leaned forward. "I'll drive him out of office if I can."

"What is it about him that fills you with such animosity? What has he done to make you so angry? This is more than politics, isn't it?"

"Mrs. Tremaine, I don't know what you're talking about," came the syrupy response.

"You certainly do. You know exactly what I'm talking about." Sandra paused momentarily. "I had to see you in person. I had to be sure of you."

"Sure of what?" Cole snapped.

She ignored his question. "I knew in person you'd not be able to hide from me." Sandra saw the uncertainty in Cole's eyes. "You're afraid of David Tremaine, afraid that if he's as good as you think, there'll be no room in government for you and others of your ilk. From what I've seen, there'll be no meeting of minds here."

Cole shifted uncomfortably. "Mrs. Tremaine, you speak in riddles. You don't know anything about me."

"I know more than you think. I know you're dishonest, and

I now know you're afraid, although you'll never admit it, even to yourself."

Before Cole could respond, Sandra stood and looked down at him. "I'm sorry for you, Senator. Dishonesty and fear are cruel taskmasters." She left the office, closing the door quietly behind her.

Mother

Nasir, Aziz and Samara sat eating around the table in Aziz's home.

"Where are you going, Master?" asked Aziz.

Samara had never heard Nasir called 'Master,' yet she realized she felt the same way toward him.

"I'm going to Jezzine tomorrow. I'm leaving in the afternoon."

"Can you see Tariq's mother this morning? She heard you were here and sent word last evening, asking to come and see you."

"Yes, let her come. I have to talk to her."

It was mid morning when, Durrah, Tariq's mother, knocked on the door. She reminded Samara of her own mother. Once more, the sorrow in Samara's heart stirred and tears came to her eyes. It seemed like a long time since she'd lost her family.

Nasir embraced the woman, then held her at arm's length and looked her over. "It's good to see you again, Mother."

"It's good to see you again," came the response in soft mellow tones.

Samara's heart went out to the woman; she knew what was to come.

"Durrah, this is Samara."

The two women greeted each other.

"Let's sit under the tree. Aziz, come and join us."

Durrah sat on the carpet that Nasir had spread beneath the tree. Her long black dress covered her crossed legs. "Have you any news of Tariq?" she asked.

"I have," Nasir said. "Samara and I saw him yesterday."

"Was he well?" came the eager inquiry.

Nasir, sitting directly in front of Durrah, took her hands in his. "Beloved Mother, your son is dead."

Samara felt the shock like a blow. She watched the woman's eyes moisten as she bowed her head.

Nasir watched as silent tears fell into her lap. Aziz knelt behind her and placed his hands on her shoulders for support. Suddenly, like the bursting of a dam, huge, racking sobs shook Durrah's frame. From deep within her came a long mournful cry.

After they'd eaten, Nasir accompanied Durrah home. He returned late in the afternoon. Samara and Aziz joined him beneath the tree, the sunlight warm in the cool air.

"Samara, I want you to stay with Durrah. I've made the arrangements. You'll take care of her for a little while. She's a fine woman, and you'll be good for each other. If you need any help with anything, you can speak with Aziz. He'll help you."

"Where are you going?" Samara asked.

"Jezzine. I have business there."

"Will I see you again?" she asked, suddenly, inexplicably afraid. She sensed something in Nasir she hadn't felt before.

"Yes, you'll see me again."

"What's happening? Something's changed. Tell me."

Suddenly chilled, she shuddered involuntarily. "You know, don't you?" she demanded.

Nasir looked directly at her. His eyes were clear and tranquil.

"My dear Samara, you are precious to me. You are like my own daughter. Destiny decreed that in this lifetime I would not have children of my own. My family has always been important to me. And now only you are left."

Samara found herself crying. Yes, she thought, you've been my family, too.

"What do you mean?" she said through her tears. "You frighten me."

"I am merely a bridge between two ways of life. Your life stretches where mine cannot go. My time is short."

"Nasir, this talk scares me. I don't want to lose you. What's happening?"

"Life is so vast that no one can ever know the whole of it. Each of us must play our appointed part. We've no say over where we're born, to whom, or the gifts we're born with. Most people live out their destiny, not knowing what is to happen. There are some, however, who have the gift of seeing. They know ahead of time what is to take place. Time is an illusion, part of the great dance we call life. Seers are not subject to time, so we know things others do not. This gift was instrumental in saving your parents' lives many years ago. It brought me to the well where we met. It's how I knew to bring you here."

"Are you going to die?"

"Yes."

"When?"

"Within a year, this body will return to the earth."

"Oh, Nasir, I can't stand to lose you. Everyone I've loved is gone. You're the only one left."

"Beloved daughter, I understand. That's why you must stay with Durrah. She's your family now." Leaning over, he took Samara's hands in his. Tears streamed down her face. "Though I'll be gone in form, the love we shared will always remain. When the time is ripe and wisdom matures, the honey of that love will drip from the hive. Then, you will feed the spirits of those whom Allah sends your way."

"Why, why?" Samara asked, despair in her voice.

"So much sorrow for one so young." Nasir said quietly, as though to himself. "It takes a hot fire to melt the ore and release the imprisoned gold. Nothing is wasted in life; all is essential. Some, however, look upon their lives with sorrow and despair. That attitude alone makes sorrow unbearable. Your destiny is to bring healing. It is Allah who has set in motion the preparation of his holy vessel, Samara." Nasir took her in his arms and held her.

"Is there no way out?" she finally asked.

"No. Even the master Jesus in the Garden of Gethsemane knew the cup of suffering couldn't pass from him. He knew there was no other way. Life is not as it seems. It's real in a certain sense, unreal in another."

"I don't understand."

"You dream?"

"Yes, of course."

"In your dreams, do you experience love and sorrow, happiness and joy, rivers and mountains? Do you see babies being born, old people dying, and people making war?"

"Yes."

"And what happens to them when you wake up?"

"They vanish."

“And what happens to the joy, sorrow and pain?”

“It’s gone.”

“Was it real?”

Samara was crying softly. “Why, Nasir, why are you telling me this? I can’t stand it! Let me die with you.”

“It’s not your time.”

“I don’t care, I can’t bear the thought of losing you.”

“Your task right now is to help Durrah. There’s a deep connection between you. You need her for a mother; she needs you for a daughter. Such unions as this are not made from flesh and blood, they’re born of the heart. Sorrow has prepared the ground. Love will flourish here. This will be. You sensed it when you first heard Durrah’s voice; it reminded you of your mother. And Durrah felt the stirring of her heart when first she saw you. It was as though she’d been waiting for you.”

“But I don’t want to lose you.”

“You can’t lose me, Samara. I am love, and love is not the form. It is the wine, not the vessel that holds it. Don’t be attached to the form. It is there that sorrow lies. Feel instead the love that is here, in Aziz; feel the love in Durrah and know that it is what I am. What we all are. The world is a dream; it’s not real because it doesn’t last. When you wake up, the sorrow and pain will ease. You’ll remember it, but it will no longer affect you. Then you’ll understand that you’ve always been home. You’ve never gone away, you’ve just been sleeping.”

They went into the house and, sitting around the table, ate in silence. The silence soothed Samara. When they finished, Nasir gathered what he needed.

“Aziz.” He embraced his friend. “Take care of my daughter.”

Aziz nodded.

“Daughter, take care of this father.”

Samara looked at Aziz and realized she had loved him when she first met him, framed in the doorway with his hair standing on end.

Nasir held her tight and then, pushing her away, took her hands. “I will see you one more time before I leave.”

Recycling

It was a few minutes to four when two men strode purposefully along the corridor leading to the Oval Office. Brock was the senior Senator from Oregon, and Prescott a Congressman from Washington State. For years they'd been staunch supporters of the logging industry. They were ushered into the room. Tremaine stepped from behind the desk to greet them, hand outstretched.

"Good to see you," he said shaking their hands. "What can I do for you, gentlemen?" Tremaine pointed to the chairs in front of the fireplace.

From the moment they entered the office, they felt ill at ease. Tremaine, as usual, was dressed casually. They, in contrast, were dressed in suits, the uniform dictated by custom for men in their position.

Senator Brock spoke first, wasting no time in coming to the point. "Most people in the Pacific Northwest who understand the implications of your plan—to have the federal government use recycled paper—are opposed to it. They know it will devastate the pulp and paper industry and the economy as a whole will suffer because of it." Senator Brock said, coming to the point at once.

"Go on."

"We agree with them; not personally, you

understand," Brock explained. "It's our job to represent our constituents and that's what we're doing."

"And what about conserving resources?"

"We support that as well," answered Congressman Prescott, "but we're more interested right now in conserving jobs threatened by your proposed policy."

Tremaine looked at the two men and waited for them to continue. They shifted uneasily.

Prescott continued, "Do you realize that if you implement this policy requiring all departments of government to use recycled paper, companies such as McClelland will have to downsize, and a large number of workers will be laid off?"

"Yes," said Tremaine. "I am aware of the situation and the changes that will have to be made."

"I don't think you realize what a negative affect this will have on employment," responded Brock. "The impact on the primary and secondary industries would be catastrophic. The lumber industry, as a whole, has been struggling for the last ten years due to environmental issues such as, for instance, the preservation of the Spotted Owl."

"You don't approve?" Tremaine asked quietly.

"It's not a matter of approving or not approving," blustered Brock. "It's a matter of the preservation of human livelihood."

"Let's cut to the real issue, gentlemen, the issue of change. I don't have time for a long discussion today."

"You don't think this is important?" Brock asked.

"I didn't say that." Tremaine's voice was steady. "It's just that I don't buy your basic premise, that's all. Your view, as I see it, is too limited. Given your stance, the problems we face cannot be solved. They'll just get worse."

"What do you mean?" demanded Brock. "We represent the needs of the people in the Pacific Northwest. We know firsthand the problems of the lumber industries."

"I know you do. What I'm saying is, you need to broaden your views to address the full scope of the problem."

"But . . ." Prescott began.

"If you give me a few minutes, I'll explain what I'm driving at," Tremaine said. Something in his tone let the two men know it was time to hold their tongues and let him speak. "Change is inevitable. It cannot be halted, but for some reason most of us have a built-in resistance to it. As I see it, we suffer when we resist change. So instead of fighting it, perhaps we'd be better off embracing it."

"Not all change is for the better," Brock interjected, unable to control himself.

"Let's just say that change is necessary and inevitable. The logging practices in this country are a sad commentary on the greed, waste and destruction of one of our great national resources. We've been poor stewards of our great forests."

"I disagree," Brock protested. "We're the most advanced nation in the world. Our logging practices are superior to those of Latin American countries. One only has to look at what's going on in the Amazon to know that."

"I won't be drawn into a conversation that has no real relevance to what has to be done." Tremaine paused and looked steadily at the two men before directing a question to Prescott. "Do you have an open mind, or is your mind made up?"

Prescott squirmed. If there was one thing he prided himself on, it was his open mind. "I'm open," he said, "I'll listen."

"Good. Now, how about you, Senator?" Tremaine turned to Brock.

Brock leaned forward. His heart was pounding and he was angry. His face was flushed, and beads of sweat covered his forehead. He disliked being talked to in this way, but a lot of people depended on him. He couldn't allow his personal feelings to override his purpose.

"I'll hear you out," he said.

"Thank you. Going back to your comment comparing our logging practices with those in the Amazon. What fools we'd be if we justified our practices by comparing them to those that are worse than ours. What's happening in the Amazon rainforest is disastrous and concerns me a great deal, but it's something I can do little about at the moment. What's happening in our forests is my jurisdiction, and I intend to do something about that."

"What do you have in mind?" Prescott asked.

"To begin with, I'm sending a signal to the country and the logging industry as a whole that we'll no longer squander our resources. We're going to be more efficient and less wasteful."

"If recycling puts men out of work, the government ends up paying for it through unemployment insurance or welfare. I, for one, am opposed to the expansion of the welfare state," Brock argued.

"On that point you'll get no argument from me," Tremaine responded. "Everything is interrelated. We must take into account all these interdependent aspects or we'll never move ahead."

"If you proceed with this idea do you know what effect that single step will have on the pulp and paper industry?" Prescott asked.

"I think I do," said Tremaine, "but go ahead and tell me what you think."

"Big companies like McClelland employ thousands of

workers. If they can't maintain their current production levels the loss of revenue will cripple them; there'll be layoffs, they might not survive."

"Those things I'm aware of. One of the problems we face here, and in Canada, comes from our attitude toward what we've traditionally considered one of our greatest assets, namely, the immensity of our natural resources."

"I don't follow," said Prescott.

"Because of the vastness of our resources, in this case trees, we've been careless and wasteful. Millions of acres of land have been stripped. The resulting problems of erosion and destruction of animal habitat have largely been ignored. We take only the best wood and discard the rest. In this way a great deal is wasted that could otherwise be used.

"Only in the last ten or fifteen years have we started to pay attention to these problems. In Norway and Sweden, lumber resources are considerably fewer. For that reason, they're generally more careful in preventing erosion, for instance, and they take better care of the land.

"One of the dangers of being a member of Congress is that you only see what logging companies want you to see. Unless you're willing and able to get off the main roads, you won't see the devastation; what to me is the rape of the land."

"You still haven't dealt with the problem of unemployment your proposal would cause," Brock interjected.

Tremaine ignored Brock's irritation. "Requiring the government to use recycled paper creates a demand. That demand, like any other, will be met by industry. The giants may not meet it because it's more difficult for them to make adjustments, but there's no doubt the demand will be met by someone willing to change. Once the big guys see that happening, you can bet they'll find ways to make the necessary changes. I want to make it clear that even with the changes we envision there'll still be jobs; paper will still have to be made, new and recycled.

"But what about the big companies?" Prescott persisted.

"Just because they're big doesn't give them special privileges. If they try to hold on to the old ways, they'll go down. When creative minds get to work, they'll find ways of diversifying, of being more responsive to the needs that arise. Perhaps they'll get smaller or break into independent subsystems. The point isn't how they'll do it; the point is, they will, or as you suggest they'll go out of business.

"We're not businessmen, we're not scientists," Tremaine continued; "it's the task of business and science to figure these things out. I have faith they will. Our task is to keep in mind the public good. To do that, we can't afford to be shortsighted, can't afford to allow segments of our constituency to dictate short-term goals, which are not in the best interests of the nation as a whole or of the planet where we live."

"It's our job to represent our constituency," Brock responded.

"I've no problem with that. You must, however, keep in mind that the interests of Oregon and Washington do not always represent the interests of the nation as a whole. My task is to keep that in mind. No single point of view can be allowed to dictate to others. It's time to develop sustainable, long-term objectives and above all, we must have confidence in our greatest asset."

"And what the hell is that?" snapped Brock.

"The creativity of the human mind," Tremaine said with a smile. "We as politicians must be creative, too. Is it not one of the tasks of political leaders in a democracy to educate their constituents? If we fail in this task, then we'll find ourselves reverting to crisis management."

"How do we educate our constituents when their livelihood is threatened?" demanded Brock.

"The practical problems will be worked out, but for that to happen, we must have open minds. We must look at things in new ways without being tied to the past, to tradition, or 'the way we've always done things.' We cannot secure the world by making change stop. Change is inevitable. The only security that exists is in accepting this fact."

"What can the government do to help ease the transition?" Prescott asked.

"One thing we're considering is developing secondary industry such as furniture factories where high-quality wooden furniture is produced. If we can expand secondary industry we'll provide more jobs and we won't have to import these items from abroad.

"We might also consider planting specialized woods that thrive in the climate of the Pacific Northwest, even other parts of the country. If we're successful, then perhaps we can produce furniture made from these highly prized woods. We're also looking at growing bamboo, large bamboo that thrives in similar climates. Bamboo is fast-growing and can be used in a wide variety of things from construction to clothing.

Another thing we've been exploring is the development of alternative energy systems such as solar and wind power. This will eventually replace energy produced from dwindling sources such as oil, and will be an integral part of a new National Energy Program. To help get it started we'll offer tax incentives and interest-free loans, for five years, to companies who want to work in this sector. Preliminary discussions have already been held with a number of businesses in the Pacific Northwest. The number of new jobs will more than make up for those lost. The government will provide funding for retraining for two years. Our aim is to provide meaningful long-term employment.

"We'd be interested in this," Prescott said, suddenly intrigued by possibilities he hadn't thought of before.

"Perhaps you'd consider serving on a committee to help bring this about? We intend to have at least some of these businesses up and running within two years, sooner if we can."

"I'd like to," Prescott responded.

"How about you, Senator," Tremaine asked, looking at Brock.

"It's not going to help us in the short term. It's not going to help companies like McClelland," Brock responded sullenly.

"Well, the opportunity's there, and I'd welcome your involvement if you're up for it," Tremaine countered. "We'll sit down with anyone who's open to ideas. Yours and Mr. Prescott's ideas are welcome. But don't make the mistake of telling me, 'It can't be done.' That's not up for consideration."

Brock was boiling. "What about the big companies like McClelland, you can't just abandon them," he concluded lamely.

Tremaine wanted to end the argument. "Look, Senator," he said quietly, an edge to his voice. "Think about what I've said: change is inevitable, time doesn't go backwards."

The room was silent except for the crackling of the fire. In the distance, a horn blared above the hum of traffic. Tremaine stood, and the two men followed. He walked to the door ahead of them, opened it and turned. Prescott extended his hand. Tremaine shook it. "We'll talk further." Prescott nodded and stepped into the hall.

Brock extended a hand, eyes averted. He wanted to escape before he completely lost control. Tremaine shook his hand and held the grip, stopping the older man from leaving. Surprised, the Senator looked up.

"Think about what I've said, Senator. Your region will need all the help it can get." Tremaine released his hand and Brock strode through the door.

The two men walked brusquely down the hallway of the Capitol building, the sound of their shoes echoing off the marble floor. Neither had spoken since their meeting with the President. Prescott had been silent in the car on the way from the White House, his mind going over the conversation with Tremaine. It was obvious the President had shaken Brock up; his usual confident certainty was in disarray. Rarely had Prescott seen the old man so steaming mad. Most of Brock's colleagues deferred to the Senator, whose white hair and dignified bearing created a carefully cultivated aura of wisdom and respectability.

"Who the hell does that goddamned asshole think he is?"

"He's the President," Prescott found himself saying.

"Don't give me that crap!" Brock turned on Prescott, his voice carrying loudly down the hall. People in the corridor turned to see what was going on.

Brock headed for his office. "We'll talk about this later," he snapped as he disappeared through the door.

Private lives

David asked Lacy Emerson to act as his unofficial representative with Jennifer Ramirez. As she drove from her home in Brunswick, Maine to Jennifer's home just east of Concord, New Hampshire, she wondered how the meeting would go. It had been a relaxed drive; she'd taken her time. Dandelions and buttercups lined the road while large thunderheads boiled in a clear blue sky. Sunshine, showers and the sweet pungent smells of spring permeated the air. Now Lacy sat across the table from Jennifer, sipping herbal tea, Jennifer drinking black coffee.

"He asked me to tell you how sorry he is for what happened. He'd like to help any way he can."

"Is he hoping to buy my silence?" Jennifer asked, her voice tense, almost harsh.

"No, Jennifer. It's a bit late for that even if he'd wanted to. He doesn't wish to intrude in your life, but if you're willing to accept assistance from him he'll happily give it."

"He trusts me?"

"He trusts you."

Jennifer seemed taken aback. She took a sip of coffee. "You mean he just accepts that Susan is his daughter?"

"He does."

"There'll be no paternity test?"

"He's not asking for one, Jennifer. As I said, he believes you. He simply wants to help both of you."

"He's not going to fight me?"

"No, he has no desire to fight you, Jennifer. If you want an agreement registered with the courts, he's open to that as well."

"Is he angry with me for embarrassing him?"

"No, he's not angry. He accepts what happened. His only regret is that he didn't know Susan when she was growing up."

"I suppose he wants to see her?"

"He'd like that; but he wanted me to tell you that he'll respect whatever decision you and Susan make. He'll not intrude in your lives. If at any time, now or in the future, Susan would like to come and see him, she'd be welcome, as would you."

Jennifer took another long sip of coffee. This meeting with Lacy was not what she'd anticipated. She'd felt trapped and on the spot when Lacy identified herself over the phone. Jennifer had wanted to hide behind the relative safety of her lawyer as the go-between in her communication with David and the negotiations to follow. Her legal fees were taken care of, there was no cost to her, and it was part of the agreement she'd made before going public. This, along with the hundred thousand dollars she'd been promised, would enable her to pay Susan's college tuition. But, there was something about Lacy that had kept her from putting the phone down. She knew who Lacy was, of course; she'd seen her on television from time to time when she was First Lady. Even then, there was something about her she'd been drawn to. The phone call had been a surprise.

"What about his wife, Sandra? How does she feel about this?" Jennifer asked.

"We talked about it. She's open to whatever happens. Sandra, like David, wants you to know that both you and your daughter are welcome to visit. If you'd feel more comfortable meeting David in private, that's all right as well. She said something that I think you'll appreciate. Loving David as she does, she said, she can well understand how you must have loved him as well. I think because of that she feels close to you. Anyway, there's no animosity from her toward you and she wants you to know that."

"Do you believe her?"

"Yes, I do. I've known her since her marriage to David. She's a good woman. I like her a great deal and consider her my friend." Lacy finished her tea and helped herself to a cookie.

Jennifer found herself relaxing, and with it she became more open. Her original wariness and hostility had dissipated, and now she found herself confronting something she hadn't expected. It was as though David had anticipated all her objections and then neutralized them. Despite her fears, Lacy had made her feel she'd be welcomed by David and Sandra if she wanted to see them.

"Let me think about it," Jennifer said with a softening in her tone.

The two women chatted for a while, sharing stories. They talked about Emerson and their children. By the time Lacy stood to leave, she felt as though they were old friends. She was glad David had asked for her help. Standing in the long hallway, the two women shared a warm hug.

As Lacy drove away, Jennifer stood by the gate waving. A sudden shaft of sunlight breaking through ominous clouds felt warm on her skin. Lacy had given her a number where she could be reached as well as a private number and e-mail address for David.

Instead of being able to generate a self-righteous anger,

Jennifer found herself having to face her own doubts and guilt. What had she done, what would she do? The truth, when she allowed herself to recognize it, was that she would like to see David again. All those years since she'd said goodbye to him had healed the old wound, but she still felt an abiding warmth toward the man she'd once loved, and now she was curious about him.

Later that day, Susan received a call from Jennifer, who described the meeting with Lacy. Susan listened, saying little. She was still angry with her mother for plastering their private lives all over the television and newspapers. When she got off the phone she found herself wondering about the man in the White House, her newly discovered father. The information her mother had shared with her before she'd gone public had come as a shock, and she still didn't know how she felt about it. After all, she thought, he hadn't been around when she was growing up. She hadn't needed him then, and she didn't need him now. Perhaps, though, this tiny seed of curiosity, which she'd barely noticed, would one day flower.

Healing old wounds

A week after her return from Washington, D.C., Jennifer drove to Durham to visit her daughter at the University of New Hampshire. She hadn't yet decided what to tell Susan. On the drive east, she found herself reflecting on the meeting she'd had with David.

She'd e mailed him five days after Lacy's visit. Following an exchange of letters, he'd invited her to meet him at the White House. She'd planned a week's vacation and prepared for her trip to Washington.

Jennifer was met at the airport by an aide and driven to the White House. Entering through the north portico, she was taken to the second floor and ushered into the Tremaines' private living room. She would never forget this meeting. David greeted her with a broad smile on his face. Reaching out his hand, he took hers and shook it warmly, drawing her into the room.

"I'm so glad to see you, Jennifer. Welcome to my temporary abode." He chuckled.

He'd retained his sense of humor, she noted.

"Come in," he said, "sit down."

They sat in front of a small fireplace in which a log glowed in a bed of white ash. David threw another log on the fire and a shower of sparks scurried up the chimney. Closing the glass doors, he took a seat opposite her. Between them, a small coffee table covered with a white cloth held a pot of fresh coffee, tea, cups and a small plate of pastries.

"You still drink coffee?" Tremaine asked.

"I do," she said quietly.

Looking around, she noticed a large desk, which occupied a prominent place in the room. An iMac gleamed in the light, and next to it two books were open on the otherwise empty desk. A couch and comfortable chairs provided ample seating; full-length bookcases lined two of the walls. It was a comfortable room, well lived-in, a pleasing combination of living room and library, she thought. Her gaze took in the pictures on the two remaining walls. One had images of waves, the other of mountains, views similar to those she'd seen in Western Canada and Alaska. A large photograph of the Taj Mahal hung above the desk.

David passed her coffee. "Black, isn't it?"

"Yes," she said.

"Help yourself to whatever you'd like."

She nodded.

"The French pastries are very tasty," Tremaine said, pouring a cup of tea for himself. He sat back and looked at Jennifer. Long black hair, now streaked with white, hung over her shoulders. She wore a red sweater and a black woolen skirt, ruby earrings and a light natural lipstick. Her blue eyes were framed by a hint of wrinkles—laugh lines, he was glad to see. The years had been good to her, he thought. He was glad.

"How was your trip?"

"It was fine." Taking a long sip of coffee, she put her cup down and, sitting straight on the edge of her chair, faced him. "I'd like you to know why I've come. I'd like to start there, no small talk."

Tremaine looked at her curiously, “Of course.”

“When Lacy came to see me, I was afraid. I didn’t know what she wanted. I wasn’t prepared for her. She came as a visitor to my home and yet she made me feel welcome. Before she came I thought I could use anger to keep her at a distance and deny or blunt whatever message you sent. But that didn’t happen. She listened to me. Somehow she made me see you were happy to do whatever I wanted.”

“Then Lacy did what I’d hoped she would.”

“She said you trusted me and were prepared to provide me with whatever I might need for Susan. There was nothing left for me to resist; you were already giving me everything I was prepared to fight you for. This forced me to see myself. I wasn’t proud of what I saw.”

David listened attentively, sensing her conflict and wondering what it was about.

“The truth is, David,” she hesitated for a moment. “Susan is not your daughter. As it turned out, contrary to what you believed about me, I couldn’t be trusted to tell the truth. I lied when I spoke before the television cameras.”

Tremaine sat back deeper in the chair. “That may be so,” he said, “but you’re speaking the truth now, and that’s what really matters. It takes an honest person to do what you’ve just done.”

“Don’t give me too much credit, David. What I said must have hurt you and your wife and certainly made things more difficult for both of you.”

“Don’t worry about it Jenn,” he said, lapsing into the name he used to call her. “Life is filled with many twists and turns and we all do the best we can.”

David reached over and took Jennifer’s hand in his.

His green eyes were quiet and held her gaze. "Tell me what happened," he urged.

Tears filled her eyes. Taking a corner of a napkin, she dried them. His whole demeanor was soft and encouraging. He was in no hurry, and she felt at ease with him.

"When I left you at the airport the last time we were together, I wished you well and I meant it. I loved you and truly wanted the best for you. At the same time, I was terribly unhappy. You may remember I'm not much of a drinker, but on my way home I stopped at the little bar down the street from where I lived. I can't remember now what it was called."

"The Griffin."

"That's right, the Griffin. Anyway, I got thoroughly drunk, for the first and only time in my life. I don't remember much of that night, but in the morning when I woke up I had a splitting headache and there was a young man in bed beside me. Then I remembered what had happened. You and I had always been careful when making love. I hadn't taken any precautions with him. I was so miserable I really didn't give a damn."

"I'm so sorry, Jennifer, so sorry."

"My mother assumed the child was yours, and over the years I just allowed her to think what she wanted. Somehow, I almost came to believe it myself. I wanted to. I wanted to have something of you; something born of the intimacy we had shared. My mother was very angry with you. Although she believed you were the father, I never told Susan about you, and I swore my mother to secrecy. Susan grew up knowing nothing about her father. The truth is, I didn't know anything about him either. In fact I never saw him after that night. It was only the week before I went public with my statement that

I sat down with Susan and told her about you. Now, what am I going to do?"

David took a moment to think about the sudden change. He took a swallow of tea. "You know Jennifer, contraception doesn't always work, so there's still a possibility she could be my child. Why do anything? Why not leave it as it is."

"You mean let her, and the whole world, continue to think you're her father?"

"Why not?"

"But you're not her father, her flesh and blood."

"That may be true, but look at it another way. The relationship we had was one of mutual love. Surely it was out of our relationship that Susan was born."

"How so?"

"Think of it this way. If you and I had not met and carried on the relationship we did, you would not have grieved when I left. If not for the sorrow of that evening, you wouldn't have gotten drunk, and getting pregnant as you did would have been equally unlikely. I'm not trying to influence you in any way. Whatever you decide is fine with me. But I'd like you to know that since your announcement, I've enjoyed the thought of being a father, and I've looked forward to meeting her someday, and perhaps helping her if I could. I still feel that way."

Tears streamed down Jennifer's face. Placing her head in her hands, her shoulders shook, and all the pent-up emotion of the past twenty years came pouring out. Tremaine pushed a box of tissues toward her and sat quietly. How often he'd experienced this for himself, the power of truth to unlock the psychological prisons that hold human beings captive.

When Jennifer had composed herself, she felt light, as though she were floating. Until that moment, she hadn't realized what a burden she'd carried all those years. A burning log in the fireplace crackled loudly, releasing another flurry of sparks.

"There's a story I'd like to share with you."

Jennifer nodded. She'd always loved his stories.

"It goes something like this. In the mountains of China there was a small village. Higher on the mountain lived a Buddhist monk, a hermit who lived alone in a small cabin. The villagers had a great respect for him. They'd bring things for him to repair. If they were sick he'd always treat them with the herbs he gathered on the mountainside. In return they brought him food to supplement a small garden he tended and the wild plants he gathered.

"One day a young girl in the village became pregnant, and when the villagers found out, they demanded to know who the father was. Afraid of identifying her lover for fear he might be beaten to death, she claimed the monk was the father of her child.

"Irate, the villagers stormed up the hill to the monk's cabin and confronted him. As was usual, he said nothing. When the child was born, the villagers marched up the hill again and handed the child to him for his care. Again he said nothing. Placing the infant in a cradle he'd built, he cared for the child as though it were his own. His love for the child was evident. From time to time the villagers came across him in the woods with the toddler on his shoulders.

"As the child grew, he eagerly accompanied the monk on his sorties into the mountain. Together they collected the herbs he used to treat the sick. The child soon learned to identify them, where they grew, the seasons when they appeared, what they were used for, the combinations, and the drying and preparation as well. Sometimes the villagers came across the monk sitting in the warm sunlight with the boy asleep on his lap.

"Years passed, and eventually the young girl, now a woman, married the young man she loved. The whole village turned out to celebrate. One day several months later the couple went to see the monk. They wanted to take over the raising of their son, who was now five years old. The monk packed the little boy's belongings in a small bag and, with the lad on his shoulders, accompanied the couple home. From that time on, it was not unusual for the child and the monk to be found visiting back and forth.

"The early upbringing and the knowledge he acquired from the monk served the boy well in his later years, while the monk's relationship with the young couple was something they treasured the rest of their lives. Neither the monk nor the couple ever felt a need to speak about the events that had brought them together."

Jennifer looked at David wordlessly, once more on the verge of tears. She sat unhurried in the silence. What needed to be said by both of them had, for the time being, been said. Somewhere she noted a clock chiming. She looked at her watch. It was nine o'clock. Tremaine stood and placed another log on the bed of coals. Several minutes passed in the comfortable silence before he spoke again.

"Let things be for a while, Jennifer, and see how you feel. There's no hurry; nothing needs to be done at the moment. You'll know what to do when the time comes."

Cole was in his Senate office when the call came through. Picking up the phone, he recognized the reedy voice of his investigator, Phil Harper. "I told you not to call me on this line," Cole snapped.

"You're not easy to get a hold of," Harper countered.

"So, what is it?"

"It's Jennifer Ramirez . . ."

"What about her?" Cole interrupted.

"She fired her lawyer."

"Fired him?"

"You heard me, fired him."

"Did you go and see her?"

"No, she refused to see me. She said our agreement was off, and she would not accept the hundred grand we promised her."

"Did she say why?"

"No, she refused to discuss it."

Cole sucked in his breath.

"Well, in that case, we just saved ourselves a hundred grand."

"That's it?"

"That's it. She's got no idea who was behind the offer. You keep your mouth shut and that'll be the end of it."

The lens of perception

With a bump, Air Force One touched down at Hanscom Field. An hour later, David and Sandra entered the packed hall at Harvard University, accompanied by Dr. Channing. As they walked onto the stage the hall fell silent. The two men wore the traditional gowns of academia, while Sandra wore a long flowing cotton dress with a floral print of burnt orange. Channing showed the Tremaines to their seats, and then stepped to the podium.

"I'm pleased to welcome David and Sandra Tremaine to Harvard. It is my intention to provide President Tremaine with a platform from which to address the nation concerning the role of the press in a free society. I was of the opinion that the ideal forum for such a conversation was the National Press Club, but they felt otherwise. I called Dr. Tremaine and told him that we at Harvard still value the realm of ideas and the ability to speak freely and respectfully with those who have different points of view. Dr. Tremaine was happy to accept." Channing paused. "Please welcome President Tremaine."

Tremaine stepped to the podium and waited for the applause to die down. "When our Forefathers declared the independence of this nation from Britain, they embarked on a great social experiment.

That experiment is ongoing, still a work in process. Regis Debrés, in his book, Revolution in the Revolution, makes the point that when a revolution succeeds, those in power, over time, become the same as those they overthrew. Debrés argued that to prevent this it was important to create an ongoing revolution, a revolution within the revolution. In this way he hoped government would continue to be responsive to the needs of its people.

"The same thoughts are expressed by the words of that great British think tank, The Who: 'Meet the new boss, same as the old boss.'"

A murmur of laughter filled the hall.

Tremaine continued. "In the American system of government, the role of the press is an essential cornerstone of our democracy. The press is an instrument by which we continue the revolution within the revolution; but when the press itself becomes corrupted, it can no longer do the job it was intended to do. I mean 'corrupted' in a generic sense; that is, it has lost its sense of objectivity and its reliance on facts. The idea of a free press as one that functions with integrity and honesty, free from the influence of government and special interest groups, is very important. One special interest group we've ignored, however, is the press itself. It has been said, not entirely in jest, that 'freedom of the press belongs to those who own one.'"

Another ripple of laughter filled the hall.

"In a democracy accurate information is essential. We, the people, govern ourselves; and to govern ourselves wisely, accurate information is required. It doesn't help when facts are distorted or left out.

"The reporting of facts has been subordinated to the blood

sport of conflict and controversy. It is controversy that drives up ratings and increases profit.

"When members of the press lose their objectivity, we find ourselves increasingly subjected to their interpretations and opinions rather than the facts themselves. This includes all involved: the reporters, the editors and the owners. In other words, any slanted perspective of the press affects their selection of facts to support their interpretations and agenda." Tremaine took a long drink of water.

A young woman near the front raised her hand.

Tremaine put his glass down and pointed to her. "Yes," he said.

"I've always been interested in the news; perhaps I'm a news junkie. Often after listening to the news I feel unsettled, even a bit depressed. I was camping in the wilderness for a couple of weeks and when I got back I switched on the television and felt my stomach churn. Nothing had changed. The details were different but the tone was the same. You'd think nothing good ever happened anymore. I find it unbalanced and oppressive and I know it's not the whole truth."

"You used the term unbalanced and oppressive. Good description. When the press focuses on the negative aspects of human nature and ignores the positive, it distorts reality and produces a kind of social malaise. Lao Tzu points out that good and bad define each other. Together they make up the whole. But when only the negative is focused on, it is not an accurate description of reality, and as such, it gives rise to depression and pessimism. When the good things that happen in life are ignored, it leaves no place for hope; and with hope absent, darkness must follow."

A question came from the press section. "What you say may

be true, but there are a lot of bad things happening in the world; theft, corruption, rape, murder and so on. Are you suggesting we don't report them?"

"Of course not. People have a right to know about such events. But is that all that's happening? No! Then why this unbalanced emphasis on the negative?"

"Couldn't we regulate the press so that it balances the negative and the positive?" came a question from a young woman in the second row.

Tremaine smiled. "I wish I had a solution to this but I don't. Perhaps with greater public awareness these changes will come about by themselves. In my opinion society is already too regulated. We have rules and laws that govern just about every aspect of life. When this happens, society becomes rigid and inflexible, and spontaneity disappears.

"Some of you may have heard of Confucius. He was a reformer in ancient China who believed in developing protocols, rules and regulations that would produce greater harmony in society. His contemporary, the sage Lao Tzu, saw what was happening and went into exile because he couldn't stand the repression and lack of freedom that resulted. I think we've already gone a long way down that road. I have no desire to make it worse by adding more regulations. I do understand your frustration, however."

A middle-aged man at the back of the press section stood up, his face flushed with anger. "You may not wish to regulate the press, but you're trying to influence it. This is just another form of regulation. I think you're afraid reporters will ask tough questions, but that's our job. The more I listen to you, the more I hear 'press censorship.' I think you want us to stop asking questions because you're afraid of where they might lead, and of the embarrassment they might cause your Administration."

"The fear you mention is in your mind; I have no fear concerning questions you or anyone may ask. I think it essential for a democracy that members of the press ask whatever questions they wish, including questions that might be uncomfortable to ask, or answer. I would suggest, however, that those questions are more likely to get a thoughtful response when they're posed with civility and respect born of a genuine interest in the truth, whatever it may be.

"When a reporter poses questions, he selects an aspect of reality to which our attention is drawn. When President Emerson held his first press conference, one of the reporters posed the following question: 'Your party has been denied the White House for twelve years. We know the Republicans exercised power through questionable means. Now your party is in power, will you resist the temptation to get even?' By the question, the reporter revealed his own thinking and introduced to the public something not in President Emerson's mind at all: the idea of revenge.

"If you wish to tarnish a man's image, it's easy. Arrange a press conference and ask him if he's stopped beating his wife. No matter what he answers, you've introduced the idea into the consciousness of those hearing the question. This, to my mind, is irresponsible journalism, an abuse of the reporter's role and the power of his position."

A slim balding man, his face unshaven, stood. "Mr. President, one of the functions of the press is to be a watchdog on behalf of the people. Our job is to ferret out and bring to public awareness corruption, wherever it is found. The press has done a reasonably good job of this when it comes to such things as politics, business and religion. But you've raised the issue of corruption in the press itself. My question is: can the press monitor itself? What happens when the lens of communication becomes distorted? Who's left to draw attention to this distortion?"

"A very good question. It's a concern I share. I see three things operating here. One is the drive for the media to be profitable, which tends to lead in the direction of sensationalism and the deliberate pitting of people against each other. Conflict becomes more important than the resolution of conflict.

"The second thing is that when the press is owned by fewer people, fewer perspectives are allowed.

"The third and most disturbing of all, is that certain large media corporations appear to have abandoned objectivity altogether. Instead, radio and television talk show hosts report opinions, not facts, and fan the flames of ignorance, intolerance and aggression. In this way they polarize the electorate, further hardening opinions and attitudes. Tabloid journalism may sell more newspapers and drive up radio and television ratings but does nothing to help address the pressing issues of the day. By polarizing the general public they foster an incipient conflict that can easily turn violent. As I see it, this is a betrayal of public trust and undermines one of the great cornerstones of democracy; namely, a free press, whose guiding principals are truth, fairness and objectivity.

"It is sad that fewer and fewer people today expect objectivity in the press. A polarized electorate leads to polarized government as representatives reflect their constituents. The result is gridlock and an inability to pass needed legislation. This does not bode well for our democracy. Democracy works best with an informed electorate whose members engage with open minds in the honest discussion of issues and ideas, carried on in an atmosphere of civility.

"Intelligent people who think for themselves understand that no single perspective holds the whole truth. As a result they are able to find common ground and collaborate in the interests of the people. But when the press foments polarization, it becomes impossible."

The lively and informative conversation continued until ten o'clock, when Dr. Channing escorted the Tremaines from the back of the hall into a warm spring night, offered his thanks and departed. A breeze blew gently from the east and brought with it the smell of the ocean. Accompanied by the Secret Service, David and Sandra walked beneath the lamps along the path leading across the quadrangle to the waiting cars just beyond the walls. Students who'd gathered on either side murmured their appreciation and joined the little procession as it passed by.

Tsunami

Levin returned to Israel while Goldhirsh, who'd remained at the embassy, met with Tremaine the following day. He brought with him an embassy secretary, a youthful and studious man called Noam, who took copious notes.

At one point Goldhirsh looked away, his face pale, his breathing shallow. A cold fury gripped him.

"Say what you have to say," Tremaine told him quietly.

The Foreign Secretary turned and faced Tremaine.

"You," he said, "are an anti-Semite. You hate Jews, that's your problem."

"Call me what you wish," Tremaine responded evenly, "but it won't change things. I'll not be party to the abuse of Palestinian people by your government."

"What gives you the right to talk to us that way?"

"The right of people to stand up and speak truth to those who would abuse others. We have many things in common, Mr. Goldhirsh, but this is not one of them. Correct me if I'm wrong. As I understand it, the term 'anti-Semite' refers to hating or discriminating against Jewish people simply because they're Jewish? Is that correct?"

Goldhirsh nodded.

"I don't hate anyone, and I don't care about your

nationality, your race, your religion. You are a human being, and to me all human beings are the same. My opposition to what you're doing is not because you're Jewish but because what you're doing deprives others of their land, their livelihood and even their lives. Surely you of all people should understand this.

"I'm deeply disturbed when Muslim suicide bombers kill indiscriminately. Does that make me anti-Muslim? I'm deeply disturbed by the acts of Christians who, despite their emphasis on peace, have a long history of intolerance and violence. Does that make me anti-Christian?"

Goldhirsh looked away.

"What disturbs me about this conflict is what it takes for a human being to forfeit his life for others; to use one's body as a weapon that will not survive the attack. What kind of desperation produces this? When there's no hope, people will try anything—what have they got to lose? Peace on the other hand requires a different attitude, a different approach. It requires softness. When I was a child there was a short poem that describes the softness I'm talking about.

Heretic rebel a thing to flout
He drew a circle that shut us out.
Ah, but love and I had the wit to win
We drew a circle that took him in.

"What kind of a circle are you drawing?"

Goldhirsh shifted impatiently.

Tremaine got up and went to the window. He stood looking over the garden. It was mid-morning and warm with a stiff wind from the southeast.

"Coming back to the issue of anti-Semitism, I have one more

thing to say. You and your compatriots drag out the charge of anti-Semitism whenever it suits you. People are afraid of being called anti-Semitic so they say nothing; they don't tell you the truth and as a result are complicit in your actions. That's the position we find ourselves in. We in the United States have blindly supported you in doing things of which we do not approve. In the past we supported you by giving you what you wanted. Now we'll support you by taking it away."

Goldhirsh changed the subject. "You didn't go through the Holocaust, and you don't have to live with the threats of your neighbors."

"What surprises me," Tremaine responded, "is that having gone through the Holocaust, you seem oblivious to what you're doing to the Palestinians. It's the same thing, the same flavor."

Goldhirsh mopped his brow. "We don't have gas chambers in Israel, we have no interest in killing Palestinians as long as they leave us alone. We do not engage in genocide."

"Genocide? Perhaps not in the same manner, but it amounts to the same thing in the end, ethnic cleansing; the forceful removal of one group and the replacement by another."

"The state of Israel is here to stay," Goldhirsh stated flatly. "You'll not change that."

"We've no wish to change that. What we're interested in is putting a stop to the depredations of your government on the Palestinians. We believe they have a right to live, where they can earn a living and raise a family in relative safety. No different from what we want for ourselves or you, for that matter."

Once more silence filled the room. Tremaine turned away from the window and, returning to the couch, sat down. He refilled Goldhirsh's coffee and glanced at Noam, who shook his head.

"If we try and meet your demands," Goldhirsh began, "I doubt the government would survive. Then you'd have a problem."

"No, Mr. Secretary, you'd have a problem."

"And if the government falls?"

"If your government falls it make no difference. What we're doing is not dependent on who's in power."

"Are you really saying that if the settlements continue by noon on the 15th of September your government will stop all assistance regardless of who's in power?"

"That is correct."

"You don't know what you're doing."

"I know what I'm doing. I don't know what you'll do."

Tremaine had given it a great deal of thought. He'd wondered what he would do if he were in the Israelis' position.

"It will be difficult, very difficult, I agree." Tremaine paused for a moment. "If a tsunami is coming, best get out of the way. No matter what you try, you'll never stop it. Unusual things can happen in a crisis. Crisis is a time of opportunity. If the opportunity isn't seen in enough time, however, it becomes a catastrophe. Best look, best understand what's coming and do what you can. You don't have much time."

Goldhirsh was struck by the quiet and even tone with which Tremaine had made his statement. "It will never work," he said lamely. For a moment he'd glimpsed the possibility to which Tremaine was pointing.

"Mr. Secretary, if there's to be peace it must work. There's no other way. Do you want peace? How about your people, do they want peace?"

"Yes, but not peace at any price."

"The price of peace is nothing less than finding a way to

share the land with the Palestinians. How you do that is up to you and up to them, but I see only two ways it can happen: either two equal and sovereign states, or two peoples with equal rights under one common law, one common government; there's no other way I can see."

Goldhirsh shook his head. "Impossible," he murmured.

"You can say it's impossible all you wish, but in September you'll have some hard facts to deal with."

Goldhirsh was like a man who had glimpsed another road, something he'd not considered before, but his trajectory was still set. "You can't follow through. You won't be able to; there'll be too much opposition."

"Perhaps you'll understand just how serious I am when I tell you informal exploratory discussions are already underway with the International Court at the Hague. Briefs have also been submitted to our own Supreme Court."

It was eleven in the morning when Goldhirsh got back to the embassy. He put a call through to Levin.

"He won't budge," he said when Levin came on the phone. "No, they've already initiated contact with the International Court.... I know, but as he said, he wanted us to know just how serious they are.... No, they've begun preparing for that too. They've submitted a brief to the Supreme Court seeking a legal opinion.... I'll be meeting with our lobbyists again over the next several days.... I told them it was urgent.... No. The Christian Zionists as well...? I'll do what I can.... I know.... Yes, all the help we can get." Goldhirsh hung up and walked slowly out of the office.

A week later Levin returned, and he and Goldhirsh once more

met with the President. Once more the Israelis tried to persuade Tremaine not to follow through on what they now called his 'threat.' Tremaine would not budge.

Facing Facts

Levin and Goldhirsh were seated across from each other in Levin's office. It was early morning.

"What can we do about this American ultimatum?" Levin asked him.

It was a question Goldhirsh had been wrestling with since the very first meeting with Tremaine, and so far all he'd come up with were questions of his own. He chose his words carefully. "Have our actions left us open to the charge of ethnic cleansing? And, will we be able to stop the settlement expansion? If we try, there'll be hell to pay and the Palestinians will exploit it."

"I think it's deeper than that."

"And?"

"As Tremaine said, its not a good idea to believe our own propaganda. Have we been serious about peace? And, if peace has been our objective, are we any nearer?" Levin paused. "I don't think we are. We've been at war with the Palestinians, in one way or another, for more than seventy years. We've been tough, some might say brutal, and the war continues. We'd be hard pressed to say our policies have worked if peace was our primary objective."

"We're not at peace, yet," Goldhirsh responded, "but our neighbors know it's dangerous to provoke us, they know they won't win. And the facts on the ground? Our borders expand with the settlements. Imperceptible as it is, we control more land every day. Encouraging settlements has been key to this expansion."

"You're right, but the level of hostility and hatred toward us has grown, and that's not imperceptible. We're in a corner, and there's no easy way out. It will cost us either way."

"Realistically, Prime Minister, the Americans have given us a deadline but they can't enforce it."

"And if they do, what then?"

"My sources in the US assure me the Administration will have to back down, they won't follow through, they'll see to that."

"I'm not sure I share your optimism, Joseph. We can't blindly hope. We have to prepare for the worst. If they withdraw their support, won't guarantee our loans and can't be counted on to back us, we'll be vulnerable and isolated."

"We're strong enough to do without them. We're technologically advanced, a first-world country and our per capita income is on a par with South Korea."

"Maybe, but we've come to depend on the Americans' largesse. The loss of financial support will make things much more difficult. It will be hard to keep current levels of defense without cutting programs and raising taxes. How well will that go over? I think you've got more faith in our lobbying efforts than I do."

"I think they'll pull it off. We've always been successful and I don't see it changing."

"You could be right, but can we afford to make that assumption?"

After the meeting with Goldhirsh, Levin went home for a late breakfast.

"What's wrong?" Rebecca asked. They'd been married for forty years and she knew her husband well. Levin for his part usually appreciated her advice.

"There was something Tremaine said at our first meeting—something to the effect that we both know only truth can resolve this conflict with the Palestinians."

"That's a rather cryptic statement. What did he mean?"

"I'm not sure; but he also said that when we believe our own propaganda it can leave us blind."

"So what did you make of it?"

"I was angry. I'd never come across this from the Americans before."

Rebecca looked at her husband. He seemed uneasy. "What makes us blind?" she asked.

"I'm not sure." When she started asking these kinds of questions it invariably pointed to something he'd missed and she was usually right. "So what are you suggesting?" he asked.

"One word. Arrogance!" She let the word hang for a moment. "As Tremaine said, we've believed our own propaganda. After the Holocaust we seem to think we're not capable of doing the same to others."

Levin nodded.

"We believe that we, as God's chosen people, have a right to this land because our forebears lived here 2000 years ago. It was our home, a place where we could be ourselves, free of persecution and oppression. The Arabs who've been living here for more than 2000 years consider it their land as well. The only difference between us is we can enforce our beliefs and they can't."

Levin and Goldhirsh rode in the air-conditioned car through the streets of Tel Aviv. Earlier in the day, they'd received warning that an assassination attempt might be made at the Independence Day rally. "We have to attend," Levin stated matter of factly.

An hour later he stood at the podium under a canvas canopy, shaded from the intense sun. Before him a vast throng of faces and bright colors stretched in every direction. Television cameras stared at him with unblinking eyes. It was hot and humid. On the roofs of the buildings, he could see the IDF sharpshooters. Security was very tight.

Levin began his address. He wanted to talk with the people, all of the people, inside Israel and beyond. "Fifty years ago we gained independence and the state of Israel was born. Peace has eluded us and we live in a state of perpetual war. Everything we've done to this point has not brought us peace. There are those who argue that peace will only come with additional force or when the Palestinians are driven out. How long have we been saying this to ourselves?

"Like my predecessors I believed we must defend our right to exist. I thought it could be done by the exercise of 'reasonable force,' and our enemies would submit. It has not worked. There seems to be no end in sight.

"The change in American policy has created a crisis for all of us. We have choices to make, but we can't make them on our own. On something as important as this we have to make them together. What are we to do? In time of war we set aside our differences and unite in a common cause. In this instance, it's not the making of war we're talking about, but the making of peace. For this we must think clearly, see and understand the facts—just the facts, not our opinions or beliefs.

"What are the facts we must now consider? The American

President means what he says. Whether we like it or not, whether we agree with him or not, we must decide what we will do with the settlements. To keep American support, settlement construction must end. The President has stated clearly there'll be no extensions. He has also said that the deadline holds no matter who forms the government: whether we form the government, another party, or a coalition; the deadline will remain."

The crowd was silent and attentive.

"What will it mean for us as a nation to lose American support? At present we receive on average 2.8 billion dollars in assistance every year. Since we declared independence we've received a total of 140 billion dollars in aid. No other country in the world has received so much. If we don't comply with the American ultimatum, all aid will be terminated, as will all other assistance, and I mean, all assistance. This includes joint scientific research, joint business ventures, as well as military cooperation and research. We'll lose our designation as a 'non-Nato ally,' which means we'd have to pay more for weapons and would lose a number of other privileges. To maintain current defensive capabilities without major internal adjustments on our part would be impossible. And should we make those changes we'll all share the cost. Without American support we'll be alone, isolated. Like it or not, America has always been our strongest ally."

The crowd was growing restless. "We don't need them," someone shouted. "They wouldn't dare." More shouts could be heard. "They're hypocrites, ignore them."

Levin continued. "This is not all. The American government has promised to assist the Palestinians in bringing their case to the International Criminal Court in the Hague." Boos and hisses interrupted Levin and he had to wait before continuing. "We don't believe it will lead to anything, but we have to consider the possibility that charges could be laid against us for crimes against humanity, the most serious of which is ethnic cleansing." The crowd had become more restless, the voices of opposition louder. Once more Levin had to wait for the noise to calm down.

"Like it or not," he continued, "we have to decide. What are we going to do about the settlements and outposts? Land swaps will work in some places, in other places it will require returning land altogether. Land for peace? We have to ask ourselves if this is what we want, you and I as citizens must advise the government on what path we will take. We have to agree amongst ourselves before we deal with the Palestinians.

"Peace will cost us but so will war. Do we want to live with the continued threat of violence without support from the Americans? Do we want to live with tension and uncertainty? Imagine instead a country at peace with its neighbors and at peace with itself, where mistrust gives way to trust, where listening has replaced deafness, an open mind has replaced a closed one and creativity and cooperation have replaced hatred and violence. Think about it. Peace! It's up to us."

Quiet and sustained clapping greeted Levin's remarks. But sounds of dissent and anger could also be heard. Levin understood that the Americans had, by their actions, brought things to a head. No longer could Israel postpone the final outline of her borders and relationships with her neighbors.

Levin and Goldhirsh left the podium and, surrounded by security personnel, made their way to the waiting cars. The crowd pushed toward them, and the security personnel had difficulty keeping the space open as they approached the motorcade. The noise from the crowd was deafening. An egg smashed against one of the parked cars, and rotten fruit landed close to the two men. Unexpectedly, one of the security men went down. There was a loud popping sound. As Goldhirsh turned, he saw Levin collapse. At the same moment he felt a burning sensation in his chest, then a bullet severed his spine. He lay next to Levin, unable to move. Everything went quiet, and he sank into the peace of oblivion.

David was seated at the desk when Jonathan Makarios pushed the door open. Looking up, he saw the shocked look on his face.

"What happened?" he asked.

"Levin and Goldhirsh have been shot. Levin is dead. Goldhirsh is in critical condition and not expected to make it."

"What happened?"

"We don't know at the moment but they're holding a young student."

The door to the office opened and Doug Kersey entered, also visibly shaken.

"Any more word on what happened?" David asked.

"The assassin was a thirty-year-old student, a member of an ultra-orthodox mystical sect from a settlement on occupied land."

The phone rang and David picked it up. He listened for a moment before putting it down. He turned to the others. "Joseph Goldhirsh died fifteen minutes ago."

Fanning the flames

"It makes me so angry!" Sandra said.

She was referring to a news item she'd just watched on CBC. She and David had been on the West Coast to spend a couple of days in Victoria with her parents. It was a little after seven o'clock on a warm summer evening. Sandra had borrowed her father's truck and they took Trapper, their golden Lab and set off for the Galloping Goose Trail. The Secret Service agents followed as usual.

"What makes you angry?" David asked.

"They showed footage of an old olive orchard in Palestine. Local people had harvested the olives for generations and the reporter said some of the trees were a thousand years old. Olives were known to have grown in the area for five thousand years. A new Israeli settlement was built nearby, a huge imposing structure with high walls and what looked like watchtowers. It loomed over the orchard which sat in a shallow valley. It was harvest time and Palestinians were picking olives when the settlers tried to drive them off. In the past week five of them were shot; two died. According to the report, there have been ten deaths in the past three years, all Palestinians, all trying to farm as they have done for generations.

"Israeli peace activists went to the valley to shield

the Palestinians while they harvested the olives. The army showed up, ostensibly to keep the Jewish groups apart. They escorted the peace activists away, drove the Palestinians out and bulldozed the trees."

"Are you serious?" Tremaine shook his head.

"Yes, I am."

"Why destroy the orchard? What was the reasoning?"

"They said trees provide cover for gunmen to launch attacks on the settlers. Did you know 2.5 million olive trees in Palestine have been destroyed or stolen since 1967? The CBC piece pointed to the fact that the Palestinians were unarmed while the settlers showed up with rifles and handguns. The cameraman caught it on film. Before being escorted away he zoomed in on the settlers. They were hostile, their faces contorted with hatred."

They came to a corner where a narrow inlet twisted toward the ocean. Crossing the bridge they pulled into a parking area. Trapper jumped out and quickly vanished down the familiar trail. David spoke to the Secret Service agent in charge.

"We're going down the trail a mile or so. I don't want the path blocked," Tremaine told him. "Local people walk here all the time." As the agent opened his mouth to protest, David placed a hand on his arm. "This is not up for discussion. Understood?"

The agent nodded. They'd had this conversation before.

Sandra and David walked along the trail. Two agents, dressed casually, a man and a woman, were already ahead of them; two were behind. Three couples out for a walk. Trapper returned to see if they were coming.

A small trail joining the path led off through the trees toward the water. Trapper had already taken it and they followed. The trees gave way to a rocky bluff twenty feet above the inlet. They made themselves comfortable on a rock covered in thick moss. Trapper had found his way to the water's edge. David picked up a broken branch and threw it. The dog leapt into the water and swam toward it.

The sun slipped behind a ridge of trees to the west and the inlet mirrored the clouds above. David put his arm around his wife as they sat and watched the changing colors of evening. A cool breeze sifted through the trees and brought with it the salty tang of the Pacific. Rose-tinted clouds darkened to purple and twilight faded into darkness.

"For a while I felt hopeful for Israel and Palestine when Levin and Goldhirsh were alive," Sandra said. "Now it seems hopeless again."

For three months since the funerals, Israel had been caught in a downward spiral of violence and counter-violence. The new Prime Minister, Samuel Herzog, seemed intent on provoking the Palestinians. "Peace through firmness," was his slogan. He'd started his mandate by visiting a fiercely contested holy site in Jerusalem. The Palestinians had taken offense, and in the ensuing riot seven Palestinians were shot and killed. Then came an attack on one of the settlements by Palestinian gunmen, followed by the closure of the borders. Gaza was locked down, water shut off, no food or medicine allowed in or people out.

Bombers from the West Bank carried out a wave of suicide bombings, which brought counter-measures. Helicopter gunships targeted Palestinian leaders and their families, and when that failed, a full-scale invasion of the West Bank followed. What Herzog meant by 'firmness' was becoming readily apparent.

"It looks like your hand is being forced, and you'll have to cut aid to Israel."

"It seems that way. Settlement construction is still going on."

"And you'll help the Palestinians bring their case to the Hague?"

"I will."

"Why doesn't Hassan do something to stop the violence?" Sandra asked. "Surely as leader of the Palestine Liberation Organization there must be something he can do."

"The escalation of violence only strengthens the position of Palestinian hardliners and they won't listen to him anymore."

"Do you think Herzog really wants peace?"

"According to his words, yes; but his actions speak louder than words."

Just then, Trapper came bounding up the embankment. They had to scramble out of way to stay dry.

The next day, David returned to D.C., leaving Sandra behind to visit with her parents.

Travis entered the Oval Office to find Doug Kersey and Jonathan Makarios already there. Kersey had just returned from Israel.

"I came as quickly as I could," Travis said as he took off his coat.

Tremaine noticed the tiredness in the Chairman. "Travis, help yourself to coffee and then join us. Doug has just begun telling me of his visit to Israel. It doesn't sound promising."

Tremaine had sent his Secretary of State to convey his concern over the siege of Hassan's compound. Israeli bulldozers had been systematically destroying the PLO's buildings and had moved on to Hassan's headquarters. They'd sealed him off, along with a dozen of his top aides. They'd cut power and water and allowed no food in for a week.

Travis put his coffee on the table and sat across from Tremaine.

"The Israelis have refused to lift the siege," David said. "Herzog is demanding a complete end to the suicide bombing and a two-month cease-fire before he'll consider resuming peace talks."

"That's impossible. Even if the majority of the Palestinians want to suspend the bombings, the militants won't let it happen." Travis responded. "He knows it. What he's doing is keeping the hostilities going, fanning the flames."

"More justification for Palestinian extremists," Kersey interjected. "They've cut waterlines and enforced curfews by killing anyone who violates them. They've stopped Palestinians from taking away their dead. According to Doctors Without Borders, there's concern over the potential outbreak of disease."

"You think the Israelis are deliberately using disease and starvation as weapons of war?" asked Travis.

"I wouldn't have believed it but it certainly seems that way," replied Kersey.

"And the suicide bombings continue," Makarios pointed out.

"Yes, they continue," said Tremaine. "Tell Travis what Herzog told you."

"The gist of what he said was: tell the President, we claim the right as a nation to exist; we claim the right of pre-emptive strikes; and we'll defend ourselves by whatever means necessary. As long as Jewish people are being killed, we will not rest. The Palestinians will pay the price. If we have to build a wall to secure our borders we'll do so. Until now we've been too soft. Our overtures toward peace have been rejected. If we're to have peace it will be peace through strength. And, he said, you can tell your President that we will not be blackmailed. Take us to the court at the Hague and see what happens. They have no jurisdiction over us."

"He doesn't leave much doubt about his position, does he?" Travis remarked.

"No, he doesn't."

The Bus

Jonathan Makarios and Doug Kersey arrived at the White House early in the morning. It was still dark. Morgan was already in conversation with Tremaine when they opened the door.

David stood with his back to the window.

"Let's start with the Middle East trip," Tremaine began, when they were seated. "Where do we stand?"

"The arrangements are made," Kersey began. "You'll visit the Jordanians, the Lebanese and Israelis."

"And the Syrians and Iranians?"

"Syria is dealing with its own crisis and the Iranians don't want to meet us right now. The Israeli Prime Minister won't be able to meet you either; he said he has 'prior commitments.' He's invited you to address the Knesset though, reluctantly." Kersey suppressed a smile.

What made him change his mind?"

"Who, not what."

"Who?"

"Rebecca Levin," he said. "She insisted. She has a lot of support in Israel."

"Well, that's interesting."

"Herzog is giving you the 'opportunity to explain yourself to the Israeli people' as he put it. He said he knew you'd take into account what he called 'the new reality, the reality on the ground.'"

"New reality? What does he mean by that?"

"I asked him the same thing."

"He said, and I quote again, 'The new reality is a state of open, if undeclared, war with the Palestinians.'"

It was August 9th. The trip had been more fruitful than he'd hoped. Tremaine had good discussions with the Lebanese and the Jordanians. In Lebanon he'd met a cautious and hopeful response. The Lebanese people, he was told, had watched the 'new initiatives' of each successive administration over the years, so they would wait and see what happened this time. "It doesn't help to raise people's hopes only to have them dashed time after time," he was told by the Prime Minister. In Jordan, he'd found considerable receptivity from the King and his ministers.

The Israelis had been another matter altogether. Tremaine had addressed the Knesset, stating his case clearly and concisely. His reception had been cool but polite. He'd explained what the United States was doing, the reasoning behind it and what he hoped to accomplish. When pressed to extend the deadline, he'd refused. September 15th would stand. When asked about opposition from the American people to what he was doing, he'd smiled, knowing what they were alluding to.

The lobbying by Israel, he admitted, had been fierce but the Administration had responded quickly to misinformation, pointing out the spin, refuting all bogus claims and inaccurate information. They were consistent and rapid with their responses. They'd tracked down and identified the special interest groups and made them public. He'd talked directly to the American people, who'd been apathetic to begin with. Exposing the lobbies and who they represented, together with his talks to the American people and news of the events taking place in the Middle East, had galvanized the public. A majority now supported the Administration's initiative. The opinions expressed by the Supreme Court had also been helpful, as had the response from the Hague.

The President had then gone on to discuss with the Knesset ways of defusing the conflict by methods other than violence. The open question-and-answer session in the Knesset following his speech had become openly hostile. He took each question and opinion seriously and made sure he'd understood the concerns being expressed before clearly and logically framing his response. By the time he left the Knesset, three hours had passed, one of the longest sessions accorded a foreign head of state.

Following the speech, which had been broadcast nationwide, Tremaine received calls for radio and television interviews, which he accepted. Two days of in-depth interviews followed. Outside the building where the last interview took place, a large and hostile crowd of settlers had to be held in check. Eggs and stones hit the car as it sped away. Three days of talking and he was beginning to lose his voice. He'd become increasingly aware that there was considerable opposition to Israeli government policies toward the Palestinians, more than he'd anticipated.

In Prime Minister Herzog, however, Tremaine had found the strongest opponent of peace. The diminutive man had been tough, antagonistic and straightforward. He had a keen mind and a pessimistic assessment of human nature. Herzog believed that peace with the Palestinians would, if it came at all, come from the end of a gun.

"We'll talk more when you visit again. I'll be curious to know how your views have changed," Herzog said when they parted. He'd managed to find time for a private five-minute discussion with Tremaine. Tremaine recognized the not-so-subtle statement as indicative of a man who believed he was right and whose mind was closed to any other possibility.

Mikel, Mera's Israeli friend, had called and asked if the President would meet with a coalition of Israeli peace groups the following morning before his return flight late in the afternoon. He'd accepted. The meeting was to take place the day after Tishah B'Av.

In the early morning Sandra and David had breakfast in their room and left with the Secret Service agents through a side entrance to the hotel. They expected to be watched by Shabak, Israel's Security Agency, but hoped they'd be left alone. Herzog, given his hostility toward him and the presence of US agents, might have felt it unnecessary to provide protection or surveillance.

Preferring not to attract attention, David had refused the offer of a limousine to take them the five blocks to their meeting. Instead the couple walked leisurely along the street. The agents, Robert Sandusky and Joan Merril, looking like tourists, walked with them. Tremaine and his wife wore sunglasses and casual attire in the hope they'd be less recognizable. The city was coming to life after three weeks of restrictions and a day of fasting. Above the mountains, a fiery sun burned in a cloudless sky. The street, in the shadow of the tall buildings, was a hive of activity. Local merchants opened their stores, sliding back the iron grates, removing shutters and wheeling out display carts loaded with produce. Along the street, traffic was becoming heavy, impeded by trucks unloading fruit and fresh vegetables from the kibbutzim.

Sandra put her arm though David's, giving it a squeeze. He looked at her and started to laugh—for a moment he'd forgotten she was wearing sunglasses with frames covered in polka dots. It made her appearance a little... unusual, he thought. He caught sight of bright red hair blowing in the breeze of an open window of a passing bus. A young girl looked out. Their eyes met, and they exchanged a smile. David waved, and she waved back. The bus continued down the street, disappearing behind two large trucks unloading produce twenty meters away.

Suddenly there was a blinding flash and a thunderous roar. Sandra was the first to regain her wits. She looked at David and the remaining agents, who'd gotten to their feet. Realizing they were fine, she turned and ran in the direction of the explosion. She raced toward the bus, now a twisted shell of metal and shattered glass. Lurid yellow flames flickered in the wreckage, giving off a pungent black smoke. Without thinking, she'd rushed to help, her training as a nurse taking over.

David and the two agents ran after her. When she climbed into the bus they were right with her. Sandra looked for survivors and checked the seriousness of their injuries. The smoke made her eyes water and burned her throat. She found the red-haired girl pinned beneath the twisted seats, a shard of metal protruding from a bloody shoulder. While David and Robert carefully lifted the seat, Sandra and Joan eased the girl off the metal spike. She groaned and passed out. Carefully, they lifted her over the side to waiting hands and safety. Climbing out of the bus, Sandra knelt beside the injured girl. Blood was pumping from the wound, and she knew it would have to be stopped. Ripping pieces from his shirt, David handed them to her. She glanced up and found herself looking into his calm green eyes. Bunching up a piece of shirt, she stuffed it into the wound and quickly bound it tight. In the distance, sirens wailed. Sandra glanced around and saw the last injured person being removed from the bus.

She noticed a woman lying on her back against a nearby building. She went over to her. Black powder covered her face and blood dribbled from her mouth. Her clothes were in shreds. Sandra felt her pulse; it was strong. She must have been shielded from the worst of the explosion, she thought. The sound of sirens filled the air. Looking up she could see a crowd gathering around the bus. She took off her coat and placed it under the woman's head. Standing up, she felt a blow to the back of her neck and then someone charged her from the side, knocking her over. As she fell, strong hands grabbed her arms and pulled her to her feet. A pair of intense dark eyes stared at her through a black ski mask. The man held a gun against her belly. On either side of her, men similarly dressed held her by the arms.

"You're coming with us," said a heavily accented voice behind her.

Before she realized what was happening, Sandra was being pushed down a narrow street between two buildings. The gun had disappeared. Then she heard a grunt, as though someone had the wind knocked out of him. She felt something heavy fall against the back of her legs, tripping her. The men on either side of her spun around, both of them holding guns. She saw David step into the man on her left. With his left hand, he grasped the wrist behind the gun and pushed it in the air. She saw him twist, striking the man's exposed side and sending him sprawling. Robert struck the other man and, knocking him down, ripped the gun out of his grip.

Six attackers, each with a ski mask over his head, materialized. One of them fired at Joan, who'd drawn her gun, and the shot struck her in the leg. She fell heavily, the gun spinning out of her hand. A third attacker lunged at David with a knife. Sandra screamed a warning.

David stepped toward the man, letting the knife pass a fraction of an inch from his face. With a fierce yank, he pulled the wrist down and then turned, sending the man flying through the air.

Before her husband could recover, Sandra watched as one of the attackers put a gun to the back of his head. As though in slow motion, she saw the hammer click back. David had begun to turn and, sensing what was happening, jerked his head down. At the same time, she heard the crack of the gun. David dropped to the ground and lay still, blood already forming a dark pool around his head. With a vicious jerk, she found herself propelled forward. She struggled, her screams no longer audible above the sirens. Before they reached the alley, the man at her right staggered from a heavy blow to the side of his head. From the corner of her eye, she saw Robert drive his heel into the man's knee and heard the cracking of the bones. At the same time, she saw a dark red stain suddenly appear on the agent's chest; his face lost all expression and he fell to the ground.

She was rushed rapidly down an alley and emerged on the other side, propelled by the men holding her arms. A small black panel-van stood nearby. As they approached, the doors opened and she was shoved roughly inside. In a matter of moments, they were speeding down a narrow street. A scarf was tied around her eyes, and rough hands secured her wrists behind her back.

At the precise moment David felt the gun at the back of his head, he knew what it was. As he jerked his head down, he heard a roar in his ears. Everything went black and silent. When he came to, he was in a hospital bed. A nurse stood in front of him, and to the right, a doctor with a stethoscope around his neck peered at his watch while his fingers felt David's pulse. David noticed the armed guards at the door.

"Where's Sandra?"

"They got away with her." The voice came from his left. He turned to see the American ambassador James MacNamara seated beside him.

"Who were they?"

"We don't know."

"Where's Robert and Joan?" David asked, referring to the agents who'd been with him.

"Robert's in intensive care, in critical condition with a chest wound. The doctors think he'll pull through. Joan's in surgery, they're trying to repair the damage to her leg.

Morgan was in his office when Travis knocked on the door. Jonathan Makarios accompanied him. They looked pale and shaken.

"Have a seat." Morgan motioned to the chairs near his desk.

"You heard?" Travis asked.

"Yes. I had a call from Herzog. He said the group that kidnapped Sandra, probably Hamas, may not know who they have. Although kidnapping isn't common, the Israeli authorities are hoping it was a random abduction— a way to bargain for the freedom of Palestinian prisoners."

"What else?"

"So far this is what we know. A bus was blown up by a suicide bomber in Tel Aviv. David and Sandra were nearby and went to help. During the commotion, she was captured. When David and the agents tried to rescue her, one agent was shot in the chest. He's in critical condition. The other agent was shot in the leg. David suffered a bullet crease to his skull—superficial but he lost a lot of blood."

"He'll be all right, though?" Jonathan asked.

"It seems so," Morgan responded. "Lines at the hospital are not secure, so I didn't speak with him directly. I did speak with the embassy, and MacNamara said the Israelis are following every lead. They've mounted a massive search, but they're trying to make it inconspicuous. I'm at the helm during his absence, but we need to keep this under wraps to ensure Sandra's safety. Jonathan, you and I will be working together. I'll need your help."

Jonathan nodded.

Travis looked up. "I'm leaving for Israel in an hour."

Hostage

When Travis and his two companions, Peter Nevis and Kevin McCloud, landed at Lod Airbase, Tel Aviv, they were taken straight to the Shabak control center for a thorough briefing on the investigation. It took the better part of two hours to bring them up to date. Afterwards, they were driven to the U.S. Embassy.

Travis showered and changed. In less than an hour he was on his way to the hospital.

He slipped quietly into the room. David looked up in surprise, and smiled.

"It's good to see you. I'm glad you came." He knew that Travis, being the kind of man he was, would do everything in his power to find Sandra. The two men talked for an hour. After the General left, David, weak from loss of blood, fell into an exhausted sleep.

Sandra lay on a rusty cot in a darkened room that smelled of rats and urine. She was gagged, her hands were bound, and a chain fastened her ankle to the wall. Her head pounded, and she was stiff all over. She was not dressed for the cold, and her captors had provided nothing for warmth. At night she was so cold she shivered uncontrollably and curled in a ball to keep warm.

All she'd been given since she'd been shoved into the cell was dried crusts of bread, a little cheese and some water. At night the door was unbarred and food was set before her, the guard remaining in the room until she finished. Whatever she did not eat or drink when the gag was removed was taken away. There was enough room to stand, and when she needed to, she could relieve herself in a battered bucket in the corner.

She had no idea where she was. Days passed, she lost count of them.

After she was put in the van, they'd traveled a short distance before changing vehicles. Twice this had happened the first day. At night she'd been gagged and hustled onto a small boat and dumped in the hold. It smelled of fish and salt. The motor was running and she heard the lines being cast off.

Once under way the hatch opened and a light shone into the hold, blinding her. Two blankets and a bucket were dropped to her before the hatch slid back with a bang. Sandra wrapped herself in the blankets and lay down. Lulled by the lapping water against the hull, the gentle rocking motion and the soft sound of the motor as it chugged quietly through the night, she fell asleep. She woke to the sound of the anchor chain rattling off the deck. Half an hour passed and the hatch was pulled back. She saw silhouettes, against a star filled sky. Hands reached down and pulled her out. Once on deck she saw a skiff emerging from the darkness. It came along side and lines were passed and secured. The dark form of a man stood in front of the small upright wheel house of the open boat. Two men jumped in and helped the female guards aboard. A crewman standing beside her, pointing at the skiff, motioned for her to get in. The skiff pushed off, heading east toward a smudge of low hills in the distance. She noticed the faint hint of light, the promise of a new dawn. When she looked back the fish boat was gone. The offshore breeze suddenly died and the sea, like liquid glass rose and fell uneasily.

They came ashore just before dawn. As she went up the beach, she looked back to see the dark form of the skiff and its lone pilot disappear, heading north. She felt a rough prod in her back pushing her forward.

The next day they travelled short distances to different homes. Sometimes they walked, and sometimes were driven. Arriving in one car they left in another. The two women had remained with her at all times. She, like them was dressed as devout Muslim women, with faces and heads covered. When walking, her hands were unbound, but she'd been shown the guns the women carried, and they'd made it clear they wouldn't hesitate to use them.

One afternoon they'd rested in a shallow cave until dark. She was given army fatigues and told to put them on. The women guards had done the same, as had the men.

For seven hours they made their way along seldom-used trails. As morning approached, they stood at the base of some low hills. Before sun rise she found herself in a large underground complex of bomb shelters, storage facilities, kitchens and rooms. That evening, they walked in single file into the mountains. Two men and a woman walked in front and the same behind her. Coming to a shallow depression between some hills they stopped. Above and to her left, a sea of stars shone through the limbs of overhanging trees. Moonlight revealed shadowy shapes on the uneven ground. A hand grabbed her arm and pushed her into a sitting position.

"Try to escape and you'll be shot!"

She stared at a short stocky man, the leader of the group.

It was the first time he'd spoken to her. He smelled of cigarettes and sweat; his eyes were hidden in shadow. At his waist was a holstered pistol and in his hands a high-powered rifle. Five men joined them an hour later. They sat in a circle and a discussion ensued, carried on in a language unfamiliar to her. From time to time the men looked toward her, dark shapes in her field of vision; the women remained at her side. An hour later they were underway.

It was five o'clock when they finally stopped. She'd looked quickly at her watch before being blindfolded. Led down a steep and uneven path she slipped. Rough hands jerked her upright. She heard the cry of a rooster in the distance and the smell of smoke. Her captors walked on either side of her.

When they stopped again, she heard hushed voices and the sound of a door creaking on a hinge. She felt herself pushed through an opening and heard the door close behind her. The blindfold was removed and one of her captors led her into a small room and pushed her onto an old bed, the springs squeaking with her weight. One man held a lantern and she watched the other one fasten a chain around her ankle, attaching it to a thick metal ring in the wall. A gag was forced between her lips and tied behind her neck. Then they'd left, the light vanishing as the door closed behind them. In the darkness she heard a bar drop into place.

Alone in the dark, dingy room, removed from the constant travel of the last four days, the sorrow that had accompanied her since being torn away from David, engulfed her. She could not stop her mind returning to the last glimpse she'd had of him before the walls of the alley had blocked her view. He'd been on his back, unmoving. Blood from the head wound had obscured his face and formed a frightening pool on the pavement beneath him.

In the intervening days, as she lay cold and shivering on the cot, the sorrow over the death of her husband left her empty and drained. Life or death, it didn't matter to her anymore.

One evening after her meal of crusty bread and old cheese she'd drifted to sleep, and was awakened by an unexpected noise. She heard the bar being removed from the door. Light from a lantern flooded the room as the door was pushed open. A man unfamiliar to her entered. His hair was white, his skin dark. At first glance he gave the appearance of being elderly, but the ease of his movements suggested otherwise.

Sandra found herself looking into eyes she would never forget. In the lantern's light they were dark and peaceful, alert, not missing a thing. For the first time in days, she didn't feel afraid.

The thought crossed her mind that she was dreaming. She sat up and swung her feet onto the floor, shivering. The man set the lantern down and, producing a small key, knelt and unlocked the chain that held her foot. He wore a soft but coarse woolen coat.

"You must be very quiet," he whispered.

Reaching behind her neck, he untied the gag and then her wrists. She could smell the lanolin from the raw wool of his coat.

"Can you walk?" he asked.

"Yes," she said, her voice a hoarse whisper.

"Then follow me. We don't have much time."

With that he stood and, taking her by the hand, helped her to her feet.

"My name is Nasir," he said, his head inclined toward her ear, "and your's, I think, is Sandra."

She nodded.

Lifting the lantern, Nasir went through the door into the outer room. The guard lay slumped on the floor facing the wall, his hands tied behind his back. As she looked up, she saw a man standing against the wall, almost hidden in the shadows. He held the door open and they slipped outside, but not before Nasir had extinguished the light.

Sandra could just make out the form of small houses in the darkness. Nasir and his friend guided her away from the dwellings and into the desert hills.

Once they were clear of the habitation, they stopped. "This is Khalil," Nasir said. In the light from the stars Sandra saw the young man bow, inclining his head in her direction.

"We've a long way to go before dawn," Nasir said. Sandra noticed his voice had a melodic tone, and an unfamiliar accented English.

"Who are you?" she whispered.

"We can talk later. Right now we must get away from here," Nasir replied.

Khalil removed his jacket and gave it to Sandra. Then he took a small flask and handed it to her motioning her to drink. She recognized the taste of honey kefir and drank it thankfully. Then they set off moving quickly. She did her best to follow. Her legs were weak and shaky, but gradually, with the renewal of hope, strength seeped back into her body. They traveled hard for hours and then, just before dawn, Khalil knocked quietly on the small wooden door of a tiny house. Quickly they were ushered inside.

Travis

"Where is she?" Abdullah asked.

"Jezzine," Harith responded.

"Is she safe?"

"Of course. Why did you call me here?"

Harith had been rushed to Beirut from Jezzine. He'd had little chance to rest and was feeling in no mood for idle talk. What he needed was sleep. He looked around the hot, stuffy room. Although it was midday, very little light entered from outside. An oil lamp flickered on a packing crate, barely keeping the darkness at bay. Harith and six of his men sat in a circle on old crates and broken chairs.

"Where did you capture the woman?" continued his interrogator.

"She was on the street, helping the injured from the bus. We knew she was American from her accent. She must be wealthy, because it looked like she had two servants with her, as well as a man we think was her husband."

"We lost three men in that action of yours. Hardly worth it for the life of a wealthy American." Abdullah spat the words out.

Harith looked up at the powerfully built Abdullah, who'd suddenly gotten to his feet.

"Whoever this woman is, she's important. In less

than an hour, my sources tell me, the Israelis launched a massive manhunt. There are rumors the American Chairman of the Joint Chiefs arrived in Tel Aviv the morning after the kidnapping. There's nothing about her in the press and that makes me suspicious. They don't want us to know who we have. We'd better find out, and quickly." Abdullah looked slowly at each of them. "Harith, get some sleep. We'll see you this evening."

"Travis, we've reason to believe she's been taken across the border into Lebanon."

"What makes you think that?"

Rotstein, the Shabak agent, paused for a moment wondering just how much he should say to Travis "We traced the vehicles. We found the last one near the border."

Travis looked at the agent. "You must have more than that."

"I wish we did!"

"They can't get across the border, can they?"

"I doubt it, but we're always finding new tunnels."

"What about the sea, could they have gone by boat?"

"Again it's possible but that's not where we found the last vehicle."

"You're not really sure it was their vehicle, are you?"

Rotstein hesitated.

"I thought so," Travis was getting irritated. "Do you have people in southern Lebanon," he asked?

"Just contacts so far but we have commando units ready."

Travis looked at McCloud and Nevis. He turned back to the Shabak agent, "Let me know what develops," he said as he picked up his coat and moved to the door.

"Of course."

They left for the Embassy, frustrated at having to sit around and wait. David had already returned to Washington. It was almost a week since Travis arrived in Israel and inactivity was not one of his virtues. But, there was nothing he could do until he was sure of Sandra's whereabouts. He had to wait. He had a feeling Sandra was now in Lebanon. He wondered how she got there and hoped she was still alive.

He was familiar with the area. In 1974, he'd spent time in Israel, working with Israeli Special Forces, Sayeret. He trained highly skilled units in techniques of counter-guerrilla warfare. For six months they worked in a section that stretched in places some sixty miles into Lebanon.

Back at the Embassy, Travis opened a map and spread it on the table. Peter Nevis and Kevin McCloud gathered around.

"This is where I think she might be," Travis pointed at the map around Sohmor in the Bekaa Valley south east of Beirut.

"Why there?" McLeod asked.

Travis straightened up and folding the map, put it away.

"It would be dangerous for them to be close to the border. If I wanted to hide someone that's where I'd do it, assuming she's in Lebanon, that is."

Travis had difficulty sleeping. He lay on the bed, drifting between sleep and wakefulness. He'd brought the two ex-Green Berets with him because of their training, because they were masters of disguise, and because they, like him, were fluent in the Arabic dialects of the area. He'd known them for years, and trusted them completely. They'd jumped at the chance to come with him, and only learned the purpose of their mission once they were airborne.

When he'd received word of what happened, Travis had immediately begun preparations to leave for Israel. Admiral McManus had warned him that, given his position, it was inappropriate for him to go. Travis knew the Admiral was right. But, as he explained, he was familiar with the area and fluent in Arabic. Travis had made up his mind and nothing would stop him. He'd become close to the President and First Lady. He liked them very much. Over breakfast, Travis told Mildred he'd be out of the country for a few days, maybe a week or so. She knew enough not to question him.

It was a long time before he drifted off to sleep. The sound of the phone jolted him awake. For a moment, he couldn't remember where he was. The loud ring came again, and he grabbed for the phone.

"Yes. ... I'll be right down. ... Yes."

He pulled his clothes on and walked quickly down the hall. He knocked on one of the doors.

"Nevis and McCloud, get down to the conference room. I'll meet you there."

"It came in this morning?" Travis asked, looking at the clock. It was zero three hundred hours.

"Yes, about fifteen minutes ago."

"And you recorded it?"

"Yes, we record all incoming calls."

"Play it again."

There was the sound of static on the line and then the voice of the Embassy operator. "U.S. Embassy. May I help you?"

"Listen carefully," came the response. The voice was accented. "Sandra Tremaine has been freed and, for the time being, is safe."

"Who is this?"

"No names," came the voice.

"How can we be sure we can trust you?" asked the Embassy operator.

"You can't, but please, listen carefully. Send some of your people to Bent Jebail; no more than three. More will only attract unwanted attention. Do not tell the Israelis, and don't bring them with you. You must look like local merchants. Go to the shop of Jabir and arrange to purchase thirty pounds of dates, then change your mind and tell him you made a mistake, it should be forty. We'll take it from there."

With a click the line went dead.

Two hours later Travis and his companions boarded the Challenger jet, which had been kept waiting since their arrival. In less than an hour he was in Jordan talking with an emissary of King Abdullah. An hour and a half later they landed in Beirut. It was just before ten. Travis had given the Israelis no useful information.

Once through customs they picked up the rental car and drove to Bent Jebail.

On the trail

"The President's wife?" Harith was stunned. "No, it couldn't be. They wouldn't be walking alone in Tel Aviv."

Abdullah responded, his voice raised. "They weren't alone, Harith, they had Secret Service agents with them. That's why you lost so many men."

"I don't believe it."

"I don't care what you believe, Harith, the woman you abducted is the President's wife."

A twisted smile spread across Harith's face. "Now we'll break the Great Satan." Harith's voice was harsh.

"We have to get her safely out of Lebanon right away," Abdullah said.

"Why?" demanded Harith.

"The Israelis and the Americans will turn the country upside down looking for this woman. No place will be safe."

"Where do you suggest?" interrupted Harith. "The leaders of Jordan and Lebanon met the American President and were impressed by the hard line he'd taken with the Israelis. They won't help us. They want peace. We need this conflict. It is Allah's way. The West has contaminated our world, and only the blood of the great Satan's children will wash away the evil they've brought on us. We have to get her out of Lebanon and into Iraq."

"How?"

The quickest route is across southern Syria. Hizballah has contacts there. I'll make the arrangements. Harith, you'll bring the woman to Ar Rutbah."

They spent the morning hastily planning. They had very little time to pull it off.

"She's gone?" exploded Harith. "How can that be?

"We don't know what happened," Faisal responded, afraid of Harith's anger.

"What do you mean, you don't know?" Harith screamed.

"When we got there in the morning to relieve Bayazid, we found him tied up and lying on the floor. The door was open and the woman gone. We've scoured the area all day. We even got old Talal to see if he could track them. It seems there were two men besides the woman. Talal was able to follow the tracks for several kilometers, before losing them."

"Bring Talal here," Harith ordered. "In the meantime, get me food."

Harith hadn't stopped to eat and it had been late when he arrived in Aanout. He just finished eating when there was a knock on the door and Talal was ushered in.

"Sit," ordered Harith.

The old man sat down and looked at Harith. "What do you want?" Talal despised the Iranian.

"Tell me all you can about the escape and where you think the woman is," Harith demanded.

"I'm not a magician, Harith, I'm a tracker."

"Don't fool with me, old man." Harith's patience was gone. "Tell me what you know," he shouted, pulling out his gun.

"Two people got her out. They were headed north when I lost their tracks."

"Why did you lose their tracks, old man?" he demanded threateningly.

"I think they were trying to lead you astray."

"What makes you think so?"

"Whoever was leading them left only a hint of a trail, not obvious to the inexperienced eye. I followed it for five or six kilometers before the trail led into some rocks and vanished completely. Whoever it was knew exactly what they were doing. They wanted you to follow the tracks in the wrong direction. They're very familiar with the terrain."

"Who might it be?" Harith was from Tehran and not yet familiar with the area. "Who, besides you, knows this area well? Think!"

"The people who live here," Talal responded.

"That's obvious! Who else?"

Faisal interjected, "There's an old shepherd who lives in these hills. His brother is retarded. They move their flocks from place to place. Sometimes he picks up supplies in Jezzine."

"What do you think, Talal?"

"I've heard of him. I've seen him from time to time. He keeps to himself, seems to be a hermit."

"I've heard it said he's a Sufi, not really a shepherd." Zahid spoke for the first time. He was one of the older men in the cell. He'd been with them for twenty years.

Harith turned toward Zahid. "Tell me what you know."

"I don't know anything for sure, but for many years some of the men disappeared into the mountains. They'd come back after two or three days. I heard rumors they went to see the old Sufi.

He seemed to have a strange effect on them. They'd become soft. I think Khalil and Tariq used to visit him."

"Khalil?" Harith snapped. "Where is Khalil?"

Faisal looked at the others. "He went to Bent Jebail. He should be back late tonight or tomorrow morning."

"He and that traitor Tariq were friends, you say?"

"Yes," responded Zahid. "He and Khalil were from the same village."

"Which village?"

"Midane."

It was mid-morning when Nasir returned. Aziz was sitting on the steps. Khalil came out of the house and joined them.

"I got through to the American Embassy. They'll send someone to Bent Jebail this afternoon. They'll contact Jabir to buy dates. That's how we'll know them."

"So we're going to meet them there?"

"Yes."

"And bring them here?"

"You and I will leave this afternoon and meet whoever comes. Sandra will remain with Samara and Durrah. She can rest. We'll bring the Americans here."

Parting

Travis and his companions entered Bent Jebail from the east. It was late afternoon when they parked and walked up a narrow side street to Jabir's small shop. Pushing the door open, they entered and were greeted by a short, potbellied merchant.

"What can I do for you?" he asked politely.

"We'd like to buy thirty pounds of dates," Travis said.

Jabir nodded. "Please, have a seat, Coffee?"

"Yes, that would be good," Travis responded.

Jabir disappeared and returned with four tiny cups of coffee on an old wooden tray.

"I made a mistake," Travis said to Jabir. "It should be forty pounds."

Jabir looked closely at him and nodded, "As you wish."

He disappeared into the back of the store and reappeared moments later. They sat on sacks of coffee beans and talked about the price of dates, almonds and olives. It seemed prices were falling—driven down, Jabir said, by the Israelis who now grew large quantities and flooded the market, making it hard for him to make a living.

Nevis and McCloud had begun to shift uneasily. But Travis, despite his impatience, knew he had to respect the process under way.

"You must come for a meal at my home," Jabir

insisted when they'd finished their coffee.

After the shop was closed, they walked up the road with Jabir. The sun was setting when they arrived at his home.

Jabir's wife, a short, plump woman with graying hair, had prepared a meal. "We'll be having guests this evening," he'd told her when he left in the morning. Her face was hidden behind a veil. She placed food on the table—lentil soup, chick peas, olives, bread and cheese. Then with averted eyes and a slight bow to the men, she excused herself and disappeared.

They'd just finished their meal when Travis heard a light tap on the door. Jabir opened it. Travis heard voices of greeting and watched as two men came into the room.

Jabir made the introductions.

"Coffee?" he asked.

"Yes," answered the older of the arrivals, the younger man nodded.

Jabir called his wife. "Coffee, for our guests," he said.

Nasir and Khalil sat across from the Americans.

Jabir's wife returned and placed the tray of coffee on the table before disappearing again. Jabir sat at the head of the table. He said nothing.

Looking at Travis, Nasir spoke in his accented English.

"Sandra Tremaine is safe and well."

Travis recognized the voice from the tape.

"Where is she?" Travis was wary. Why would these Palestinians help them? Travis, without being obvious, had been observing Nasir carefully since his arrival. He saw an old man, upright, slim and wiry, his body fluid and relaxed. Even in the dim light he could see his face was open and his eyes calm. Travis made the decision that Nasir was someone he could trust.

"We'll take you to her." Nasir responded.

Jabir had followed them outside as Khalil led them to a dark battered van parked beside the rental car.

Travis looked at Nasir.

"It's less conspicuous" Nasir said, answering the unspoken question. "Jabir will arrange the return of the rental car"

"The documents are in the glove box," Travis had turned toward Jabir as he handed him the keys.

"Thank you for your kindness and generosity." Travis said shaking Jabir's hand. "Please thank your wife for our meal." Nevis and McCloud nodded and thanked him as well. Nasir took Jabir aside and talked with him briefly. Then, kissing him on both cheeks, he said good bye.

Travis was sitting in the front beside Khalil who was driving. He turned to Nasir. "What happens next?" he asked. It was hard to hear in the van. The road was rough and the engine noisy.

Nasir leaned forward. "We're going to Midane. We'll leave the van with a friend and take you to Sandra. There's a young woman with her called Samara. She'll guide you through the mountains. She knows them well." Nasir paused. "I must ask a favor of you."

Travis waited in the dark, not knowing what to expect. Had he misjudged Nasir, he wondered. Did he want payment for helping Sandra.

"The guerillas who captured Sandra will soon know that she's been helped by a friend of mine called Durrah. Both she and Samara's lives will be at risk. I want you to take them to America with you and help them get settled."

Travis didn't need to think about it. "I'll be happy to arrange it," he said, "I can arrange for you to come with us, as well."

"No." Nasir replied. "Thank you, but I won't be able to go. I have a meeting in the mountains. My time here is all but over." He continued, "I've arranged for you to go to Deir Quanoun, not far from Tyre."

"Why there?"

"An old friend of mine lives there. His name is Omar, he's a doctor at one of the hospitals in Tyre."

"Omar?" Travis was surprised.

"You know him?"

"I don't know him personally but if it's who I think it is I've heard of him. He's a friend of Chris Heatherington, the Vice President's father in law."

"Captain Heatherington?" It was Nasir's turn to be surprised.

"That's right. He was a captain in the British Army."

Nasir smiled to himself, marveling at Allah's handiwork.

"You know him?" Travis asked.

"I do. It was a long time ago. We were in Acre together."

Travis shook his head, not understanding the reference. It was difficult to hear Nasir's voice over the sound of the van.

"When you get to Omar's home," Nasir continued, "he'll take you to the airport in Beirut."

"We have a plane waiting for us at the airport." Travis said. "We flew to Beirut this morning. But getting them through security might be a problem.

"I don't know the details," Nasir said, "Omar is taking care of it."

The van shrieked to a halt. A flock of sheep blocked the road.

It was past midnight when Khalil, Nasir and the Americans turned east several kilometers from Midane. They drove up an unpaved track for five kilometers before stopping in front of a small home. Khalil parked the van beside it.

"Tell Hilmi to be ready," Nasir said as Khalil went inside. Moments later he reappeared.

Leaving the van where it was they followed a well-traveled goat trail up a gentle valley with steep sides. Nasir set a fast pace. When they reached the head of the valley they stopped. Nasir and Khalil listened intently. The night was dark and overcast. High clouds hid the stars. There it was, the sound of stones being dislodged somewhere above them. The sound carried easily in the cool night air. The trail from Aanout entered a few hundred meters ahead of them. It was unusual to find someone on the trails at this time of night.

"Nasir, take the men to Durrah's. I'll meet you there," Khalil whispered. "I'm going to see what's happening. If I don't catch up, get the Americans away quickly." Before Nasir could respond, Khalil vanished up the trail. Nasir and the others took the trail to the right.

Khalil made his way to where the trails met. He waited. A few minutes later, he heard the distinct sounds of men traveling at night. They moved cautiously, but the weight of their equipment and the darkness made it difficult for them to be completely silent. Khalil watched and counted the dark shapes as they emerged onto the trail. There were ten of them, all well armed. Once on level ground, they put their equipment down and stopped to rest. Khalil listened carefully. He heard the murmur of voices and cautiously moved closer to catch the words.

"Which way is Tariq's home?"

"About three kilometers down this road there's a small trail which enters from the east. It's at the end of that trail, about six kilometers altogether," came the hushed response.

Khalil recognized the voices of Harith and Zahid. This was his cell. He knew at once why they were here. Turning away from the voices, Khalil moved silently along the trail. He had to get to Durrah's home and get everyone out. Suddenly, he froze. He sensed someone directly in front of him, almost within arm's length. He held his breath, listening. A light flashed in his eyes, blinding him.

"So, Khalil, what are you doing here?"

Nasir and the Americans arrived at Durrah's home and knocked on the door. Durrah appeared and held the door wide while they entered, closing it behind them.

Once inside Nasir introduced them. "Durrah, this is Travis, McCloud and Nevis. They've come for Sandra."

Eyes averted, Durrah welcomed the men to her home. A small oil lamp burned in front of a picture of Tariq.

"Sandra's sleeping," she said.

"You must wake her at once."

"Nasir," a woman's voice said.

Nasir looked up to see Samara standing just inside the door. Sandra, hidden in the shadow, stood beside her. The two women had been sleeping. "You've come at last," Samara said to him.

"Yes."

"This is what you spoke of, isn't it?" Tears glistened in her eyes.

"Yes. Samara, you and Durrah must go with Sandra and these men. They'll take you safely away from here. I told you that one day you'd go far away across the sea to another land. Now is the time for it to happen. You must help Sandra and Durrah. There's not much time so get ready at once."

Samara and Durrah left the room.

Sandra had watched the interaction between Nasir and Samara.Travis had watched as well. Shifting his gaze, he saw Sandra looking at him. He hardly recognized her. She'd lost weight, and her hair, tied back, looked short. She wore long pants and a loose-fitting shirt. In the subdued light, Travis had at first taken her for a man.

"Sandra, is that you?" Travis stepped forward.

Sandra turned toward him in the dim light. "Travis?" She stared at him in disbelief. Suddenly she was in his arms. Like a giant bear, Travis held her. "Is it really you?" she said, looking into the big man's face.

"We've come to take you home."

"Has David been buried yet? Have I missed his funeral?" she asked, almost choking on the words.

Travis looked at her, momentarily taken aback. Then he said slowly "He was in hospital in Tel Aviv. He returned to Washington several days ago."

"He's alive?"

"Yes, he's fine."

Sandra stood transfixed. Her mind had difficulty adjusting, but her heart leapt with joy at the news. Her legs suddenly weak, she sat down on a nearby chair.

Samara and Durrah returned, dressed and ready to travel.

"You must hurry," Nasir said to Samara. "You must go to Hilmi's house. Don't take the trail leading to Aanout. It's too dangerous. Go the other way, toward Midane, then take the trail over the hills. You remember the way?"

She nodded. "You're not coming?" Samara directed her question to Nasir.

"No, daughter, I'm not. You must hurry. There's not much time. Great danger is approaching."

"Are you ready?" Nasir looked at the women.

"Yes."

"Then you must leave at once. Under no circumstances are you to return, no matter what happens. Understood?"

They nodded.

Durrah suddenly knelt in front of Nasir and kissed his feet. "Master, I will ever remember you."

Nasir gently reached down and, taking her by the hand, helped her to her feet. His eyes looked long and deep into Durrah's, and she returned the gaze. "Goodbye, Mother. Take care of this daughter of ours."

Nasir turned and placed his hands on Sandra's shoulders. "You must take Samara and Durrah with you when you return to your country," he said in English. "If they remain here they will die. They'll need your friendship."

"You needn't worry," Sandra responded. "I'll take care of them." Impulsively she hugged Nasir, kissing him on both cheeks. "Thank you," she said.

He smiled at her, then turned and shook hands with the Americans. "Take care of them," he said. "The guerillas are close."

"They're in safe hands," Travis said.

Nasir smiled. "God be with you."

"And with you," Travis responded.

Samara stood in front of Nasir, wiping away the tears. He took her in his arms and held her. Then, he gently pushed her away.

"You must go. Remember I will always be with you, my daughter. Now go." Nasir gently turned her around and, kissing the top of her head, pushed her toward the door.

Once outside, it took a few moments for their eyes to adjust to the dark. Samara looked back and saw Nasir silhouetted in the light from the door, hand raised in a gesture of parting.

Release

Nasir traveled hard all night, just far enough ahead to keep the guerrillas following, never close enough for them to catch up. At first light, he entered a stand of ancient cedar, the glade carpeted with the droppings of the great trees. The scent of cedar filled the cool air.

Nasir had moved rapidly ahead of the advancing guerrillas for several kilometers, knowing it would be easier for them to follow his trail as the light of morning dawned.

The stand of trees grew against the side of the mountains that rose in giant ramparts seven hundred meters above and to the west. Before him, the land fell away in great rifts and valleys that opened to the foothills. Silence permeated the landscape.

Nasir jumped onto a low ledge against the rock face, a meter off the floor of the glade. With the blanket around his shoulders, he sat quietly with his back to the mountain and waited. For the last time, he watched the soft colors of dawn bathe the surroundings in purple and gold.

Savoring the beauty of this remote place, Nasir bid a silent farewell to the mountains and the life he'd loved, glad to be going home at last.

He heard the sounds of the men approaching long

before they arrived. Unmoved, he watched as they slipped into the glade along the length of its curved perimeter, rifles at the ready, searching him out. It took only a few moments for their eyes to adjust to the subdued light in the grove. Then they saw him. They advanced quickly and surrounded him, not more than five meters away.

"Where are they?" Harith hissed. He was furious.

Nasir said nothing.

Seeing Nasir confirmed his suspicions. The old man had been alone and had led them away from their quarry. He'd outsmarted them.

Harith knew the President's wife would now be far away. This round in the battle with the Great Satan seemed lost; opportunity had slipped through his fingers. He, of all people, had failed to do the bidding of Allah.

Harith's men were unsettled. There was something strange about the man before them. He sat unmoving, seemingly unafraid, his eyes alert, taking everything in.

The fury in Harith suddenly burst. In three swift strides he stood before Nasir. He raised his rifle. The only thing in his mind was to smash the face of his enemy. As Harith moved to strike, Nasir's eyes glittered. Harith stopped. Something in the gaze of the old man caused Harith's mind to suddenly go blank. He lowered his rifle.

"It's over," Nasir said quietly, as though to himself.

"What did you say?" Harith demanded.

Just then, a shaft of light from the rising sun struck the rock face above the trees to the west. The reflected light suffused the glade beneath it in a soft golden glow.

"It's time to go," Nasir said, his voice barely audible.

“You’ll never leave here alive,” Harith screamed. Spittle flew from his mouth, rage once more taking hold. Jerking his rifle up, he leveled it at Nasir’s head and started to squeeze the trigger.

Looking past the gun, Nasir fixed his eyes on the would-be killer. Raising his hand, he pushed the gun aside. “You’ll not defile the temple of Allah this day,” he said quietly. Then, shifting his gaze, he looked into each man who stood before him. He felt their fear, anger and frustration; he saw in them the never-ending disturbance of the wind over the vast silent depths of the ocean.

The boundaries of normal consciousness melted away and, as the men looked on, Nasir closed his eyes, a slight smile playing across his lips. His breathing slowed, becoming fainter until at last it stopped. The men stood waiting and wondering, lost in their own private thoughts, eyes fixed on the figure before them. Then, one by one, they lowered their rifles and bowed their heads while Harith stood silently watching.

Just an ordinary man

They followed the path from Durrah's home until it joined a narrow track. A dog barked behind them, a desultory bark. They turned east leading away from the homes and suddenly the dog barked again but this time it was intense and urgent. The road wound through low hills, which got taller the further they went. Samara, in the lead, was moving fast. After several more kilometers she turned south into a ravine and started climbing.

They climbed for an hour.The ravine was covered in loose rock and sand. It was hard in the dark to avoid the thorny plants scattered in clumps. Sandra caught her foot on a sharp rock and felt the blood running into her sandal. Samara, ahead of her, continued climbing and the rest of them followed close behind. Sandra was having difficulty but knew she couldn't stop, they had to keep moving.

On the way to Durrah's home earlier in the evening it had been overcast, but now clouds flew across the moon, driven by an upper wind, while all around them was stillness and complete silence, except when they dislodged rocks which tumbled down behind them. With guerillas near by Travis was concerned about the noise and the intermittent moonlight.

At the top of the ravine Samara stopped to give the

women a chance to catch up. They came out onto a rounded ridge that stretched into the distance. The ground was firm and the slope considerably less. It reminded Travis of the desert country in the hills east of San Diego.

Suddenly they froze. They listened. There it was again, the sound of someone climbing over the stones in the ravine below. Stones knocked loose could be heard bouncing into the darkness below. The moon flashed through the flying clouds. Everyone was flat on the ground. Nevis and McCloud had crawled to the edge of the ravine, Travis between them, was five meters back from the rim. They formed a wide semi circle. Darkness reappeared and thick cloud covered the moon. Then Nevis saw them. Two dark shapes just below them and coming fast, jumping from rock to rock. McCloud who by this time had seen what was happening, pulled back. They peered intently at the edge, waiting, ready. Clouds slid off the moon as two dark shapes leapt to the ridge and came straight at the waiting men. Splitting in two directions they bounded away.

"Goats! It was goats." Travis started to laugh. The surge of adrenalin had left them weak with relief.

Travis looked below them to the southwest. He could see a single light in the distance.

Samara pointed to it. "That's where the van is."

When they got to the bottom of the hill Samara led them along the trail until she reached the house where a light streamed from a small window. Beside the building Travis recognized the van they'd driven in from Bent Jebail.

It was a little before six when the van pulled up in front of Omar and

Hana's home. The eastern mountains were a black silhouette against the approach of dawn. They saw a simple and elegant building of white stone, which seemed to glow in the early light. It rose above an arched compound that encircled it, making it appear larger than it was. On the top of a hill it over looked a terraced valley that disappeared in the darkness below. The drive had taken them three hours and they'd travelled eighty kilometers. Quite a feat, Travis thought, given the narrowness of the roads that had snaked their way through the steep mountains.

"Excellent job," he said in Arabic to Hilmi, a short wiry man who'd done the driving.

Travis eased himself out of the front seat and helped the others unfold themselves from the cramped space. As they approached the arched entrance a slim elderly gentleman appeared, accompanied by a short, white-haired woman of slight build.

"Welcome, welcome," Omar said, smiling broadly in greeting.

Travis bowed to Omar and his wife. The party of six stood in a half circle as Omar and Hana greeted each of them, obviously pleased to see them. They were in a leafy garden hidden from the road. Turning, the couple ushered them into the house where the smell of fresh coffee came wafting on an early breeze. Just then the sun broke free of the night's tight grasp, flooding everything in a rich golden light.

Hana and Omar had breakfast ready on the table. Homemade creamed cheese, fresh mint, diced tomatoes, sliced cucumber and olives with pita bread and a sauce made of thyme, turmeric and sesame seeds in olive oil. "A traditional Lebanese breakfast," Hana told them.

After breakfast Hilmi left for the return trip. When he was gone Omar and the three Americans took their coffee and went into the courtyard. They sat at a round marble table overlooking the terraced valley below, which shone vibrant in the fresh light of the new day. Irregular white flagstones covered the open floor of the patio while honeysuckle and roses hung in great profusion from the arches that surrounded the house.

"I talked with Heatherington, whom I think you know," Omar began. "He's been in touch with the White House. I understand you have a plane at Beirut, fueled and ready to go?"

"We do." Travis paused. "We're taking Durrah and Samara with us so will there be any problems at the airport? What about passports and immigration permits?"

"Heatherington has made arrangements for when you arrive in America. I have friends at the airport and since it's a private plane you won't go through the usual airport screening. I'll take you to Beirut as soon as you're ready."

Travis felt a sense of relief.

"I had a call yesterday from President Tremaine. He's notified the Israeli authorities of Sandra's release."

"Good, that was one of my concerns."

"When we finish coffee, we should leave," Omar added.

"How long does it take to get to Beirut? Two hours?" Travis asked.

"Three should be enough." Omar finished his coffee and stood. The others followed.

They heard laughter coming from the kitchen. They found Sandra seated on a chair with her foot in a bowl of warm water. Durrah knelt beside her bathing the blood away, revealing a deep cut to her toe. Hana sat beside her holding a small medical kit, and Samara was watching. This moment of laughter and lightness made Travis aware they were still not out of danger. He'd be glad when they were safely aboard the plane and headed home.

Samara turned away and looked out the window. Hana watched her. Samara put her hands to her chest and bowed her head as though in pain. Hana knew something had happened and also knew to leave the young woman alone.

"When you're finished," Travis said gently to Sandra, "we need to leave. We have a three-hour drive ahead of us."

It was 10:30 when they entered the parking area at Beirut International Airport. Omar took them to the office of the airport manager, who was expecting them.

Sandra had fallen asleep almost as soon as the plane was airborne. She'd had very little sleep since her escape, and during her captivity, very little food. She seemed to have lost her usual stamina. She woke, startled, and for a moment didn't know where she was.

She looked around and relaxed. She was safe. Durrah was still asleep. Nevis, McCloud and Travis were at the back of the cabin talking quietly. Samara was staring out the window. Sandra looked closely and saw Samara's face was wet with tears. Sandra pushed the seat upright and went over and knelt beside her.

Samara wiped away the tears. "Nasir has gone," she said. "He died at dawn, just after we arrived at Omar's."

Sandra felt as if she'd been hit in the stomach. It was less than a day since she'd looked back and seen him silhouetted in the doorway. Although she'd not known him long, she'd sensed a deep peacefulness in him. "How do you know?" she said, feeling unsettled.

Samara touched her heart. "I know it here," she said sadly.

Sandra bowed her head. Samara's words were a terrible shock.

When she looked up she found herself looking into the quiet dark eyes of the young woman who'd helped her escape. This woman, she realized, had lost the man she loved, the man she referred to as Master. She recognized in Samara the same peacefulness and strength, the same ineffable quality she'd found in Nasir.

Samara looked over Sandra's shoulder.

Sandra turned. Travis came from the back of the plane with a tray of coffee. Nevis followed with muffins. McCloud, she noticed, had brought Durrah's seat upright and was helping to swing her table into place. He took the cups from Travis and handed them out. "I always wanted to be a flight attendant," he laughed.

"We land in fifteen minutes," Travis said, taking the seat across from Sandra as she sat down. He leaned toward her. "While you were asleep," he said in a low voice, "David and I talked by phone. We're taking Samara and Durrah to Maine. The White House would be too much of a culture shock for them. Mera and Morgan have arranged for them to stay in Ali's home at the farm. No one has lived there since he died, but it's furnished and would be ideal for them. Mera has gone to Maine to get things ready. Heatherington and Nadia have gone to help too. They'll look after them when Mera returns to Washington."

"That's good," she said. "Nadia knows what it's like to come here from Lebanon."

"David thought you'd want to stay with them for a couple of days, so we'll be landing in Portland instead of Washington."

Her relief at learning the women would go to Maine was tinged with disappointment. She'd been looking forward to seeing David again. The last time she'd seen him, he was lying on the pavement in a pool of blood, and she'd thought he was dead. She wanted to feel his arms around her. To feel that life was real again.

They sat quietly for a while. Travis sensed her disappointment.

"Before we left Durrah's home," he said, "Nasir took me aside and talked to me. He asked me to act as a kind of godfather to Samara. That's the nearest word in English I can think of."

As Sandra looked at Travis he suddenly seemed uncomfortable, almost embarrassed. "What is it?" she asked.

Travis seemed to be searching for the right words. "He knows things," Travis finally said. "I never thought I'd say this, but he knows things people don't know. He knew about you, he knew where to find you, and he knew to call me at the American Embassy in Israel when he did. He asked me to take Samara and Durrah to America. He said it was their... 'destiny,' was the word he used. He said Samara would go to university and asked me to help. I told him he could come with us, but he shook his head. 'I have a meeting in the mountains,' he said, 'and when it's over I'll be gone. My time here is all but over.' I was so taken aback by his words I didn't know what to say."

"Samara just told me Nasir died after we arrived at Omar's."

"How did she know?"

"She said she felt it in her heart. She knew he was gone, that he was dead."

Travis sat back in the chair. He seemed shaken.

"She's a lot like him," Sandra said quietly. "I think he was her teacher and had taught her about the inner world." Sandra looked at Travis, wondering at the strangeness of life. "We will help her," she said finally. "Both of us."

Travis nodded. "We will."

They felt the engines throttle back and the plane banked, slipping sideways as it prepared to land. The captain's voice came over the intercom. “Time to fasten your seat belts, folks. We’ll be landing shortly.”

Sandra got up quickly and helped Durrah with her belt. When she turned to help Samara she saw Travis beside her talking to her in Arabic. She wondered how it was for the women to get into a plane for the first time. She knew Samara had a terrible fear of them.

When the plane came to a stop she stood up and stretched. Her foot was sore. She found herself recalling the climb up the ravine. She’d been in sandals and it had taken all her strength to keep up with Samara. Travis had helped her as best he could but they hadn’t stopped until they were on the top of the hill. They were driven by the same urgency with which Nasir had ushered them into the dark.

She felt a catch in her chest. Nasir had known he was going to his death. She hadn’t known him long but she had loved the short time she’d had in his presence.

A low sun shone in their eyes when the door opened. She turned to make sure Durrah was all right. Samara stood beside her, the older woman holding her arm.

David watched as Sandra emerged from the plane. She was wrapped in a long white cotton shirt which came to her knees, partially covering a pair of army pants with one of the legs badly ripped. Her clothes were covered in red dirt. She looked beautiful to him and somehow vulnerable. Travis was beside her helping her down the steps. She was limping and looked as if she’d lost weight. When she got to the bottom of the steps she looked up and he saw the surprise on her face. Then she was in his arms nearly knocking him down. They stood to the side of the ramp, oblivious to what was happening around them. Both of them had thought they might never see each other again.

Sandra pushed away from her husband and looked at him. It felt unreal, as if she was in a dream.

“Wow,” he said. “You smell terrible.”

“Thanks a lot,” she said. “And how do you think you smell now?” She laughed and hugged him again.

Travis, who’d been talking to the women in Arabic, introduced them to Tremaine. “I’m glad you’re here.” he said, “I thought you were still in Washington.”

Tremaine winked at him before turning to the women. He was delighted to meet them and thanked them profusely for bringing Sandra to safety.

Travis translated.

The nervousness they’d felt about meeting the President of the United States had vanished. He was just an ordinary man, someone really no different from anyone else.

Circles

Mohammed would never forget that night. It had been hot all day but as evening approached it began to cool. Customers in his father's coffee shop stared silently at the television. The tiny space was packed with men watching the news. Flames flickered across the screen, and the sound of sirens set everyone's nerves on edge. A suicide bomber had entered a crowded nightclub in Tel Aviv and blown himself up. Fifteen Israelis had died, and more than fifty were injured.

"The Israelis won't let this pass." Ismael sighed. "There'll be reprisals, and they'll come fast. And directed at us." Since the death of the Israeli Prime Minister there'd been three bombings, which claimed the lives of forty Israelis and injured hundreds. The loss of Palestinian life in the reprisals was already over nine hundred, and the numbers wounded, in the thousands.

Ismael pushed through the crowd to where his son Mohammed was standing. He was only fourteen but tall for his age. "Go upstairs and tell your mother what's happening. I want you and your brothers to go and get water," he told him.

"At this time of night?" Mohammed asked.

"Go," he said, and pushed his son out the door.

Mohammed bounded up the stairs at the side of the

building to the cramped quarters where he lived with his parents, his grandmother, his two brothers, Mustafa and Mahmoud, and his sister, Sarah. Sarah was three, Mahmoud eleven, and Mustafa thirteen, a year younger than Mohammed.

"There's been another bombing," he announced to all as he burst into the room. Jamilah, his mother, sat at the table with his grandmother, Farah. Both of them were mending clothes by the light from two candles. "We're going to get water," he told his mother. He went to wake up his brothers, who were already asleep on their mattress.

Jamilah got up from the table. "How bad is it?" she asked as she emptied the water bottles into containers.

"It looks bad. I think father expects a curfew again," Mohammed responded.

Farah continued sewing, but took everything in. She was a slight, frail woman with gnarled fingers who worked the needle without effort or thought.

Mahmoud and Mustafa stood by the door, yawning and rubbing the sleep from their eyes. They picked up the water containers, handing two to Mohammed.

"Be careful," Jamilah said as she opened the door for them. "Don't take any chances. Get back as quickly as you can." Pushing the door shut, she listened as the boys thundered down the stairs.

The room was stifling hot. Jamilah was short, about five foot two, with a solid, stocky build. She checked on Sarah, who was asleep in the corner on one of the sleeping mats. Jamilah, though she loved her boys, felt a deep affection for her daughter, who, even at this young age, bore a striking resemblance to her husband.

Jamilah returned and, sitting down, resumed sewing. Her

dark hair, tied up during the day, now hung about her shoulders. The unsteady light from the candles revealed streaks of white. She was attractive, but hard work and the raising of four children had taken its toll on her. Despite the hardships of her life, the wrinkles around her eyes and mouth suggested an irrepressible sense of humor. It was something her family appreciated because it lightened even the most difficult times.

Farah reached over and turned on a small battery radio. The announcer was saying that Israeli troops, accompanied by tanks and helicopters, had mobilized and were preparing to enter Palestinian-controlled areas. The Prime Minister of Israel had delivered a brief statement, which the station now played.

"Tonight's killing of innocent Israelis is an act of barbarism that will not go unavenged. Since those behind the attacks target civilians and show no respect for the conventions of war, they cannot expect us to do so, either. We assert the right to use whatever means necessary to defend the sovereignty of Israel and safeguard her people. We'll root out this cancer of terrorism, wherever it is found. We serve notice to all those nations who've lent support to terrorism that we hold them responsible for this bloodshed. The time for talk is over; it is now time for action. We will not waver in bringing safety and security to the State of Israel."

Farah turned off the radio. The two women looked at each other, knowing that what was coming wouldn't be good.

Mohammed and his brothers picked their way over the uneven ground in the darkness and ducked down a narrow alley. The Israelis had cut the waterlines in the neighborhood. For six months, the residents had to fetch water from a well in a small market square a kilometer away.

Five minutes later, they came into the square. People had already gathered, waiting to fill their water containers. Most of those waiting in line were women and young boys. An elderly man pumped furiously at the squeaking pump.

"Hurry," hissed a woman behind him.

The boys could feel the fear and tension around them. As they waited, they caught snippets of conversation, none of which were reassuring. Then, in the distance, over the sound of the pump, came the dreaded sound of helicopters.

"Hush," someone said. Everyone listened to see whether the sounds were coming closer. They weren't; not for the moment, at least.

It was the boys' turn. Mohammed worked the arm of the pump as hard as he could. He'd just finished filling the containers when the night sky to the west lit up. The sound of the explosions shook the ground.

Walking fast, arms straining, Mohammed and his brothers headed for home. Twice they stopped to rest before turning back onto the street where they lived. As they rounded the corner, more flashes lit the sky, followed by the deep booming sound of high explosives.

When they arrived they could see by the flashes of light that their father was boarding the windows. The small generator he used for the shop was now quiet. Mahmoud and Mustafa carried the water up the stairs while Mohammed went to help his father. Neither said a word. They worked in unison, aware of the gathering storm.

The sound of helicopters could be heard in the distance, the volume steadily increasing. After midnight the sound had become so intense it was impossible to sleep. One of the helicopters came very close. Suddenly the apartment was illuminated by a high-intensity light. Ismael could see the helicopter hovering above the buildings across the street. The noise from its motor was deafening, and the downdraft from its rotors tore through the windows and filled the house with dust and debris. Plates rattled on the shelves and came crashing to the floor.

Jamilah and Farah held Sarah between them, trying to shield her from the fierce winds and deafening sounds that raged all around them. The boys cowered beneath one of the windows on their sleeping mats and covered their heads.

Ismael saw the danger they were in. The wall was flimsy and provided scant protection. Crawling on his hands and knees, he grabbed them and, in the intense light, moved them to the side of the room and away from the windows.

Heavy-caliber machine gun bullets tore through the front of the building, sending splinters flying in every direction. Ismael watched as the wall disintegrated, leaving them completely exposed. He was struck in the chest with such force it threw him against the far wall. Then, as suddenly as it began, it was over. The light shifted, and the sound of the helicopter receded into the night.

Mohammed would never forget that night. In a few hours, he'd be reunited with his family again. Soon, the sorrow that had sapped his life and the hatred that had filled it would be exchanged in the miracle of death. Once more he would see his mother's face and hear the melodic tones of her voice. His father would be there, too; his siblings, and his grandmother with her comforting wisdom. This time they wouldn't be separated. This time, they'd be together and enjoy the blessings the Prophet promised, blessings the Israelis could not understand and could never take away.

Mohammed had gone to the road just before dawn. He could see the settlement above him; it was well lit and well guarded. He'd said his goodbyes earlier to those who'd trained him, those who'd nurtured and molded the hatred in his heart and turned it into an unstoppable weapon.

He sat in a depression, hidden from the light, his back against one of the few remaining trees. At last, the sun pushed back the stars and a pink glow lit the eastern horizon. He was at peace again. He felt possessed of a strange lucidity, something he'd never known before.

Mohammed was tall for his age, and slim. The stubble of his beard was dark and made him look older than he was. He was dressed in an oversized uniform of the Israeli Defense Forces. By the time the sun slipped above the horizon, he was in position.

The Jerusalem Post

Bomber Strikes Again:

Nine Dead, Thirty Wounded

Early this morning, a suicide bomber attacked a bus filled with passengers from one of the outer settlements in the West Bank. According to reports from the scene, the bombing took place as the bus was leaving the settlement. One of the survivors said a young man jumped out of a ditch and ran at the passing bus. The resulting explosion was so powerful it blew the bus on its side and tore a hole in the road.

At press time, the number of dead stood at nine and was expected to climb, as several passengers suffered severe injuries. Twenty passengers were taken to a nearby hospital for treatment. The Al-Aqsa Martyrs Brigade claimed responsibility stating, 'our attacks are a direct response to Israeli brutality and will continue for as long as Israeli occupation makes Palestinians prisoners in their own homes.'

The Israeli Prime Minister stated at a mid-morning news conference, "We will not tolerate these acts of barbarism and will take whatever steps necessary to bring them to an end. If we must enclose the Palestinian areas in a ring of steel, concrete and fire, we will. If it means we must lay siege to them and starve them into submission, we will do that as well. If it means we must root them out and kill them one by one, we will accomplish it. We will destroy the nests of these terrorist rats and those who support them."

A young Saudi boarded a jet in Turkey, bound for Boston. He was dressed in traditional white clothes. He was alone and carried only a small bag; his suitcase had been checked through earlier. He had an eight-hour stopover in London before continuing on his way. At Heathrow he took a taxi into the city. The weather was unusually hot and humid. The taxi dropped him off at a small outdoor restaurant. Two men were already seated at the table, both Saudis. They stood when the traveler arrived, and one of them whispered, "Greetings from the Sheik." Two hours later the men parted and the traveler returned to Heathrow to resume his flight to Boston.

Maine

Nevis and McCloud returned to Washington, while Travis, Samara and Durrah drove to the farm. Sandra and David would come later.

It was evening when Travis and the women turned off the road into the drive that wound its way beneath a canopy of trees to the farm. Mera was there to welcome them. She showed the women around their new home while Travis translated. She explained that her grandfather had lived there until his death a year ago. It was dark when Sandra and David arrived, accompanied by their usual retinue of agents.

In the morning after a late start they had breakfast seated around the large wooden table in the kitchen. When they were finished Mera showed them around the farm. They spent the day in quiet conversation and short walks.

That evening they drove to Mera's parents leaving Sandra and David at the farm. Durrah and Samara were deeply moved by the elderly doctor and his wife who welcomed them warmly in their own language.

Nadia and Heatherington had prepared mezze, a traditional Lebanese food. They sat on the deck in the fading light and leisurely enjoyed their meal. After supper Mera and Travis did the dishes before rejoining the others. The night was still and cloudless, the air clear and the stars brilliant. In the distance a lighthouse flashed. The sound of waves rising and falling against the rocky shore came soft on the warm evening air.

Heatherington had plied the women with questions, wanting to know more about what had happened. He was astonished to learn that they knew his old friend Nasir. For years he'd assumed Nasir was dead. "Tell me about him," he'd said. "How is he?" And with a great deal of emotion they described the last days they'd spent with him.

When they left that evening Heatherington invited himself to the farm the next afternoon. Mera jokingly 'twisted his arm,' with the promise of supper. He and Nadia wanted to know more about Nasir, the man they called Master.

David returned to D.C., with Travis the following evening. After some discussion it had been decided that Sandra would stay in Maine. Being in the countryside among friends would give her a break before being thrown back into the whirl of Washington. She also wanted to help Samara and Durrah get settled. The experiences of the past week had brought the three women close.

A week later it was arranged that David would fly up from Washington and Sandra would join him at the airport in Boston. From there they'd fly to Victoria to visit Sandra's parents on the West Coast, arriving on the eighth of September and returning the evening of the tenth. It had been a long time since she was with them and she wanted to see them before winter set in.

The first days of September in Maine were unexpectedly and unusually cold. One morning the four women woke to find that frost had brushed the leaves with the fresh colors of autumn. In the afternoon they drove to Camden for food and supplies. Samara, with considerable effort, had made a list. They parked the car and walked to the harbor. It was a cool, bright sunny day, with white cotton clouds that hung unmoving in an intense blue sky. Samara and Durrah were fascinated by the river, which flowed from under the bakery on main street, forming a large still pool, before it fell over the weir for its brief hectic rush to the harbor. Mera, seeing their interest, took them to the bakery where they sat drinking coffee in front of the window and watched the river emerge beneath them.

By the time Sandra left to meet David in Boston, she was happy to see the women were settling into their new home. Durrah and Nadia had become friends. They'd discovered Durrah's father had come from a village close to where Nadia was born. Mera and Sandra were impressed by Samara's quiet acceptance of her new life. Both at the farm and at the Heatherington's, laughter spilled into the passing days.

September

It seemed like a long time since David and Sandra had been able to go for walks on their own, to be silent together.

They drove to Whiffen Spit in Sooke and took Trapper with them. The Secret Service agents remained at the entrance, giving them freedom to walk alone. It was an hour after dawn and there was almost no one around. They saw two people in the distance, walking their dogs. At the end of the Spit they followed the trail beside the lighthouse to the sloping pebbled beach and sat on a large driftwood log. The air was still and the tide had turned, pushing inland and creating great roils of water, shining and moving as though alive.

A blue heron came drifting by, wings spread wide, its raucous voice trailing behind it. After landing it stood on its stilt-stiff legs and waited. Watching the heron David was struck again by the stillness of the bird as it fished. Like a lightning strike its long beak pierced the water. For a moment a fish could be seen struggling and then as quickly as it appeared it vanished down the birds long gullet.

Sandra, who'd also watched the heron, snuggled closer to David; a cold wind had sprung up and she felt chilled. David put his arm around her. Trapper trotted over and flopped at Sandra's feet with a grunt.

The wind freshened coming off the open Pacific, creating small choppy waves. The heron spread its wings and, lifting on the wind, drifted over the Spit and vanished leeward. Dark threatening clouds appeared from the southwest and the wind intensified again. Four-foot swells came rolling shoreward, white spray streaming like a horse's mane flying in the wind. Without a word Sandra, David and Trapper stood and made their way back to the truck.

They left at midnight and were scheduled to arrive in Washington, D.C. a little after nine a.m., local time. Once Air Force One was airborne, David and Sandra, who were still on Eastern time, went to bed and quickly fell asleep.

Tremaine was up at seven-thirty. He showered and dressed. When he finished he went to the galley to get tea. He'd just sat down in the lounge when the phone rang. He picked it up and listened to the voice on the other end.

"I'm sorry to disturb you," Travis apologized, "but we just got word that communication has been lost between the ground and four commercial airliners, two originating from Boston, one from Newark and one from Washington."

"Is it a technical problem?"

"It's hard to tell; they're running tests and everything seems to be working from the ground."

"Any idea what's going on?"

"Not at the moment."

"All right. Let me know when things change."

"Will do."

Tremaine put the phone down, puzzled. He looked at his watch. It was eight twenty-five.

Sandra came into the lounge, yawning, cup of coffee in hand. She came over, set her cup down and put her arms around him before sitting down in one of the soft leather chairs, pulling her legs up beneath her. David sat opposite and sipped his tea.

"We'll be landing in about an hour. Do you want breakfast?"

She nodded. "Do you know when …?"

The phone rang again, the sound startling them. David picked it up. "Tremaine here."

Travis was on the other end. "We still haven't been able to contact the four aircraft. They simply don't respond to the ground and their transponders are no longer working. The one from Boston is off course and heading toward New York instead of Los Angeles, its destination. … Hold on a second. … I've just been informed that the second flight from Boston is also off course and heading toward New York. I'll call you back. Something's not right."

David replaced the phone.

Sandra knew by the look on her husband's face that something was wrong. "What's going on?" she asked.

"We don't know," he replied. "There's something…"

The phone rang again.

Tremaine picked it up. It was Travis. He could tell by the sound of his voice the General was shaken."The first airliner just crashed into the North Tower of the World Trade Center."

"What?" Tremaine was stunned. "And the other airliners, where are they?"

"The second one from Boston is still airborne and holding a course for the New York area."

"Thanks, Travis. We should be on the ground shortly."

Tremaine cleared the line and then spoke into it. "Jonathan, meet me in the conference cabin." He turned to Sandra. "One of the planes just crashed into the World Trade Center."

Sandra jumped up and followed Tremaine into the large central cabin where wide-screen televisions stood at each end. He clicked on the television just as Jonathan entered. The three of them stood transfixed.

It had been a long day. Tremaine diverted Air Force One to New York after the second plane struck the South Tower of the World Trade Center. On the way, he ordered American airspace closed; nothing was allowed in or out. Incoming planes that could not return to their point of origin were diverted to Canada. Shortly afterward, the Pentagon was hit and fifteen minutes later, news came of the final plane crash southeast of Pittsburgh. Air Force One landed in New York shortly after the collapse of the second tower.

By helicopter they'd gone to the site of the World Trade Center, where they'd been appalled by the destruction. Smoke and dust covered the area and, through it all, they could see crowds of people filling the streets.

On the way back to Washington, Tremaine had been in touch with Travis several times. Now he sat quietly with Sandra and Jonathan in the lounge.

"This is what I was afraid of," he said quietly as if to himself.

Phoenix

Tremaine addressed the Nation and the world at seven o'clock on the evening of September 11.

"Today, Tuesday, September 11th, is a day we will all remember. Today, thousands died in the worst attack in our nation's history. Unlike the Japanese attack on Pearl Harbor, those who attacked us today are unknown.

"My heart is heavy with shock and sadness. What happened this morning is hard to comprehend. To those of you who've lost loved ones, know that our hearts go out to you and we will do all in our power to ease your suffering.

"This attack was the work of terrorists, men willing to sacrifice their lives to do us great harm. In light of these events, we must ask ourselves: Why were they willing to make such a sacrifice?

"Twenty-five hundred years ago the Chinese sage Lao Tzu asked the same question. His words are still as relevant today as when he first uttered them. 'Why,' he said, 'do people care so little about death?' He answered: 'When life becomes intolerable, death is welcomed. And he who has embraced his death lives without fear. A man like this makes a formidable enemy.' It's important we understand this, for if we don't, we'll find ourselves engaging an enemy who cannot be defeated by force of arms.

"When events of such magnitude happen, the impulse is to strike back, to use force against those who attack us. This is understandable, it is a natural response, a human one, but it does not in the end bring us what we want: peace. At a time when the urge for revenge is overwhelming we must show restraint. How we respond will determine whether killing continues or comes to an end.

"The ancient sage understood this well. He cautioned those who would listen, 'Repay bitterness with kindness and force with softness.' Christ made much the same point when he said, 'Resist not evil,' and 'love your enemies, do good to those who would do you harm.'

"History shows that we have lived more by the code of Hammurabi, 'an eye for an eye and a tooth for a tooth,' than with the guidance offered by Lao Tzu and Christ. The events of today have shown us where it leads.

"No one in their right mind wishes to continue this cycle of violence. Most Americans want peace. For that reason, I say: Let this be the end of it. Let those who died earlier today be the last to die. What more fitting memorial could we make on their behalf than to remove the causes that led to their deaths and find a way to live in peace with one another?

"For that reason, I direct my remarks to those who wish us ill, to those who attacked us. You have our undivided attention. As the representative of this nation, I am prepared to meet with you or your emissaries, without preconditions, at a neutral location. Our purpose is simple. To listen. To hear what you have to say, to understand what drove you to these acts, and to uncover the underlying causes, whatever they may be. When we're satisfied we have understood, we will do all we can to eradicate them. To this

I give my word.

"Life is always uncertain. We never know when it may end. It is our love for those who've gone that fills our hearts with grief and loss. Human beings are resilient, capable of passing through loss and suffering, capable of foregoing the desire for revenge, capable of arriving at a place of greater understanding and greater compassion. Our own loss may help us to better understand and appreciate those beyond our borders, our brothers and sisters, from every corner of the earth, who've lost loved ones through starvation, genocide, war and terror.

"Citizens of the world, it is at times like this that opportunity presents itself almost as compensation for what has happened. It is at times like this that compassion comes to the fore and the softness in our hearts invites us to take a different path, one less familiar to us than the one of revenge and retaliation so often taken.

"This planet upon which we live is our spaceship through time. Unlike a train, however, there's no getting off. The earth is our home, it is the home of all of us. Would we not be better served when we find ways of getting along? When differences arise and lead to grievances as they inevitably will, we can learn to resolve them. We know how to do this. To begin with we must listen, with open minds, and metaphorically walk in each other's shoes, before things get out of hand.

"The fact is we already share a common goal, summed up as follows: the right as human beings, regardless of our color, creed, religion or nationality, to earn a living, to have a roof over our heads; and the freedom to raise a family in relative safety.

"It is time for us to make a departure from the actions that have perpetuated this cycle of suffering. If we truly desire peace, lasting peace, then what alternative do we have but to identify the roots of terrorism; to understand how we have contributed, wittingly and unwittingly, to the events that took place this morning. This, if we have the will, we can accomplish. It will be neither an easy task, nor one that will happen quickly. It will take patience, persistence and perseverance. Thank you and good evening."

The way

In the morning Tremaine and Sandra went to the Pentagon. The day afterwards, they were in New York. They moved from place to place, serving soup and sandwiches, listening to people, hearing stories; just being there and offering encouragement. Each afternoon they returned to Washington. Travis, Kersey and Morgan stayed in the capital to keep abreast of events; they were able to be in touch with Tremaine at a moment's notice.

Tremaine was approached for an interview by James G. Whitfield, the chief BBC foreign correspondent in Washington. Known for thoughtfulness and objectivity he didn't hesitate to ask direct questions; it was his job. He had a polite efficient manner, a gentleman in the way only the English can be.

Tremaine accepted and the interview was broadcast on Saturday evening by all the major networks.

Tremaine sat across from a man in his seventies, bald except for short hair graying at the temples. He was tall and slim, with wire-rimmed glasses, blue eyes and an open and welcoming presence.

JGW: "Mr. President, I would like to say to you and the American people how shocked and saddened I am by Tuesday's events. To the families now grieving

I would like to extend my heartfelt sympathy."

DT: "Thank you, Mr. Whitfield."

JGW: "Mr. President, we've recently witnessed the worst attack on American soil since the attack on Pearl Harbor. There are those in this country who believe you should respond with all the military might at your disposal. Would you comment, please?"

DT: "Were we to do so, people would think we were the terrorists. Retaliation is always the first impulse. It's what we usually do and I'm not just speaking of Americans. Violence provokes violence in an ever-tightening spiral of destruction. We know the result of violence from experience. More innocent people will die. There is enough suffering already. I don't want to add to it. Why try the same thing and hope for a different result? It doesn't make sense."

JGW: "Isn't retaliation a natural response?"

DT: "It is. It's reflexive, fueled by emotion. But, even if we were going to retaliate we don't know who was behind the attacks."

JGW: "Whoever they are, surely they must be considered evil, misguided men who should be punished?"

DT: "It depends on one's perspective. Men and women we consider terrorists might be considered patriots and martyrs by our enemies, and vice versa. To England, George Washington and the fathers of Confederation were traitors, but to the rebels they were heroes. It's one's perspective that determines who is called a traitor, who a patriot, who a terrorist, and who a victim.

"As far as punishment goes, the Government is required to bring those responsible to court, where they'll be tried by a jury of their peers. It is the jury who determines guilt or innocence. If found guilty they'll be punished."

JGW: "Some may construe your remarks as condoning violence."

DT: "I do not condone violence. It is important that the events of Tuesday signal an end to the violence, not the next step in it. I want those who died to be remembered as the last to die in this cycle of violence."

JGW: "What do you think was behind the attacks?"

DT: "When I ask what kind of mental state would bring me personally to create an event like this, the answer is clear. It would be an act of last resort, an act of desperation, an act that would only occur when I had nothing left to lose, when I couldn't be hurt anymore, when life had become so crushing that death was preferable and by my death people I care about might live."

JGW: "The men who flew those planes into the buildings gave their lives for what they believe. How do you fight that?"

DT: "We can't. There's no way to fight against an attack like this. But, perhaps we can understand it, understand our enemy's perspective. It's likely our enemy believes they've been poorly treated, that we've hurt or harmed them; and this would extend to people they care deeply about. We in America have to consider the possibility we might have hurt them in some way. We can change that, and make sure it doesn't happen again, but we don't have the power to change their actions. Better to exercise the power we have than try to exercise power we don't. Why force a locked door when we can walk through an open one?

"Let me rephrase this in another way. Our neighbor may have a garden filled with weeds but we have no jurisdiction there. The only jurisdiction we have, is to remove the weeds in our own garden. By doing so we stop the spread of our weeds to other gardens.

"In the body, pain serves as a warning that all is not well. It draws attention to the problem and we take remedial action. The same is true in the global body politic. We must discover first the underlying causes and do all we can to eliminate them, if we can."

JGW: "Do you have any idea who the enemy is?"

DT: "You mean who attacked us, the people who flew the planes?"

JGW: "Yes."

DT: "As far as we can tell there were fifteen Saudis, two citizens of the United Arab Emirates, one Lebanese and one Egyptian."

JGW: "So this was not an attack by one nation on another?"

DT: "No. We think it was an attack by Muslim militants."

JGW: "Since the hijackers originated in the Middle East could it have something to do with previous administrations' support of Israel?"

DT: "I think so. The Middle East is the focal point where a conflict between the Israelis and Palestinians plays out. It is also the one place in the world where extreme power meets extreme powerlessness, extreme wealth meets extreme poverty, where West meets East, where Christianity meets Islam and Jews meet Muslims.

"The conflict between the Israelis and Palestinians is like an infected and open wound that never has a chance to heal. Not able to heal, the infection spreads."

JGW: "What, in this case, is the source of infection?"

DT: "Injustice!"

JGW: "What is behind the injustice?"

DT: "Man's inhumanity to his brothers and sisters. That inhumanity appears in many different guises; one of which, for instance, takes place in Gaza, where people are held in what could be called the largest concentration camp in the world. Where one and a half million are confined to one hundred and forty square miles; where they're enclosed by bombs, bullets and barbed wire; where electricity, sewage, food and medicine are withheld at the will of the Israeli government. There's no peace here. Without hope, real hope accompanied by real action, the contagion spreads.

"A great wrong was committed against the Jews during the Holocaust, a great wrong is being committed against the Palestinians today. The victims of yesterday have become the oppressor of today. Just as the crimes against humanity perpetrated by the Germans had to be acknowledged before healing could begin, the crimes against the Palestinians must be acknowledged or there can be no healing. What happens in this conflicted area becomes the template for what happens elsewhere. If that is the case, let it be a template for how we resolve our difficulties, rather than a template for what doesn't work."

JGW: "Some are suggesting the events earlier this week point to an epic struggle between two opposing religions, the Muslims on the one hand and the Christians on the other. What are your thoughts on this?"

DT: "I would suggest it's more a reflection of a growing disparity between the wealthy and the poor, between the powerful and the powerless. It is the Christian West that is predominantly wealthy and powerful, when compared to many Muslim nations where people are, on the whole, poor and powerless."

JGW: "Is religious fundamentalism not at the root of the problem?"

DT: "I don't think so. The root of the problem is poverty and injustice. When things become increasingly difficult, when people are desperate, they look for answers they can understand. Some look for an explanation of their circumstances and find it in religion. They may conclude God is punishing them. Why? Because they have not obeyed the letter of His law. What then must they do? They must return to the fold and this is done by a total obedience to the literal interpretation of scripture. In return they hope God will bless them and things will improve.

"Poverty and injustice feed the violent fires of fundamentalism. Addressing those grievances is like removing oxygen from fire. When poverty and injustice are removed the world becomes a safer place for everyone.

"You asked me earlier who the enemy is. Is it not greed and selfishness? Yet, greed and selfishness are human attributes, and no group or nation has a corner on that market. The Chinese sage Lao Tzu sums it up this way when he says:

Today, men have little mercy
And try hard to be generous
They tell others how humble they are
And always find a way to be first
This is the way of ordinary men
It is a way that leads to death.
It is not the way of the wise.

JGW: "The approach you're suggesting requires a complete shift in perspective. You're pointing in a direction we rarely go. What guarantees are there that this approach will be any more effective?"

DT: "Other than death there are no guarantees in life, so why would anyone expect guarantees for something like this?"

JGW: "Do you think this approach is realistic?"

DT: "It may or may not be. We have yet to see. What is not realistic, however, is expecting the poor and powerless to stand by while the wealthy and powerful become more so, at their expense. As long as we think this way, we'll continue deluding ourselves, and the events of Tuesday will serve only as the first salvo in a global war unlike anything we've seen before.

"As the discrepancy between rich and poor increases, so does the potential for global conflict. And as that potential increases so does the possibility—perhaps necessity is a better word for it—of moving beyond conflict to a world that works for everyone. For this to happen, however, requires generosity of spirit, compassion, kindness and an open mind.

"If we want peace for ourselves we must offer it to others. Despite cultural, national, religious and social differences we belong to the same family, the family of man. This planet is our home, the home of us all. Lao Tzu said: 'When one loves the world as oneself, everything is taken care of.'"

JGW: "Thank you, Mr. President. I appreciate what you've had to say. I wonder, now, if we could address a number of specific issues we've not dealt with so far."

DT: "Certainly."

JGW: "Today is September 15th, the deadline your government set for the Israelis to end settlement construction in the occupied territories. Can you tell us what is happening?"

DT: "As of noon today we ended all financial support for the Israeli government."

JGW: "So the settlement expansion continues?"

DT: "I'm afraid it does."

JGW: "How much does that support amount to?"

DT: "Since the founding of the state of Israel in 1948, our country has provided 140 billion dollars in foreign aid altogether, which averages 2.8 billion dollars a year. This includes both direct military and non-military aid. With the agreements currently in place the aid would have continued up through 2018. Israel has been the largest single recipient of U.S. foreign aid, and it amounts to one fifth of our entire foreign aid budget. Our tax dollars have been subsidizing one of the most powerful foreign militaries in the world."

JGW: "Could you tell us what other steps you'll now be taking?"

DT: "The United States of America officially recognizes the State of Palestine. By doing so we affirm the right of Palestinian people to exist and live in their homeland, in the place in which their families have lived for a thousand years and more."

JGW: "There are no clearly defined borders at the moment; so isn't that a problem?"

DT: "The fact that there are no clearly defined borders with Palestine also means not all Israeli borders are clearly defined either; and haven't been since the state of Israel was declared in May 1948. That didn't stop us from recognizing Israel as a state and it doesn't stop us from recognizing Palestine as a state either."

JGW: "Are you going to play a role in the process of defining borders?"

DT: "That's up to the two governments to work out for themselves, not up to us. The United States will offer assistance if it's requested by either side, but in the meantime we'll take steps to remedy the damage we've done to both sides by our blind support of Israeli expansion. This is our moral crisis.This is what we must deal with."

JGW: "Does this mean you'll help bring the Palestinian case to the International Criminal Court in the Hague as you earlier stated?"

DT: "Yes, it does."

JGW: "And the issue to be brought before the court has to do with 'Crimes Against Humanity.' Namely 'Ethnic Cleansing'?"

DT: "That's correct."

JGW: "Are their any further actions you are contemplating?"

DT: "There are. By withdrawing all financial support for Israel it will free up almost 3 billion dollars a year. There are better ways to spend this money, ways more in line with our objective; to contribute to a climate of peace in the region. We'll provide funding for peace groups in both Israel and Palestine. We'll have more to say about this by the end of September."

JGW: "Is there anything else we should know about?"

DT: "There is. There are serious problems in Gaza caused by retaliatory attacks and incursions by Israeli forces. We'd like to do what we can to alleviate some of these problems. As I'm sure you're aware, there are 600 schools in Gaza, all of which have been damaged; some seriously. Sewage treatment is an ongoing problem and the system needs to be rebuilt. Israel has not allowed the material for these repairs to cross the border. We will provide the material to rebuild the schools and the sewage treatment facilities."

JGW: "What makes you think the Israelis will change their minds and allow the construction material to cross the border? As you pointed out, they haven't allowed it so far"

DT: "We'll bring it in ourselves."

JGW: "How will you do that if the border is closed?"

DT: "We'll bring it in directly from the sea. Using helicopters and smaller boats, supplies will be offloaded from American ships anchored off the coast. We'll enter through Palestinian territorial space, which does not require permission from the Israelis; although of course, we'll inform them of what we're doing."

JGW: "Do you have any concern that other countries in the Middle East might use the changed circumstances to attack Israel?"

DT: "We've been talking to all the parties in the region and it's my sense they want the initiative to work. These governments want an end to the instability and volatility in the region. They'll support our actions if they are fair. Besides, they're well aware of Israel's military power, that even without American help, Israel would be able to withstand any attack."

JGW: "It might look to some as if you favor the Palestinians over the Israelis. What would you say about this?"

DT: "Some people will think that, no matter what we do; and there's nothing that can be done about that. Our concern is injustice. If the injustice is resolved the conflict will end and peace will be a reality. Withdrawing financial support on the one hand and contributing on the other lets all parties know we mean business and are only interested in justice."

JGW: "Coming back to the issue of terrorism and the attack Tuesday. What practical steps will you be taking?"

DT: "As we've stated publicly, I'm prepared to meet those

behind the attacks without preconditions at a neutral place of their choosing. I can't think of anything more practical than this at the moment."

JGW: "And what do you want to say to them if they'll listen to you?"

DT: "As I've said, our purpose is to listen to them: to find out from their perspective what led to the attack. Then, we'll see what we can do to remedy the situation."

JGW: "They must have been aware of your public stand concerning Israel and the Palestinians, and yet that didn't stop the attack."

DT: "That's true, but the planning must have been underway for years. The first attack on the World Trade Center took place in February of 1993. That attack did not bring the buildings down. I think it quite likely that after this failure new plans were formulated years before the election of this Administration.

"We in America have for many years, blindly supported the Israelis despite our claim of neutrality. So why would anyone believe us? Why would they pay any more attention to what a new Administration had to say? Why would they stop an attack years in the planning for what must have seemed like faint hope?"

JGW: "Recently your nation's words and actions have been congruent. Yes means yes and no means no."

DT: David smiled. "That's right. It might take a while for the parties concerned to recognize we mean what we say and don't say what we don't mean."

JGW: "The Israeli government didn't believe you."

DT: "So it would seem."

JGW: "The Israeli government has argued that your financial support over the years was primarily for peaceful purposes and had nothing to do with their relationship and policies toward Palestinians. What do you say to this?"

DT: "First, as I told Prime Minister Herzog, this is not accurate. Without going into details, we consider this statement disingenuous. Even if some of our financial assistance didn't go directly to support the Israeli military, it enabled their government to help finance the illegal building of settlements on Palestinian or disputed land."

JGW: "Despite what you've said there's still a possibility that some may want the peace process to fail."

DT: "That's true. Hard-liners will feel threatened by what we're doing, but people themselves will be less inclined to support them. I hope they'll see that the United States, through its actions does indeed support justice and peace for everyone. I think most of us want to live in peace. That being the case what would we have to give up for it to happen?

"George Santayana famously said, 'Those who refuse to learn from history are condemned to repeat it.' So, I wonder, do we learn from history? I don't think we do. What we learn we often forget. Anyone who's ever written exams knows this. But, understanding is of a different order altogether. When it happens, it's permanent. It cannot be forgotten. So what we need is understanding, which exists beyond blame and beyond national stories"

The two men sat quietly for a moment. Then Mr. Whitfield extended his hand. "Thank you Mr. President," he said, and turning to the camera bowed slightly, "and from the Oval Office, here in Washington…Goodnight America."

Softness

Many years ago, two Kings ruled neighboring countries. When one of them died his son Kabir came to the throne. He was a young man of thirty-five. Rashid, the neighboring King, was greedy and power-hungry. When he came to the coronation of Kabir, he saw how prosperous the country was, and how vulnerable. Kabir was young and inexperienced.

Six months after the coronation, Rashid sent a message to Kabir. When the messenger arrived, he was shown into the King's presence. The message was delivered as follows: "You will hand over the reins of government to me, Rashid. If you refuse, I will cross the border with my army and take the country by force. If you abdicate I'll assume the throne without bloodshed."

Kabir sent the messenger away and told him to return in an hour. The King convened his advisors and presented them with the demands of King Rashid. The advisors urged him to refuse the demand of their neighbor. Kabir listened carefully and then asked them, "What difference does it make who rules? What difference does it make if I step down and let Rashid take over? Surely he's right in thinking it will save a great deal of suffering, death and bloodshed."

"That's true," they countered, "but you're our King. He has no right to rule this land."

"That may be, but Rashid governs his country well and there's no reason to think he'd do otherwise here."

When the messenger returned, he was told that Kabir had accepted Rashid's demand and would step down to avoid bloodshed. By the time Rashid entered the capital Kabir had vanished. Stripped of his wealth, he lived among the people in relative anonymity.

As the years passed, Rashid realized he did not have the allegiance of the people. They still revered and respected Kabir. Rashid realized he would not have their allegiance as long as Kabir was alive. So he put a price on the young King's head. "One hundred pieces of gold will be given to the man or woman who turns him in," Rashid proclaimed. He then sent his soldiers out to spread the word. Years passed and still Kabir remained in hiding, free, and more highly regarded than ever. Rashid increased the price on Kabir's head to five hundred pieces of gold.

One evening, Kabir was traveling through the forest high in the mountains when he saw a fire and heard voices. As he was about to enter the clearing, he heard his name mentioned. He paused and listened. Peering through the branches, he saw an old man and his young wife sitting around a campfire over which the evening meal was being prepared. The old man said to his wife, "I'm getting old and may not be able to take care of you much longer. Today when I was in the village buying food, I heard that a huge reward is offered for turning in our King. I was thinking I should look for him. The reward would be more than enough to take care of you after I'm gone."

"You can't do that!" exclaimed the young wife in horror. "The King has done nothing to hurt you and has done so much to make sure that none of his people are hurt. How could you think of such a terrible thing?"

"What you're saying is true but we're on the verge of starvation and I'm worried what will become of you when I die."

Kabir stepped into the firelight. Without identifying himself, he asked if he could spend the night with them. They agreed, and shared their meal with him. Later that evening, Kabir revealed himself to the couple and told them he'd overheard the conversation. "To help you in your predicament, I'm surrendering myself to you. Take me to king Rashid and receive the reward."

Faced with this possibility the old man refused. Kabir insisted. "If you don't take me to the king, I'll say you hid me, and for that you'll be killed." The old man capitulated.

The next day they went to the capital. Some of the people recognized the King and followed along to see what would happen. By the time they reached the palace there was a large crowd. Stopped by a sentry, the crowd was asked who'd captured Kabir. Two of those who were in the crowd claimed it was them. Kabir interrupted and pointing to the old man said, "He's the one who brought me here, it is he who should get the reward." Kabir was taken and thrown in the dungeon to await his fate. The King called the old man before him to pay the reward.

"What really happened?" Rashid asked. The old man told him. Rashid realized he'd never command the allegiance of Kabir's people. He'd seriously underestimated Kabir's wisdom and courage.

Calling Kabir before him, Rashid bowed at his feet and asked forgiveness. The next day Rashid withdrew and Kabir resumed the throne. The two Kings became good friends, and their countries prospered.

POSTLUDE

The long birth of the novel Stillpoint.

It was the eve of the Gulf War some 20 years ago and George Bush senior was preparing to attack Saddam Hussein. Saddam had promised 'the mother of all wars.' Saddam, it appears, didn't realize he was poking a hornet's nest.

As I listened to the news, Lao Tzu's words came whispering through time. Lao Tzu, or "Old Gentleman," as he was called, was a poet sage who lived five hundred years before the birth of Christ. We know him today as the author of the *Tao Te Ching*. Listening to him was like listening to a running commentary on what was happening.

Weapons, **he said**, *are instruments of violence*
and fear.
The wise have no use for them
Except in the gravest necessity, when compelled
And, only with restraint.

In Victory
After the slaughter of men
How can anyone rejoice? **He asked.**

That's why the wise enter a battle gravely
With sorrow and compassion in their hearts
Like those attending a funeral.

I thought of the US military and those who lobby for war as a first response and Lao Tzu's words answered my unasked question.

When weapons are created, he said,
The temptation to use them
Is overwhelming.

As the buildup continued I felt a deep sense of foreboding. It seemed we were starting down a road from which it would be hard to turn back. Although we hadn't yet realized it, that road was leading to a place of greater violence and polarization.

The commentary from Lao Tzu became more intense and I found myself wondering what he would do if he had lived today and found himself in a position to advise those in power.

Thus began *Stillpoint*, 'though at the time it bore the name, *Mr. President*. I quit my job and went on the road to sell the book.

I flew from Hawaii, where I lived at the time, retrieved my truck from the docks in Seattle, bought a used camper and began a ten month journey. Loaded with fifteen hundred books I drove north to south and west to east.

But, as it turned out, I was from the country, and by natural inclination more solitary than social. I gradually withdrew from people and moved into remote areas of the mountains east and north east of San Diego. Needless to say I didn't sell many books, although some are scattered all over the south west, left in bookstores on consignment and never retrieved.

Not long after my return to Hawaii, I moved to Vancouver Island to care for my mother. At the time I shared an office with a psychiatrist. We had interesting conversations over tea in the kitchen. I still lived in my camper, and paid a dollar each morning at the fish wharf for a hot shower.

Besides seeing clients I was writing *a contemporary version of Lao Tzu's Tao Te Ching*. When I completed the several drafts I put them in the waiting room on the table with the magazines.

The title read, Something to ponder while you wait. When it was published it became *Something to Ponder, Reflections from Lao Tzu's Tao Te Ching.*

Years later a man introduced himself to me. "You don't know me," he said. "I read your book, *Something to Ponder*, while waiting for my appointments with the psychiatrist. What I found in that book stayed with me."

In the meantime *Mr. President* languished in a friend's basement. Events moved on, the war was over and the "Old Gentleman" began whispering to me again. There was an edginess to life, nasty violent clashes like boils bursting with toxicity, erupted throughout the world. It seemed to reflect the new undercurrents unleashed in human consciousness.

I re-wrote *Mr. President* and called it *Uncommon Reason.* Despite the fact that it won several awards it contained a lot of lectures and discussions and had a limited appeal.

Lao Tzu continued whispering, he wouldn't leave me alone and *Stillpoint* emerged on the scene.

I wanted *Stillpoint* to take readers on a journey through history, into a world most knew little about. I wanted them to understand what it would be like to live through those times, not just intellectually, but emotionally as well.

In the process characters emerged that I fell in love with, others I disliked. Through it all I hoped they would give voice to the suffering and loss, the beliefs and assumptions that lead to war and have done so for as long as man has roamed the earth.

I wanted readers to be so immersed in the events they were no longer bystanders but engaged participants in an unfolding conversation about war and peace.

I wanted them to be able to say they learned some things and understood others and as a direct result the complexity of the events taking place in the Middle East would seem somehow, not so complex. I wanted readers to see from a different perspective, a perspective the poet, T S Elliot, identified as the *still point of the turning world*: a perspective quite different from the one defined by propaganda, the one with which we're all well acquainted.

I wanted readers to have a deep sense of compassion for the suffering of those caught in the tightening spiral of violence. And most importantly, glimpse, if even faintly, a path that could eventually lead to peace in the region; and, to understand we, you and I, are part of what happens in the Middle East, either through our ignorance or through our awareness.

Lao Tzu continues whispering to me from time to time; I've learned to pay attention. We are friends now, well acquainted with one another. In writing *Stillpoint* he was always looking over my shoulder reminding me that:

When a sage governs a nation
He does not place himself above others
Their difficulties and humiliations are his own.

This is what makes a great leader, he concluded.

Colin Mallard

do we learn from history?
probably not.

experience shows us
what we learn we often forget.

anyone who's been to school knows this.

but understanding
is of a different order.

when it happens it's permanent.
it cannot be forgotten
or remembered.

it just is.

Bibliography

Abuelaish, Dr Izzeldin. *I Shall Not Hate.* Vintage Canadian Edition, 2011.

Carter, Jimmy. *Palestine Peace not Apartheid.* Simon and Schuster 2006.

Mallard, Colin. *Something to Ponder, reflections from Lao Tzu's Tao Te Ching.* Advaita Gems Publishing. 2009

Marcus, Amy Dockser. *Jerusalem 1913 The Origins Of The Arab-Israeli Conflict.* Viking Penguin. 2007.

Mearsheimer, John J. And Walt, Stephen M. *The Israeli Lobby and US Foreign Policy.* Viking Canada Penguin Group. 2007.

Pappe, Ilan. *The Ethnic Cleansing of Palestine.* One World Publications Ltd. 2006.

Sand, Shlomo. *The Invention of the Jewish People.* Published by Verso 2010.

AIDA The Gaza Blockade: Children and Education Fact Sheet. Various reports from UNRWA. United Nations Relief and Works Agency.

Mc.Arthur, Shirl. *A Conservative Estimate of Total Direct U. S. Aid to Israel: Almost $114 Billion.* Washington Report on Middle East Affairs, November 2008, pages 10-11

Palestine Remembered. http://www.palestineremembered.com/

Colin D. Mallard

Colin Mallard, was born in England during the Second World War and immigrated to Canada in his teens. He was deeply interested in Eastern Philosophy, particularly, Taoism, Advaita Vedanta, Zen and Sufism. He was trained as a psychologist and, for a number of years before his retirement, worked with families of abused children.

Colin has written a number of books. "Something to Ponder" and "Understanding" are about peace on a personal level. "Stillpoint," his most recent book, explores the nature of peace on a collective or global scale.

His books have won a number of awards.